For The Love of Jazz

Elke Feuer

CRIMSON
ROMANCE
F+W Media, Inc.

Crimson Romance
an imprint of F+W Media, Inc.
10151 Carver Road, Suite 200
Blue Ash, Ohio 45242
www.crimsonromance.com

ISBN 10: 1-4405-6141-9
ISBN 13: 978-1-4405-6141-2
eISBN 10: 1-4405-6144-3
eISBN 13: 978-1-4405-6144-3

Cover Art Credit: 123rf.com

Dedication

Big thanks to my husband and kids for giving me time to do what I love, and my wonderful parents for watching the kids during football season.

Acknowledgments

First, I'd like to thank Crimson Romance for giving me the chance to fulfill my dream and editors, Jennifer and Ashley for your help with the book.

My best friend and star critique buddy, Katie, who read the story again and again, without complaint (well, just a little) and encouraged me to submit even though I was expecting another child.

To an awesome teacher, Leigh Michaels, who provided stellar advice in her classes at Gotham. Also, the writers I met at Gotham, whose friendship I value along with their continual encouragement: Chauncey, Cecily, and Hope.

My fellow Ass Cheek Angels bloggers for the inspiration they provide.

And last, but certainly not least, my friends and fans on Facebook, Twitter, and WordPress. You guys rock!

Prologue

CHICAGO 1959

Please meet me, it's important! Lola pulls her knee-length coat closer to her petite frame and suppresses the tickle of fear at the base of her spine. It's late, but she can't ignore her friend's urgent request.

Cool night air rustling through the trees is the only noise. Visitors to the park are gone, leaving behind dark empty walkways and overflowing garbage bins. Crunching leaves and strange noises in the black distance start her heart racing. This is a bad idea.

She sees her friend coming and smiles in welcome and relief. As they draw closer, there is no smile in return. Normally cool but inviting eyes shine with malice. Lola's eyes widen in surprise as a gun is pointed at her. Before she can scream she feels the sting and burning of flesh as bullets from the outstretched gun enter her shoulder once, twice. She falls to her knees.

Her eyes fill with horror as reality sets in. "Why?"

Silent hate glares from behind the barrel of the gun and another bullet fires, this time hitting her leg.

"Help!" she screams. Her gaze shifts frantically down lonely sidewalks. No one is coming. It crushes her like the pain tearing her apart.

Another shot fires and hits her other leg, and Lola knows she is meant to suffer first. She raises her hand in a frail attempt to stop the bullets. It doesn't make a difference. The gun fires again and blood pools around her and on the icy ground beneath her fingertips.

Hot tears spill as she thinks of William. If she'd listened to her intuition, she could be spooned against him instead of dying in the dirt like an animal abandoned by its owner.

She doesn't want to die and leave him, or the happiness she's found. She screams until her lungs burn with the sensation they'll burst from the strain.

Anger boils the blood still running through her veins. She longs to take the gun and shoot back. Have them feel her pain. Feel the agony of regret; words left unspoken, unshared kisses, things left undone, the fear of the unknown that lies in the darkness swirling in the distance, and the anguish of the unanswered question. 'Why?'

She remembers the offered friendship, smiles, and the laughter shared. It was all a lie! Heartache crushes her, dulling the pain of her physical wounds. "This isn't over," she vows, even as life begins to drain from her weak frame.

"You're over," is spat back at her.

Images of the moment she met William, their first kiss, and their lovemaking flicker like a movie before her closed eyes. She won't share the rest of this life with him, bear his children, or grow old with him, but she takes comfort in knowing she'll see him again, love him again, and no one will take it away. She clings to the hope she can wait for William until they are together again. Yes, she will wait. Silent calm seeps in as her life slips away.

Chapter 1

CHICAGO
Fifty Years Later

"This is it." Josie Fagan took a deep breath. "Moment of truth."

She got out of her car, ran shaky fingers through her hair, and smiled when it tickled the back of her neck. The curls would return to their original state, but the gesture gave her comfort.

Each step to the chestnut brick house made her heartbeat escalate. She'd felt a connection the moment she saw it advertised for renovations—even dreamed about the house and a man standing in the upstairs window, waving her inside. She looked up, but no one was there.

Emotional connections, as her father used to call them, were as natural to her as breathing. Since her childhood, she'd felt strong connections to things like jazz music, old buildings, and, just recently, Chicago. Like being black, it was a part of who she was.

She made her way along the sidewalk to the crimson front door and, with a shaky hand, rang the doorbell.

When it opened, she looked up to meet cool emerald eyes and neatly combed ebony hair. If not for his suit, she'd have guessed he was a construction worker, with his strong square jawline, and shoulders that were barely contained beneath his expensive suit. Icicles of recognition jumped across her vertebrae.

She extended her hand. "Patrick Pullman?"

When he took her hand, memories sparkled in his daunting stare before he released her hand reluctantly, as though breaking the grasp would stop the wheels turning in his mind. "Yes. Josie Fagan?"

Interesting. He felt it, too. She nodded, but pretended not to notice. Her interest was in what lay behind him. She was about to see the inside of the house that had taunted her the last two days. The intensity of the connection to it surprised her. Other than jazz music, no connection had been stronger.

He gestured her inside.

When she stepped into the entryway, warmth surrounded her like the coverlet her mother had given her on her eighteenth birthday. It started in the pit of her stomach and spread prickles over the surface of her skin. It was the thrill of waiting for the sun to set, then watching it explode into brilliant hues of red, yellow, and gold. It was being curled up with her favorite book by the warm glow of a fireplace with the faint sounds of jazz in the background. It was home.

"Thanks for coming on short notice." He came to stand next to her in the entryway.

"My pleasure." Her voice creaked, still feeling the sensations awakened by the house.

"I've selected three restoration architects to bid on this job. I'm looking for someone to handle all aspects of the job, from the restoration to providing design ideas. I will expect a design and estimate from you by the end of the week."

His curt business tone was a dose of cold water, reminding her why she was there. "Let's get started."

Nodding, he walked into the next room.

Thick mahogany moldings trimmed the middle and tops of each corner of the room, and brown water stains crept halfway down one of the corner walls, peeling the faded wallpaper—a hint at plumbing problems. An imposing white mantel framed the fireplace in the middle of the room; it was a looming fire hazard. Built-in mahogany bookcases with glass shelves flanked it. She wanted to laugh when she saw the television, from the seventies, along with the mocha recliner positioned carefully before it; she'd stepped back in time.

Moving toward the chair, she grazed one hand over the surface. Soft leather tingled her fingers as she caressed the top of the chair and along one side to the arm, taking in each crevice that had aged it. The urge to know the history of each crease seized her and the thought—*shouldn't it be on the other side of the fireplace?*—intruded.

"Ahem." The word pulled her from her trance.

"Shall we continue?" she said as nonchalantly as she could muster. *What was that?* She'd never had a connection like that before.

Placing her large black portfolio on the cushion, she took out her camera and started taking photos of the front door, snapping her way back to the living room. "I recommend keeping the original cut of the crown molding. It will add value to the house if you decide to sell."

"I don't intend to sell."

She paused mid-click. The passion in his voice surprised her. She turned her attention back to the room.

In the kitchen, just off the living room, she took panoramic views of the room, the oak flooring and beamed ceiling. "What would you like done here?"

"Modern appliances are a must, but I'm open to suggestions on everything else."

An open mind, huh? Good trait for a client. "Okay," she said and followed him up the staircase. "Did your family always own this house?" She knew the answer because she researched potential clients, but their answers were much more fascinating.

"Yes, my uncle had it built in the nineteen fifties and was the only owner."

"What happened?" She continued to take photos to give the impression of a casual conversation. The Pullmans valued their privacy, and she didn't blame them. They were public figures, after all.

"He died a couple of weeks ago."

Sadness hit her unexpectedly, along with questions about his uncle, but she ignored them. She didn't ask personal questions, especially during the bidding stage. Following him to the next room, she said quietly, "I'm sorry."

A half smile pulled at his lips, showing hints of a dimple. She was a sucker for dimples.

"You stay at the house?" she asked, peeking inside the next room on his tour. It was the only dust-free and relatively clean room she'd seen so far.

"I moved in a few days ago."

Her eyes moved about the room with renewed curiosity. There was a nine-drawer mahogany dresser adjacent to the bed, with two cologne bottles sitting on its top. The remaining surface was bare. A blue polo shirt was draped across the chair in front of the small desk at the end of the bed. On the nightstand, a modern digital clock flashed the time in flickering red, and behind it sat a silent, cheap wooden one. An elegant, welcoming four-poster bed, with a silver oval crest nestled in the middle of the headboard, anchored the room.

Heat rushed to her cheeks, making her painfully aware of the narrow doorway and of Patrick, who stood only inches away. She stepped out of the room into the doorway and one side of his body brushed against hers. As she looked, his intense gaze met hers. What she wouldn't give to read minds. Okay, maybe just his mind.

She took a quick step back.

"Sorry," he mumbled.

She smiled politely, afraid if she opened her mouth the words, *bump into me anytime* might fall from her lips and embarrass her, him, and give a prospective client the wrong idea. "How many bed and bathrooms?" Focus, Josie!

"Three, and one bathroom." He led her down the narrow corridor to the next room. "I didn't have the other rooms cleaned, since I plan to renovate them right away."

She nodded, despite the urge to lecture him on the dangers of dust and mildew. The other two bedrooms were sparsely furnished and as dated as his; however, the pine flooring was one good thing going for him. The bathroom was old-fashioned but large, and had a marble countertop.

"I'd like another bathroom. Is that possible?"

"It's a challenge given the age of the house, but possible."

"Good."

"It might mean giving up space in one of the bedrooms, or losing one completely."

"Good to know."

The rest of the tour consisted of a basement with cracks in the foundation; rickety, leaking plumbing; dents in the roof of the attic; and an electrical panel with wiring from the Dark Ages. The outside gave the illusion of a stable structure and possibly mediocre electrical and plumbing, but it was worse than she thought.

"It's a lot of work, but that's why I advertised for a restoration architect and not just a designer," he stated as they made their way back to the first floor.

His words regained her attention; her thoughts had strayed to the snug fit of his pants.

"What do you think?" he asked when they reached the kitchen.

Her head snapped up. Had he had read her thoughts? She cleared her throat and realized she'd stopped taking pictures after seeing his bedroom. She hadn't asked questions about his expectations for renovating the rest of the house. Nothing! Merely moved about each room in a daze as if it was her first renovation and nerves had paralyzed her silent. "It's beautiful," she choked out.

"Beautiful?" He snorted. "That's not a word I expected anyone to say. I was thinking in terms of renovations."

"Forgive me, Mr. Pullman." She pulled out her notebook. "It's not often I come across a rarity like this house." *Or such a cute butt.* "The built-in mahogany bookcases and stained-glass trim above the pocket doors and bay windows are in good shape; however, the walls will need to be stripped, and the electrical and plumbing redone to facilitate the upgrades to the kitchen and the new bathroom. It's a crumbling mess..." she said with delight before her voice trailed off.

Stop talking, Josie! The last thing any owner wanted to hear was that their house was falling apart. Just because you love old buildings that doesn't mean everyone else does. Next you'll be boring him with its structural history. She cringed inwardly when she imagined the words 'cute butt' falling out during her ramble, but his unchanged expression meant it hadn't escaped. "Did you have other expectations, either with the renovations or the design?"

"I was going to gut the place and completely renovate it to a modern style."

Her heart almost stopped and the smile slid off her face.

"I changed my mind."

Her smile returned.

"Is there a way to incorporate modern elements without compromising the historical integrity?"

"There is," she declared. "I can restore its original beauty while combining modern touches that won't change the charm and uniqueness of the house. I've done it with other houses. Excuse me."

After retrieving her portfolio from the recliner, she placed it on the countertop and flipped through before and after photos of other renovation jobs. "These places were completely renovated inside and out in most cases. However a lot of the original architectural structure and accents that made the homes unique were restored to their original grandeur."

"These are fantastic!"

"Thank you."

He closed her portfolio.

"How long will it take to finish?" he asked, his business tone returning.

"My first guess would be eight to twelve months, but I'd have to check a few things to be certain."

"I need it finished in six months," he stated matter of factly.

"Why?" The word slipped before she could stop it. An invisible wall went up around him. Wow, he did that faster than she ever had.

"Do you really need to know?" His tone was that of a politician who'd just been caught in an awkward situation, but was adamant he had good reason.

"Not unless it affects the job. There's always the possibility of delays, Mr. Pullman, especially with a restoration as extensive as this one, so I can't make guarantees. I can promise you that I'll do everything in my power to meet the final deadline."

Tension, that had held him as straight as a rod, softened. "Thanks for not telling me what you think I want to hear."

"You're welcome."

Silence crackled between them.

It was now or never. She squared her shoulders for added courage. "Mr. Pullman."

"Patrick," he supplied.

"The truth is, Patrick, I came here to make you an offer."

Surprise flickered in his green eyes and a devilish grin took over from his polite one. She suppressed the urge to roll her eyes. His tabloid reputation with women wasn't exaggerated after all. "It's purely professional." She gave herself a mental high five at the disappointed look on his face before continuing. "I could draw this out, but beating around the bush would be a waste of our time."

When he didn't respond or change his expression, she continued. "I want you to hire me."

One eyebrow rose in suspicion.

She bit her lip nervously. "My company is new and having a job with you would help establish it." She left off that it was failing miserably. Her old boss was making it difficult to drum up business since she left him six months ago. Calling him a jerk would be a compliment.

"What about the clients for these jobs?" He pointed to her portfolio.

"They're outside of Chicago. More importantly, those jobs are affiliated with the company I used to work for, not my own company."

His laughter didn't reach his eyes. "Let me get this straight. You want me to give you this job knowing it's the first your company has done?" He shifted from one foot to the other. "I like what I see, but as I mentioned, I'm on a tight schedule and I can't take a chance. A proven company is my best choice."

"Those other companies have more than one project. You'll be my only client, so you'll have my full attention." It wasn't going to be easy—she had known it the moment this idea had come to her—but this was her only chance to set herself apart. Being overly confident was a risk she had to take.

"And please call me Josie." She gave him the smile she used on clients to persuade them to use her design ideas. "I've been in this business for fifteen years and my abilities as a restoration architect are evident from my previous jobs." She pulled out work references from a pocket in her portfolio. "These are statements from satisfied clients that confirm my reliability. My personal references verify my integrity, and I've known my construction crew for years. They're the best."

The intensity of his gaze didn't change.

Okay, this guy was going to need a little more coaxing than usual, but what did she expect? He was a lawyer. "I can attempt to dazzle you with wit and charm to convince you I'm the best choice for this job, but I'd rather let my work speak for itself." She held her breath when he closed the gap between them.

Emerald eyes tried to read her mind, see if she was telling the truth. She welcomed it; whatever it took for him make him consider her offer.

"Accept my offer, Patrick. You won't regret it." She ignored her racing pulse. She wasn't sure if it was nerves or his closeness. The smell of his cologne that had tickled her nose when she first inhaled it now engulfed her senses, along with the faint scent of his skin. It was spicy, exotic, and masculine.

He leaned closer and their faces almost touched. "Maybe you'll regret your offer."

His intimate tone made her toes tingle. "Not a chance."

"Two other companies are bidding on this job."

"You'll choose me." She squared her shoulders. "I'm the best at what I do. Neither have my experience or the diversity you need."

He took a step back and her senses recovered. Oh, he was good. Too good.

His face remained expressionless as his eyes studied her further. What could be left? He'd stood close enough to hear her heart race and check her bra size.

Gone were his mischievous eyes. In their place were the professional ones that greeted her at the front door. "I'll call you when I make a decision."

"I have some final checks to make that I'll need for the estimate."

"All right."

She smiled and quickly shook his hand, ignoring the pull to be close to him again, and left. Well, that certainly hadn't played out how she planned.

Half an hour later, she resisted the urge to slam the car door and, instead, threw her clipboard on the seat. She took a deep breath and squeezed the steering wheel tightly. A job with a powerful Pullman would not only give her business the boost it needed, but open the door to high-end clients. If he didn't choose her, she'd have to renegotiate with the bank and wait for another suitable client. She could lose her business by then. "Damn it!"

Another client was probably better. The unexpected attraction and connection she had felt with Patrick could make working with him—distracting. She had too much at stake for things like getting involved with clients...possible clients.

• • •

Patrick watched Josie's blue Honda pull away from the sidewalk and frowned. He knew her, although he couldn't put his finger on how or from where. He'd searched through the sea of faces he'd dated since Sharon, but none matched hers.

When they shook hands in the doorway, something strange had happened. Heat spread over him; his senses were bombarded by her presence and visions of her looking up at him, smiling and reaching out to touch his face.

He was stunned and struggled to find his voice to ask her inside. She had walked past him so calmly she couldn't have seen or felt what he had. That alone was enough not to hire her. He didn't like complicated relationships.

Then there was her unwavering look when he attempted to intimidate her. She hadn't backed down or had the decency to stammer, the way most people did. Instead, she stood there and let him study her like an open book. The problem was, he liked what he saw, and not just the sincerity and confidence in her eyes, but the soft curve of her face, delicate caramel skin, and sexy, kissable lips.

He sat in the recliner she'd touched earlier and ran a hand through his hair in frustration. He'd flirted with her. It was... unexpected. *Decorum always!* his mother's words reminded him.

Josie's offer had surprised him. He knew all about people wanting to use him or his family's name. He swallowed the bitterness rising in his throat. At least Josie had the decency to offer him something tangible in return.

She had over fifteen years of experience, so that would make her well into her thirties, but she didn't look a day over thirty. He hadn't noticed a wedding ring on her finger, or signs that one had been there. Not that it mattered.

Her passion for restorations was evident, along with her pride of prior projects. He'd watched her smile and caress pieces of furniture in a way that had unnerved and excited him at the same time. Another stroke against hiring her.

She was right. With her diverse background, she could handle the restoration, the contractors, and the designing. She was the best person for the job. He loved this old house as much as his uncle had and didn't want just anyone handling the restorations. It was his playground as a child and a place of comfort as a teenager.

Sadness squeezed around him. With his uncle gone, the last of the happy memories lingering in the house were being choked out. Sorrow had plagued his uncle for as long as he remembered. The cause was a dirty secret no one could speak out loud, even behind closed doors.

The knot in his stomach—and each complication that raised its head—said he needed to hire someone else. He hoped to God one of the other companies was just as qualified.

Chapter 2

"Mr. Pullman will see you now." Patrick's secretary hung up the phone and motioned her to his office.

"Thank you."

His secretary contacted Josie for the meeting the same day she had sent her estimate and proposed designs. Josie was certain she had the job. He wouldn't meet just to tell her she didn't get it, would he?

Her breath stopped when she walked into his office.

At home, he'd been imposing with his broad shoulders and confident, arrogant air. In the courtroom, he was known as "Calculating Pullman" for the way he won cases. Seated behind his large mahogany desk, he was a frightening force.

"Please have a seat." He pointed to a chair in front of his desk.

Her heart dropped. She hoped he wasn't going to give her a long speech like the ones his father gave. Just give me a straight yes or no, don't sugarcoat it. She sat calmly in the black leather chair, smiled through gritted teeth, and, for a moment, regretted her blatant confidence when they met.

His fingers played with the onyx paperweight on his desk. "Did you get new clients?"

Her heartbeat raced as she shook her head slowly.

"Good. I want you to do the restoration." His eyes rose to meet hers.

Oh man! There was a catch, and she wasn't going to like it.

"I want you stay at the house during the renovations and not take on any other jobs until mine is done."

"What?" He couldn't be serious. She searched his face. He was. "Why do I need to stay at the house?"

"I need this project finished on time and that will mean having you close to discuss designs and restoration changes. Living at the house is the best option." He leaned back in his chair. "Room and board is free. You don't want to waste money your business needs, do you?"

Damn. He knew about her finances and was going to play hardball. Well, she had no intention of letting him use it against her. She was the best candidate and they both knew it. If she wasn't, he would've hired another company. "I want a flattering personal reference," she countered.

A cocky grin curved his lips. "Then I want guarantees."

She held his gaze.

"You'll get your reference if you meet my six-month deadline, if I'm satisfied with the quality of the work, and if the job comes within budget." He moved his chair back into the upright position.

"That will not include any changes you make to my original estimate or if you select inferior products," she added quickly.

His smile broadened and a boyish dimple winked at her.

Is he enjoying this?

Damn him, he is!

She didn't like it one bit. He was taking away the control she wanted—needed—to have. The excitement she'd felt when he agreed to hire her vanished. The masculine atmosphere floating in the air like cheap cologne when she arrived squeezed around her, making her uncomfortable.

"Do we have a deal?" His confident tone implied he knew her answer.

Behind his desk were bookcases lining the back wall filled with perfectly aligned law books and neatly labeled black binders she assumed contained client cases. Matching storage cabinets extended from the left side of his desk and had no photos, like the rest of the room. The framed law degree hanging on the wall adjacent to the bookcases was the only clue they sat in his office.

It was as clinical as a hospital ward. "Calculating Pullman" was not exaggerated.

You could walk away. It flared, unwelcome, in her mind, but it was not an option she would entertain. His offer was too good to pass up. She could settle with the bank and not lose her business loan.

Behind his desk, his arrogant smile still mocked her and her resolve toughened for no other reason than to knock him off his self-erected pedestal. He'd be just another client she won over with her talent, minus the wit and charm—he didn't need them.

Relaxing her stiff posture, she shifted to the edge of her seat and met him with renewed conviction. "I'll agree, if you accept this as a business arrangement and being close doesn't mean you knocking on my door at inappropriate times of the night," she said, choosing her words carefully. "I'm a professional and will be treated that way, understand?"

His arrogant smile wavered. "Agreed. I don't mix business with pleasure."

She ignored the twinge of disappointment that gnawed at the back of her neck.

"The new contract with the changes will be emailed to you shortly. We'll sign it tomorrow and I'll transfer the deposit into your account." He stood up. "I'll expect you at my house this weekend, moved in and ready to start working first thing Monday," he informed her.

Her head snapped up.

Before she could open her mouth to argue, his secretary came on the phone and informed him his next appointment had arrived. She stood up, quickly shook his hand, and gave him an icy smile before leaving.

Instead of the elation she anticipated, her legs grew heavy with each step toward her car. She didn't mind the house; the occupant was going to be the problem. *At least I have somewhere to stay*, she thought dryly. It was one less thing to worry about while moving her business from Detroit to Chicago.

This company had been a dream since the seed of architecture was planted by her father at the age of twelve; it became her whole life after her mother died three months ago. Taking on this job meant leaving her mother's house in Detroit for good. Signing the papers tomorrow was only a formality; there was no turning back.

•••

"It's done," Patrick told Gary, the lawyer handling his uncle's will. "I chose Ms. Fagan." It was better to remember her as Ms. Fagan, his restoration architect, and not Josie with caramel eyes and inviting lips.

"Good. She was the best."

"How do you know that?" Patrick asked. Of course he knew. Her company was the one Gary recommended out of the three.

There was silence on the other end of the phone.

"I see." He ran a hand through his hair in frustration. Was there nothing in his life someone didn't know before him? "And if I'd chosen another company?"

"I know you want this to go as quickly and smoothly as possible, and that's going to happen with Ms. Fagan," Gary replied, not answering his question.

He was right, as much as Patrick hated to admit it.

"Was she unpleasant?" Gary asked.

"No."

"Then what's the problem?"

"No problem." What could he say? He didn't want to work with her because of the images he saw, or the strong attraction he felt toward her? It was ridiculous when he thought about it, and would sound stupid out loud.

"Good. And the schedule?"

"If there are no delays, it will be completed on time," Patrick confirmed.

Gary didn't respond.

Patrick didn't like anyone in charge of any part of his life. He had enough of that with his family. The sooner it was over, the sooner he would be rid of Gary, get his inheritance, and move on with his life.

"We'll talk again soon," Gary said quietly.

"Uh-huh."

Patrick slammed the phone in its cradle. "Damn you, Uncle," he cursed. He regretted the words the minute he said them. His uncle didn't put him in this situation; he had, the moment he signed the documents.

Soon the other conditions of his uncle's will wouldn't matter. He'd have a home—an empty one, but a home nonetheless. His uncle's house was his sanctuary growing up and would be again when the renovations were done. From the time he moved in after his uncle's death, the house had comforted him. His apartment in Oak Park had never felt like home, any more than his parents' home had growing up. *Home, love, and family are all that's important.*

His uncle had been his source for those things, but now that he was gone, so were they. Pain traveled up his throat, threatening to choke him. He thought Sharon would be his source, but he was horribly wrong. That he found out before they had married should have made him feel better, but it didn't.

He thought back to his uncle's passing just a few weeks ago. *"Restore my house, Patrick. She'll come back."* *Strange* words for a man on his deathbed, but it didn't matter. Patrick gave his word and nothing and no one would get in the way of the promise he'd made, not even his strong attraction to Josie and the recent strange dreams of her, and of people and places he didn't know.

He smiled, remembering their negotiation. She'd been irritated, but had matched him with her own demands. Despite his reservations about her and the sparks that lingered between them, he was excited to return the house to the state he remembered as a child.

Chapter 3

Josie parked her car at the edge of the curb. Just beyond the window stood her latest restoration project and her place of residence for the next few months. Two miles off Lake Shore Drive, the street was private, one you would find in any suburban neighborhood. Kids played ball and moved out of the street for the occasional neighbor's car coming home or heading out. Couples holding hands and people walking their dogs passed on the sidewalks. Old men sat in lounge chairs on the edge of the grass close to their homes.

Large elm trees lined both sides of the road: ageless, beautiful and covered with new leaf growth, a hint of spring. The branches, extending high above the tops of the houses, were spaced several feet apart and reached out to each other—lovers with their hands outstretched in welcome. She hadn't noticed them the first time, too excited to get inside the house and speak with Patrick about the job. Her passion was old houses and neighborhoods, especially those that sustained their quiet existence and original homes.

She got out the car, took a box out the backseat, and headed to the house.

Bright orange in the shrubbery of the neighboring house caught her attention. When she looked closer, a woman with a straw hat emerged and glared at her earnestly, making her feel like she was sneaking into the house for a rendezvous or to steal something.

"I'm here to restore the house," she said loudly.

Sharp eyes inspected her and then as quickly dismissed her, and the flower-covered hat returned beneath the rose bush.

Another perk of quiet neighborhoods—nosey neighbors. Josie grinned. She would introduce herself to the neighbors before the renovations started.

After the shock of Patrick asking her to stay at the house wore off, she found she was excited about staying there. What she didn't like was his being there with her. Why he wanted to stay at the house during such an extensive restoration when he had an apartment downtown was beyond her. Renovations were messy and inconvenient. He must be more of a control freak than her. God help her if he was.

She opened the door and the house greeted her as warmly as it had the first time she visited. She smiled. "Hello to you, too."

"Need help?"

She shrieked and nearly dropped the box in her hands. Turning, she saw Patrick standing in the doorway to the kitchen, his expression solemn. "You scared me." *Did he hear me talking to the house?*

"I didn't mean to."

"Help would be great." She smiled, placed the box in his arms, and hoped he wasn't thinking he hired a crazy person. "Did you decide which room I'm staying in, or do I get to choose?"

"I picked one."

Each time they met, he had been dressed in a formal suit. Today he was dressed in khaki shorts and a baby blue polo shirt. He was no less imposing, but she felt more at ease as she followed him upstairs.

Flirtatious Patrick was not present today and she was thankful. It would make their working relationship easier. *Liar!* So what if his ridiculously sexy smile hadn't left her thoughts since the moment it showed itself?

"It's next to yours?"

"Is that a problem?"

"No," she mumbled and walked inside the room where she'd be staying. It wasn't the same room she'd seen her first day there. The surfaces of the furniture shone like new, instead of dulled by dust. All the personal items had been removed and only an oak dresser and matching nightstand remained, with a queen-sized bed in the corner of the room. A new cream and violet flower print bedspread covered it. A small crystal vase with a bouquet of spring flowers adorned the dresser. Like the rest of the house, it made her feel at home. "Thank you," she said softly.

After their interaction at his office, she didn't expect a room so nicely prepared. He was full of surprises. She didn't like surprises.

"Don't mention it," he said with a shrug. "Are the rest of your things in the car?"

"Yes."

She headed back downstairs and tried to ignore the heat of his gaze on the back of her neck. When she reached her car, she opened the trunk for him to take out another box.

"Is this it, or do you have more trips to make?" He looked in the back of her car before coming to stand next to her.

"No, those are all my things, except for my work desk. Why?" she asked, a handful of clothes on hangers draped across her arm.

He shrugged. "Most people I know couldn't fit all their clothes in this car; not in one trip, anyway."

"Accumulating things isn't a priority for me." She adjusted the clothes to a more comfortable position on her arm. "Besides, I'm here to work, not move in." Way to make the client feel uncomfortable, Josie. Just keep your mouth shut.

"Right," he mumbled before following her inside.

"What things are?" he asked.

"Are what?" She turned from her task of putting clothes in the closet to face him.

"Priorities for you?" He stepped closer.

"To gain experience and knowledge in my field, and, of course, have a steady client base to sustain my business." She eyed him warily as each step brought him closer.

He chuckled. "That sounds like something my father's PR office had me say in college." He towered over her five-foot-six frame when he reached her, which didn't take much effort. "Nothing else is important to you?" His tone was low and his interest seemingly genuine.

Why did he want to know? Her internal alarm sounded off as she remembered how her old boss used personal information to take advantage of her.

"No," she whispered. *Damn.* As she looked into his inquiring eyes, the room closed in around her, made smaller by his large frame, the stack of boxes beside her, and the closet behind her. She took a step back, hoping to put space between them, tripped on a stack of books she'd forgotten was there and fell backwards into the closet. Good one, Josie!

Laughter bubbled from her throat. She'd just ended up in the closet trying to avoid him. So much for thinking she could handle anything he threw her way. She couldn't muster being a foot away.

"You okay?" He extended his hand and chuckled with her.

"I think so." She took his hand. "This is what happens when I'm interrogated by clients," she joked.

His laughter died. "I didn't mean it that way," he said quickly.

Liar, she thought, but held her tongue. Suddenly she was closer to him than before she fell into the closet.

Her gaze moved over his lips before it headed back to his eyes. She gulped down the nervous lump at the back of her throat. The heat from his hand engulfed hers and ignited sensations that spread throughout every pore of her skin until it tingled. It was more intense than any connection she'd felt in her thirty-five years. She tried to pull her hand from his. Her breath stopped when he didn't let go.

Fathomless green eyes searched hers before he broke the spell and released her hand.

Disappointment etched his face before he went to stand by the doorway. *Did he feel something?* Excitement and turmoil swirled in her stomach.

"Well, if that's everything, I'll let you get settled," he said from the doorway.

"Thanks for helping."

"Sure. I'm heading into work, but I'm back this evening."

"You're working on a Saturday?" she asked, then caught herself. "Sorry, I shouldn't ask such personal questions."

He laughed and the dimple on his face winked at her. "If you consider that a personal question, Josie, I'm getting off easy."

His laughter was a deep, erotic rumble that tickled the back of her mind and the base of her spine. She managed a feeble smile. This was bad, real bad.

"Any chance we could meet later to discuss the renovations?" he asked.

"Of course." So much for letting her get settled.

"Good. See you then." He smiled intimately, reminding her of the feel of her hand in his.

She released the air in her lungs she didn't realize she was holding after he left the room. Walking over to the small stereo system she'd brought, she pressed the Play button and the rustic sound of Billie Holiday's voice filled the room.

"Damn!" She'd forgotten to tell him that Danny, her contractor, was stopping by. Keeping her wits about her on this job was going to be a challenge with a client as...distracting as Patrick. Words she never thought she'd hear herself say. Professionalism, always, was her motto. It had never been a problem before. Reaching into her handbag, she took out a Post It note, wrote down the words and stuck it on the mirror of the dresser. "So you don't forget," she told her reflection.

Looking around the room, she reached for the box labeled 'Business stuff' and pulled out a picture frame and smiled. Beneath the glass was her business license.

The doorbell's loud ring interrupted. She checked her watch and made her way to the front door. Right on time.

"Welcome, Mr. Stanley." She greeted him formally after opening the door.

"Hey there, JoJo," he answered, sidestepping her formality.

She smiled. Danny was anything but formal. That was evident from his paint-stained jeans, checkered shirt, and the tool belt hanging from his slim hips when she'd deliberately told him he would be meeting the client. Ever the clichéd construction worker, the clipboard with his inspector checklist was the only indication he was anything more.

He followed her past the entryway and let out a low whistle. "Wow, this place is a time-warp dump!" he exclaimed after circling the living room, his deep blue eyes taking everything in.

She laughed. "That's why you're here."

"Yeah, you need all the help you can get if the rest of the place is as bad as this living room. Hope you still remember how to take down a wall," he teased.

She grinned. That was how they'd met. He'd mistaken her for a construction worker and ordered her to knock down a wall. Luckily, she'd worked in construction for two years during college and was able to take it down in a time that impressed him. They'd been friends ever since.

"Let me give you the rundown before we start the grand tour," she said excitedly. "There are three bedrooms, one bathroom, an attic, living and dining room, and a kitchen."

"Okay, now give me the real statistics," he said, leaning against the wall.

"The electrical wiring needs redoing, and most of the plumbing needs to be updated. He wants another bathroom, which will mean wall removals upstairs, and I won't even start with the work needed with the fireplace—special cutting for the crown molding and built-ins—and then there are the cracks in the foundation and mysterious gaps in the roof frame, and it all needs to be done in six months."

He ran a hand through his sandy blond hair. "I see—so the usual, then." He grinned.

"I just wanted you to know what you were getting into before you made a firm commitment."

"Really? So you haven't already told the owner you have a hardworking, reliable crew who is willing to do anything to get the job done?"

She avoided his gaze.

"I thought so."

"Do you want the job or not? I can find another contractor if you're not interested."

He pushed his lean, six-foot-two frame upright and walked toward her. "You weren't nearly this cocky when I was still in Detroit." He stared her down.

"Yes, I was," she attested. "You've been away from me too long."

A crooked grin pulled at his mouth. "I did forget how arrogant you were."

"Arrogant? Me?"

He shook his head. "Let's get on with it."

Josie led him to the kitchen, where he proceeded to check out the condition of everything there.

"Did you find somewhere to stay yet?" he asked from underneath the sink.

"Yes." How would she tell him without him raising that infernal disapproving eyebrow of his?

"Oh, where?"

"Here."

Danny lifted himself off the floor.

"Here?"

"Yes."

"Why?" He moved to stand in front of her.

"The project has a stringent deadline and the owner wants to make sure we work together closely to avoid delays or complications that could be easily resolved because I'm on site."

"Are you sure shacking up with a client—especially one with a notorious reputation like Patrick Pullman—is a good idea?"

"I'm not shacking up with him!" She put a hand on her hip. "You know me well enough to know that I don't mix business with my personal life, and this situation is no different." Well, at least he didn't give her the eyebrow.

He shook his head. "It's not you I'm worried about."

"He promised a personal recommendation at the end of the job," she stated with conviction.

"What does he want in return?"

She pursed her lips at him in annoyance. "He's getting my restoration services and doesn't expect anything but to have the job done on time, within budget, and to his design specifications."

He remained silent.

Gritting her teeth, she stared at him sternly. "It's really none of your business."

He shrugged. "You're right."

She relaxed, relieved that he was dropping the subject. Their conversation returned to the work ahead.

• • •

A zesty aroma and the sound of laughter welcomed Patrick when he walked into the house. To his surprise, Josie was in the kitchen, a wooden spoon in her hand as she stirred a steaming pot. Seated at the countertop was a man he didn't know.

"I knew you couldn't say no if I got the stove working," the man said, wiggling his eyebrows at Josie. Patrick suppressed the urge to pull the barstool out from under him.

Josie laughed out loud.

He stood, transfixed. It was intoxicating, and different from the laughter they had shared today. That was out of nervousness and embarrassment at falling into the closet. He had held onto her hand longer than needed to see if he would have the same visions as the first time they shook hands. He was both disappointed and relieved when nothing happened.

More laughter interrupted his thoughts and he mentally shook himself. It was dangerous to let her wander into his thoughts as anything more than someone who worked for him. "Ahem."

She shrieked and the man turned around.

"Is scaring me going to become a habit?" she asked, bringing her laughter under control.

"Are after-hours guests going to be a habit?" The moment the words left his lips, he cringed inwardly. He sounded like his father.

Putting down the wooden spoon, she walked over to stand next to the man. "This is Danny Stanley from Stanley Construction. He's the subcontractor for the renovations. I wanted to get a jump start on the renovations, so I invited him here to get familiar with the site before he and his crew got started Monday," she finished in a professional tone. "I forgot to mention he was stopping by. Sorry."

"Nice to meet you." Danny extended his hand.

Patrick shook Danny's hand and changed his tone to one he used to charm new clients. "Guess I'll be seeing more of you."

The glint in Danny's eyes as he sized him up reminded him of junior high and the bullies who thought beating up the senator's son would be fun. This wasn't the schoolyard, but it sure felt like a stand-off.

"I promise not to keep her," Danny said in a way that made him wonder if there was something more to their relationship. Jealousy sliced through him. He avoided Danny's eyes and the challenge that was there.

"Come get me when you're ready to meet," he said to Josie before turning to leave them. She wasn't his to have or even think about, beyond work, and that's how he intended to keep it.

• • •

Josie raised her hand before Danny's face to stop him from saying whatever was about to come out of his mouth.

"What?" he asked with wide-eyed innocence.

She gave him a sideways glance that said his comment wasn't needed or welcome.

He shrugged and turned back to his plate to finish eating. As soon as he was done, Josie ushered him out the door with a quick good night.

She felt unprofessional for not telling Patrick about Danny, but there was nothing she could do about it now and kept her fingers crossed that he would like the changes she had made to the original designs. She went upstairs to Patrick's room, ready for their meeting. She took a deep breath and knocked on the door.

When it opened, he stood in the doorway, naked from the waist up, his wet hair dripping onto his bare shoulders. He held a shirt in his hands. "You ready?"

She stood frozen as droplets of water made their way down the front of his smooth chest, down the taut muscles of his stomach to the trail of bare skin leading to his dark blue shorts. Images of him standing naked under a steaming shower flooded her mind and her nipples tightened, straining against her purple T-shirt, and she prayed he wouldn't notice.

The tightening turned to warmth as it made a painful trip between her legs until she tingled in anticipation. It was a sensation she hadn't felt in a very long time. Her nose filled with the smell of soap and his cologne. Mixed with his skin, it was playing havoc with the muscles along her back, already in motion from the sight of him. She took a strangled breath and averted her eyes as he slipped the shirt over his head.

"Let's meet in the kitchen. The island will give us more room and it's a lot cleaner and sturdier than the dining table." Thankfully, her voice didn't betray her and remained level, despite her feeling otherwise.

Agreeing, he followed her down the hallway to the kitchen, seemingly oblivious to the reaction he'd had on her.

"What's that?" He pointed at the plate of food on the other side of the designs.

"Seafood ravioli."

Dark brows knotted in question.

"Think of it as an apology for not telling you about Danny," she said with a shrug.

He pulled the plate toward him. "Thanks."

"Yes, I cook, too," Josie stated when he looked at her in surprise after taking a bite.

Before him, she spread out the renovation ideas for the kitchen she'd prepared. "As discussed, the electrical and plumbing for the entire house need updating. I plan to start with the kitchen first, if you don't mind."

Shaking his head, he took another bite.

"I made some changes to the original designs you saw. I thought a gas stove would be a better choice for you. There are a couple of models that will fit the style I'm proposing." She continued when he didn't object, merely nodding between chews. She flipped the presentation board over to reveal his new kitchen.

No words left his food-filled mouth, but his eyes said what she wanted to know. He liked the design. Nailed it!

"Is that glass for the backsplash?" he asked when his mouth was empty and he touched the sample.

"Yes. I think it will add something extra, and it comes in a range of colors."

"Good. I'm not a fan of red." He turned the board around to look at it from another angle.

"It seems overwhelming when you see it by itself, but with the ebony cabinets and speckled black countertop, you'll need some color."

"I guess." He wasn't convinced.

"If you really don't like it when you see it all together, then we can change it. Nothing is set in stone."

She reached across the counter to move the cabinet sample out of the way and their hands brushed. Sensations tickled her spine and she ignored them, but couldn't ignore the green eyes watching her. Her eyes wandered to his hands—long, thick, masculine fingers with manicured tips, but there was nothing metro-sexual about them. They said way more than she wanted to know, more than she needed to.

Neither of them moved for several minutes as his eyes found their way to her mouth. She felt the caress of his gaze over her lips, and it was dangerously delicious. Her thoughts wandered to the daydream she'd had earlier of his naked body, but they didn't get far.

"I'll be working from home during most of the restoration." He shifted his position subtly and removed his arm from the countertop. "I'm between cases right now, and I want to take advantage of our time together while I can."

The distance he put between them should have put her mind at ease, but instead it grated her nerves in a way she hadn't expected.

She attempted to keep her tone devoid of annoyance while replying. "Good, that will help."

"I want to be here, especially in the early days, in case you need me."

That's what phones are for—hello? "Are you sure the noise won't be too distracting? It can get pretty loud with walls coming down."

"I'll be in my room behind closed doors, but I have noise-reducing headphones if things get bad," he declared.

She twisted her fisted hand into her leg under the table. It was bad enough having him half-naked in the next room, but now he would be at the house all day, every day. *Seriously?* She longed to grab the ravioli she'd made him and dump it in his lap just to remove the smug look on his face. Instead, she showed him the rest of the samples for the flooring and color ideas for the walls.

Half an hour later, Josie closed the door of her room and leaned against it. This was going to be a long project and it wasn't just the timeframe. She sighed with relief before making her way to her bed and sitting on the edge.

The door next to hers closed.

Boxes piled in the corner of the room needed unpacking, but it was the last thing she wanted to do. What she wanted was a stiff drink to drown out thoughts of her new client and the challenging job ahead.

She grabbed her dark blue silk throw covered in silver elephants, a thick candle and the book she was reading, a glass of red wine from the case she bought on the drive down, and headed downstairs.

The leather recliner called to her when she reached the living room. She didn't know why she was drawn to it. Its weathered condition made it a death trap, ready to close her into it, but she didn't care. It welcomed her in a way none of the other seats did. She covered it with her blanket, lit the candle until the room was a soft glow, and set the wine and her book on the table next to the chair.

She eased tentatively into the recliner to make sure it would hold her weight. It did. She pulled the handle to slowly release the leg rest and held her breath as she leaned back. Once again, the chair didn't disappoint. Picking up the glass of red wine, she took a sip. "This is better."

The room around her was a neglected mess, but she saw it for what it was—a beautiful challenge. Despite her confident proposal to Patrick, this job unnerved her in ways no other had. Fifteen years of experience gave her the skills to handle what needed to be done, but the stakes scared her. Her life savings, her only real friend's business reputation, as well as her own—and then there was Patrick's deadline. Six months was not a lot of time to finish an entire house; she knew how quickly and badly things could get delayed, and how expensive it could become.

His plan to stay at the house during the beginning of the job was an irritation, and she prayed it was only at the beginning. It would be worth it in the end, she knew that, and would make sure to remind herself every day.

The thought of her first night in a room next to him unsettled her nerves, which was another reason for a drink. She'd noticed good-looking men before, from clients to contractors, and occasionally had to deter them from wanting more than a professional relationship, but he was different. With him, she wanted to make the dimple in his cheek wink at her again and have him wrap her in the breadth of his shoulders.

Those kinds of thoughts were dangerous. Answering the door half-naked didn't make things easier, either! At the end of the day, she wouldn't have the luxury of going home to clear her thoughts. He'd be in the room next door, showering naked and sleeping, possibly naked.

Flickering light at the corner of her eye interrupted the candlelit room. Next to the grandfather clock, a silhouetted figure without substance created shadows that danced on the wall behind it. She opened her mouth to scream, but fear suffocated it. Her heartbeat deafened her as the figure glided toward her.

It came to stand at the tips of her bare feet and the face of a man materialized, making the goose bumps on her exposed arms jump in a frantic attempt to leave her skin. She sat frozen as he watched her with profound intensity.

Something that resembled a slow smile came across where his face should have been. It was not made of flesh, which made it difficult to see his features clearly. His transparent hand reached out toward her and her heartbeat, which had slowed during his careful scrutiny, leaped back to a frenzied pace. She wanted to run, but the position of her body in the recliner made it impossible.

What would happen if she did run or scream? Would he turn into a decaying corpse, screaming at her despite the smile? Before she could contemplate it more, he slowly dematerialized, leaving behind a floating trail of condensation similar to talking in cold weather.

Had she really seen a...ghost? She looked at her wine glass. No, she'd only had one glass, but since when did drinking produce ghosts? Never! Blood pulsed wildly against her temple in fear at what she'd seen—or hadn't seen. The clock on the other side of the room struck one o'clock, startling her. Had an hour really passed?

"Time is the least of your problems, Josie." Pushing the recliner back to its upright position, she looked around frantically to make sure it was really gone. The dimly lit room suddenly closed in on her, casting dark shadows in corners that weren't there earlier. She shot out of the chair and headed to the light switches, turning them all on. Light filled the room, with the exception of the odd missing bulb, and revealed nothing but dust bunnies. She breathed a deep sigh of relief.

Now what? She could knock on Patrick's door and tell him what she had seen, but what good would that do? The last thing she wanted was her new client to think he'd hired a psychotic person. Besides, what would she say? 'Hey, I just saw a ghost. Can I sleep in your room?' Yeah, that would go over well.

She blew out the candle and picked up the glass of wine from the table, her liquid courage to sleep. She made sure the lights in the stairwell were turned on before the ones in the living room were turned off.

She closed her room door and pulled the chain across the newly installed deadbolt lock. Reason told her the lock couldn't keep the ghost from coming into her room, but it gave her some comfort anyway. What the heck had she gotten herself into?

Chapter 4

Josie woke to the smell of coffee the next morning, stretched, and got out of bed. Peaceful sleep instead of nightmares with ghosts had been her bedmate.

Looking down at her striped long-john pajamas, she decided to change. Being covered from head to toe would help to remind her and Patrick that she was here in a professional capacity. *Then why are you combing your hair?* She placed the brush back on the dresser. Quick fingers through her tresses was her usual morning routine. Giving herself a once-over in the mirror, she headed downstairs.

Patrick was in the kitchen, whistling and pouring himself a cup of coffee. To her dismay, he was naked from the waist up, a pair of plain green pajama bottoms hanging precariously on his hips, giving her a view of the muscles on his back and other curves on his body. Her imagination took off, starting with her fingers running down the length of his back and tugging playfully at his pajamas while she took a mischievous bite of his...

"Good morning."

Josie's head snapped up. He was facing her now, a hand moving quickly through his hair to get it under control.

"Morning." *Oh God, did he see me staring at his lower body?* So much for reminding him of her professional capacity.

His friendly expression said he didn't notice.

"Coffee?" he asked, a cup dangling from his hand.

"Yes, thanks," she mumbled.

His eyes moved over the length of her body, then at his own apparel. "I wasn't expecting you up this early."

He turned to pour her a cup of coffee, and she averted her eyes to keep her imagination from running wild again. She kept her eyes above his neck when he handed her the coffee. "I'm an early riser. My mother..."

She started to say she'd gotten into the habit for her mother, but took a seat at the island instead. She added two sugars and took a sip. Her eyes met his with surprise. "Good coffee."

"Only good?" he teased.

Looking at him over the rim of the cup, she smiled. "Okay, it's really good."

"It's my one skill in the kitchen," he said with a grin.

Her eyes dropped for a quick glance down to his waist and then back up to his chest to watch the muscles of his arms flex as he took a drink from his cup. Green eyes were watching her when she found them. Her breath stopped in her throat. They said 'I caught you' and he was enjoying it.

His eyes darkened before they made their leisurely way down her fully covered body. She might as well have been standing before him naked, as he'd stripped her right down to her pink cotton polka-dot underwear. Heat rushed to her cheeks and she adjusted the collar of the blouse around her neck. Well, there was one more thing he was good at in the kitchen—undressing her with his eyes.

He came around the island and she kept her eyes on the kitchen wall behind him, away from the sexy, flexing muscles walking towards her. Her senses were bombarded with the intoxicating smell of his skin before he even reached her. She felt herself grow moist. *Oh God.*

He took the seat next to her.

She didn't dare turn and look at him, afraid he might see the evidence in her eyes that her body was betraying her, which was ridiculous.

"Sleep well?" he asked in a low husky tone.

The distance between them suddenly disappeared and his words were right next to her ear, seductive and sensual. She wanted to move her chair, but remained still.

"Fine," she croaked.

"Good. I was worried the house would keep you awake with its noises."

"Noises?" she asked, remembering the ghost. Had he seen or heard something last night, or since he moved into the house?

He shrugged. "Creaking floors, wind through the windows. You know, the kind of noises old houses make."

"Oh."

"What noises did you think I was talking about?"

The mischief in his eyes told Josie she had to make a choice. Continue to let their relationship become informal, or set ground rules, as she did with all her clients.

They'd be living under the same roof for the next six months and rigid interaction would make things more uncomfortable than the sexual tension between them, but she didn't want to give the impression she was open to a 'casual' relationship.

Under normal circumstances, she might consider it. It had been a long time since she'd been this sexually attracted to a man, but she had too much at stake. "I think we should set some ground rules, don't you?"

Patrick's expression turned solemn after a spark of disappointment. "What kind of rules?"

"For one, the dress code." Her gaze ran along his naked chest, then back to his face.

He pulled his pajama bottoms farther up onto his hips, removing the tantalizing view she'd had since coming downstairs.

"No half-naked bodies before noon," she said with a playful grin.

He nodded curtly. "What else?" he asked.

She groaned silently at his solemn tone. Her smile hadn't helped the way she hoped. "We'll be under the same roof for a long time, so we'll need boundaries. We'll let each other know if we pass them, okay?"

"Okay."

His pensive eyes traveled over her face. "I'll make the coffee. You do breakfast, as well as dinner?"

"You're expecting me to cook, too? That'll cost you extra," she teased.

"I'm sorry, I didn't mean to imply..."

She laughed. "I was kidding. I don't mind cooking. I'm here rent free, after all."

Serious eyes held her. "It's not expected."

"I know. I don't mind; I enjoying cooking as much as eating." Her gaze became mischievous. "I'm getting the better end of the bargain. The kitchen is being renovated first, remember?"

A frown creased his lips, along with disappointment.

"Don't worry. I do wonders with a toaster oven. Just be prepared to gain a few pounds."

He pulled at his side muscles. "I'll risk it."

Waves of warmth flowed between them and their mutual gazes lingered a little longer than necessary before they looked away at the same time.

"So." He interrupted the silence. "What's on the agenda for today?"

She looked him over. "How about you put on a shirt, then we'll talk?"

He laughed. "All right. Give me five minutes."

She was glad things remained civil and she wouldn't be tortured by his naked flesh every morning. *What a way to go!* Shut up! It was better this way. She didn't need a relationship with anyone right now, especially a client.

• • •

A week later, Josie watched the back of Patrick's neck as he inspected the progress of the kitchen's demolition, and she wished she could reach out, put her hands around it, and squeeze until he stopped breathing.

"How much longer before we get started putting in the cabinets and appliances?" he asked, blocking the doorway.

Taking a deep breath, she pulled him out of the way so a worker with dismantled cabinetry could get out. It was becoming a constant habit for both of them, him getting in the way and her moving him.

"Well, Patrick, as you can see, we're still doing the demolition. The new plumbing and electrical need to be done *before* we can start fitting out the kitchen." It was the second time this week she reminded him.

He frowned. "Why is it taking so long?"

She suppressed the urge to tackle him to the ground and shake him violently while shouting, 'We just started three days day ago!'

She guided him out of the kitchen to let another worker by. "We'll go today and pick out your appliances and your backsplash, but it will be another two to three weeks before we put them in. Until then, you'll have to be patient." *And get off everyone's back so we can work.*

"We'll be working on the living room at the same time, so that'll keep us to your deadline," she assured him. "We start moving stuff to the attic tomorrow morning—"

"I want to be here so nothing gets damaged," he interjected.

"That's fine." She forced a smile and nodded before continuing. "The paint store is on the list. We'll pick up samples of the colors you selected so you can make sure you like them on the walls."

His expression perked up. "Good."

Finally! He'd been so serious since the demolition started that she was beginning to wonder if pod people had taken over his body. "Great!" Now she wouldn't have to strangle him—not yet. "I'll call you when I'm ready to leave."

She pushed her way through the layers of plastic blocking the entrance to the staircase to keep out the dust from the demolition downstairs. Patrick was still hot on her heels when she reached the top. When he didn't head to his room but continued to follow her, she turned. "Were you planning to follow me to the bathroom?" she asked without a hint of the agitation she felt.

His cheeks darkened with embarrassed. "No."

"Good." She continued down the hall as Patrick veered into his own room.

The man was incorrigible! It was early to start picking out some of the items she planned for today, but it was the only thing she could think of to get him out of the house. She didn't have the luxury of avoiding him, but she could ensure the crew was able to work without him getting underfoot.

Back in her room, she reviewed the designs they'd agreed on and got the samples they'd need. She picked up her handbag and keys, and then cringed when the door creaked as she opened it. That creak had been her nemesis from the day she moved in, telling Patrick of her comings and goings. She grabbed a can of WD-40 and was in the process of spraying the lower hinges when she heard a voice.

"Planning on sneaking out?" Patrick asked looking down at her.

"Yeah, I've got a hot date tonight, and I don't want my...client hearing me leave." Mischief filled her eyes as she stood up.

"That statement sounds like it's missing a word or two."

'Pain in the ass' wasn't appropriate; at least not to his face. She smiled. "I'll be ready in five minutes."

"I'll wait for you downstairs. We'll take my car."

The grandfather clock loomed in the corner of the living room when she got downstairs and she shivered when she remembered the ghost. Thankfully, it hadn't reappeared.

She smiled with professional satisfaction at the progress they'd made, even with his constant comments about the slow progress. Clients!

So far, the only issue was the electrician, who failed to show up. She and Danny kept a list of backup contractors, though, and a replacement electrician was slated to be on site later that day.

Patrick backed into the living room to make way for two men moving out the kitchen sink. They bumped into the wall, taking a chunk out, and then banged the front door against the wall to get to the dumpster set up outside. "Ready to go?" he asked when he saw her.

To her surprise, he opened the door for her. Did men still do that? No one she knew. "Thank you." The soft, neat interior of his BMW welcomed her frame. "No leather?" she teased.

"I don't like leather."

"Really?"

He gave her a sideways glance. "Yes."

"Are you okay?"

"Yes." He shifted in the seat and sat up straighter and stiffer.

"You're doing a terrible job of hiding it." She shook her head and laughed.

He gave her a strange look. "Why'd you say that?"

She turned in the seat. "Well, you're sitting straight enough for me to iron a shirt on your back."

He laughed and shivers ran up her back at the intimacy of it within the small confines of the car. The smell of his skin—which she tried to forget each night before going to bed—invaded her nose.

"Not convinced, huh?"

She shook her head.

He grinned and his dimple winked at her. *Damn! I could seriously get used to that.* She hadn't seen it much the last couple of days and hadn't realized how much she missed it.

"I know I can be...controlling," he said.

Silence.

"Okay, I can be very controlling," he confessed.

"Yes, you can," she agreed, "but you're the client and you're on a tight deadline." She suddenly felt guilty for thinking about choking him earlier.

After running a hand through his hair, he returned it to the steering wheel. "I didn't realize renovations were such a..."

"Challenge?" she supplied.

"I was going to say 'pain in the ass'." He grinned.

She laughed. "Few people do. It doesn't help when you're staying at the house, with the noise and people handling your things in your space. Personally, it would drive me crazy."

"I thought it was just me."

"No, it's extremely stressful. There's still time to change your mind and stay downtown," she suggested, mentally crossing her fingers. To her disappointment, he shook his head.

"It's too far to commute and I need to be hands-on with this project."

Chills attacked her back at the thought of him being hands-on with her. Pushing them aside, she changed the subject. "Why did your uncle let the house fall apart?"

A sharp look cut across her before his eyes returned to the road. *Wrong topic, Josie!*

His face crinkled in pain before returning to his calm, Pullman expression. "He just did."

She longed to ask more questions, but his politician look said 'don't bother'. "So, growing up a senator's son must have been difficult." She hoped this topic wasn't off limits.

'What do you think?' his eyes answered, but he said, "It still is."

"I sympathize; I couldn't do it."

He looked at her in surprise. "Why? Most people don't think so."

"Well, you're in the public eye all the time. Your family is constantly scrutinized, and criticized. You would never know who your real friends are, if they wanted you for your name or what they could get from you." Oh crap, that last statement applied to her. She blushed.

A cynical smile curled his lips.

"Sorry, I hadn't thought of it until now."

He shrugged. "Don't worry about it. At least you're offering something tangible, and you don't want anything illegal. That's better than most."

Words didn't come, so she touched his arm. The heat of his skin sent a delicious shiver up her arm and across her chest. A quick glance at him showed his eyes had darkened. *Does he feel it too?* She didn't have time to dwell on it.

"So, where's the first stop?"

"Tiles Incorporated." She rattled off the directions before she looked out the window. The tingles that started with touching him lingered. Her other connections usually passed, but this one hadn't. It grew stronger each time they touched.

She breathed a sigh of relief when he pulled into the parking lot. "Here we go," she whispered when she got out the car and headed toward the store entrance.

"Are you hungry?" she asked hours later after they visited the last store on her list. She'd thought being in public places with him—picking out appliances, color and tile samples—would make it easy for her to keep him at a distance. No such luck. Their time alone had been more intimate than at the house, crowded with people working. Every brush of their hands and glance at each other drove her crazy.

She wanted to get home and find solace in her room and in Billie Holiday's calming tunes, but it wasn't five o'clock and she'd promised Danny when he called that she'd keep Patrick out until then.

Surprise flickered in his eyes. "Sure. You pick the place."

"Not a good idea. I've only eaten at two restaurants since I moved here—the deli and the pizza place. Both are within walking distance of your house."

"Pizza it is." He started the car and pulled out of the parking lot.

She smiled when he opened the restaurant door and pulled out her chair when they got to their table. "Your mother taught you well. I can't remember the last time a man held out a chair for me who wasn't a waiter."

His dimple winked at her when he sat across from her. "Actually, it was my father. He's old-fashioned about things like that."

"Really? Does that mean you got your charm from your mother?" she teased.

He chuckled. "No, that's mine." His gaze softened when it reached her. "We can't all be as sweet as you."

She glowed under his compliment before she saw the sarcastic smile tugging at the corners of his mouth. "Cute, very cute."

He let out a boisterous laugh, drawing the attention of the people at the next table.

She was mesmerized. He'd never laughed outright before; it was usually controlled. His face transformed. Gone were the hard lines around his eyes, and it made him look cheerful. His lips moved across his even white teeth with each laugh and her stomach shifted uncomfortably. It made him more attractive—something she hadn't thought possible.

Black and white images shimmered softly before her of his mouth smiling and his eyes filled with playful wickedness as he looked down at her beneath him.

I am in big trouble. The end of this project needed to come, and quickly.

•••

Miles Davis tunes flowed through the speakers, breaking up the awkward silence that had lingered in the car after they left the restaurant. Shadows of buildings and trees passing outside the car ran like a movie across the windows.

"So, you really like jazz music, huh?" He'd selected this radio station because it had drifted through the walls of the house the first night she moved in.

Some nights it distracted him from the fact she was right next door, while other nights the soft, seductive music made it painfully obvious she was there, under his roof, and he was flooded with thoughts of her long elegant neck, or a wisp of hair that'd fallen in front of her face earlier that day that he longed to brush aside. Thoughts of her wouldn't bother him so much if they were just of the sexy curve of her ass or her breasts in the T-shirts she wore, but they weren't, and that was the problem.

"I didn't realize you could hear it. I'll turn it down."

"I don't mind. It reminds of visits with my uncle as a child."

Her warm gaze met and held his before returning to study the scenery outside.

His insides tightened. She had been quiet for most of the meal in the restaurant and he searched his mind for something that had upset her, but he came up with nothing. She had recently lost her mother, so maybe that was the reason. Whatever it was, it wasn't his concern, and neither was making her smile again.

"Why jazz?" He tried again. She hadn't answered him the first time.

She shrugged. "The connection is stronger for me than with any other music."

"Hmm, my uncle used to say that. It was the only music he listened to, other than the occasional tragic opera." *Why would I tell her that?* Sharing personal things with her was becoming a bad habit. One he needed to break.

"Really?"

He nodded, but let his conversation stop there. She had a knack for making him talk without asking. If he wasn't careful, he might accidentally spill his guts, or a family secret. Silence was better.

He parked the car along the curb.

She was out of the car and halfway to the front door before he got to the walkway, but she didn't go right in. No lights were on inside the house. "My keys are inside," she called out.

The entryway closed in around them as he fidgeted with his keys to get the door open. Light from the street provided only a soft glow. He felt her eyes on him, caressing his face and neck, but he didn't look at her. The control he'd held onto all night might disappear, and the urge to pin her against the side of the entryway and run his hands over her curves while he kissed her would win.

He cursed when he couldn't find the keyhole, and he vowed to have Danny replace the regular lights with motion sensor ones tomorrow. He wanted to shout in relief when the key finally went into the lock. Their night had felt like a first date, from the quiet dinner conversation to the awkward silence in the car and the lingering sexual tension, but it wasn't a date.

"Good night, Patrick." Her voice was barely a whisper.

"Night," he said quickly, afraid if he said more, he would say the wrong words. Words like "wanna come to my room?" The sooner he got away from her, the better.

* * *

Nine o'clock flashed from the clock on her nightstand. Josie leaned back in the chair and glanced down at her desk. The surface was covered in stacks of paperwork with design sketches and various paint color, wood, and tile samples. She looked down at the work scattered before her and knew she needed a break from the giant monster ready to consume her room, and the enjoyment she felt with new projects.

The jazz club she'd seen the day before while walking the neighborhood for design ideas came to mind. She took a quick shower and slipped into a black dress.

When her door opened silently, she smiled victoriously; her nemesis had been defeated. The light under Patrick's room door said he was still awake, so she walked quietly down the staircase and out the front door.

Cool night air washed over her when she stepped outside. Wind rushed past her and blew through her hair as she made her way to the sidewalk. Stress from the past few days fell like rain at her feet with each step she took away from the house, down the street, and around the corner, revealing one beautiful building after another.

As she got closer to the downtown area, the people passing her on the sidewalks thickened, like ants flowing from a disturbed anthill. Enticing smells came from the restaurants and lights flickered from the other shops lining the street.

Within the crowd, the Jazz Joynt was a beacon of orange neon. Anticipation seared her as she headed down the gray concrete steps leading below the street. On impulse, she ran her hands along the wall and was mesmerized by the electric sensations running along her fingertips, then her arm. They spread to the rest of her body the closer she got to the bottom. The intensity of the connection was the same she'd felt walking into Patrick's home. But where his house had felt like home, this place was like an old friend welcoming her back. *I've been here before.*

The noise of shoe clicks and stomps on the sidewalk faded, along with the murmured voices and scattered laughter. As she neared the bottom of the steps, the noise transitioned to the faint sounds of instruments in the distance, as if coming from the other side of the wall. The stairwell opened onto a large room before her and she stood in the entryway until her eyes adjusted to the dimmed lighting.

Quick, sharp laughter and muffled conversations filled her ears, along with the clinking of glasses not only at the bar. Neon lights flickered from two corners of the room, casting colored shadows against the walls and floors onto the people seated at small round tables.

A wooden bar, off to one side at the back of the room, provided minimal seating. The size of the club was difficult to determine, even as her eyes adjusted to the poorly lit room. Steps led up to a second level of the club, bordering one edge of the compact wooden stage below.

The atmosphere reeked of cheapness and a time before No Smoking signs, and manifested every idea of jazz clubs that formed in her mind the moment she had first heard Billie Holiday's voice. The age and character of this one did not compare to the modern clubs she went to in Detroit. It was jazz club heaven.

If you didn't smoke, it didn't matter; the air was filled with it, drifting around the ceiling of the club like shifting clouds as each smoker blew more smoke into the already thick air.

She headed tentatively toward a table close to the stage; taking a seat, she blended in with the sights and sounds.

The band was playing "Ain't Nobody's Business," and although no one was onstage singing, the words formed in her mind. She closed her eyes and a smile tugged her lips as she heard Billie's voice echo in her mind.

Someone touched her lightly on the shoulder. "Would you like a drink?"

Looking down at her was a dark, wrinkled face; someone, she was certain, who had had the privilege of hearing Billie sing in person. His eyes held hers for a moment and a sharp twinge ran up her back. He smiled and showed even white teeth, which she suspected weren't his.

She nodded nervously.

"Red wine, maybe?"

"Thanks." She watched the weathered old man make his way behind the bar with an agility she wished she could bottle up and store for when she got to his age.

He returned with her drink and waved his hand at her money. "It's on the house."

"Thanks." *Did he feel the same recognition I did?* "You're not from Detroit, are you?" She leaned closer across the table to get a clearer view of his face.

He chuckled. "No. Lived here all my life. Just move here?"

"About two weeks ago."

"Welcome back," he said, then frowned at his choice of words.

"Thanks." He had felt something. First there was the house, then Patrick, now this club and the bartender. What other connections would she make?

He headed back to the bar.

Taking a drink of her wine, she leaned back in the chair and smiled at the choice of song by the band—"Them There Eyes." Her eyes closed and the sound of the instruments flowed over her skin and her mind until she was a part of them. The words formed silently and she mouthed them, surprised that she didn't care if anyone saw her.

"The stage is open if you want to go up and sing."

The friendly bartender was smiling down at her. She shook her head. "Thanks, but I don't sing."

"Really? Too bad. I bet you're good."

"I'd rather eat nails." The words slipped out before she could stop herself. Heat rushed to her cheeks. Like everyone else, she sang in her car and in the shower, but anything more terrified her.

He chuckled. "Pearl is singing the next set." He nodded toward the willowy, dark lady at the edge of the bar.

Straight out of a black-and-white movie, she was dressed in a knee-length, blue-sequined number, complete with several rows of long string pearls and short, wavy, heavily greased hair. She wasn't as old as the bartender, and he was easily in his seventies, but she wasn't far behind. Strange, Josie hadn't noticed her earlier.

Josie smiled at her, but the woman watched her with wary eyes that narrowed into slits the longer they looked at each other. A chill of recognition ran down the back of her neck; this lady's glare was ice.

"She could show you a thing or two." Joe said with a toothy grin.

She doubted Pearl wanted to show her anything but the street outside. "I'm Josie Fagan." She extended her hand to him and hoped it would distract him from the topic.

His pleasant face underwent a series of expressions that made waves in the wrinkles around his eyes and mouth before he reached out and shook her hand. "I'm Joe, just Joe."

"Nice to meet you, just Joe." *What was that?* His reaction was significant. Did he know her parents? She didn't remember them ever visiting Chicago, but maybe they did before she was born.

"Enjoy the music," Joe said. He headed toward the stage and whispered to one of the band members.

Part of her wanted to leave after Pearl and Joe's reactions, but another part was enjoying the music too much to leave just yet. Another song started, one she recognized immediately, because it was her favorite. "*Lover Man.*" Instead of hearing Billie's voice in her head again, the urge to sing slammed into her. She shifted nervously in her seat, crossed her legs when they moved to stand up, and glanced around the room to distract her from the sensations overtaking her body.

A burning awareness spread out across her skin, as if heat was passing through her body. Someone, or something, was trying to get inside her. Prickles of fear raced up her back. Her connections had never tried to take over before. *Stand up!* The command radiated through her body and the corners of her mind. *NO!*

Her knuckles hurt and she realized she was tightly gripping the edge of the table. She nearly jumped out of her skin when warmth touched her shoulder. A man with his hands outstretched stood next to her.

"Want to dance?"

Whatever had tried to disturb her was suddenly gone, leaving no trace; only her own anxiety remained. She took the stranger's hand and let him lead her to the dance floor.

• • •

Patrick looked up from his book when he heard the front door open. Twelve o'clock flashed on his watch. He held his breath and waited for Josie to walk into the living room. He heard her leave earlier and decided to wait up for her. It hadn't stopped him from thinking about her or wanting her. *Pathetic!*

Her humming filled the room and when she reached him, his closed jaw creaked open. Before him, she stood in a thigh-length black dress that clung to shapes of her body in ways not even his imagination had conjured up.

"Hot date?" he choked out.

She laughed throatily and he gripped the book in his lap tightly. It was sexy, intoxicating—different from her usual laugh. Her sultry gaze moved from the top of his head to the tips of his toes and back up again, undressing him. *Oh God!* He felt himself harden painfully.

"Hot, yes; date, no," she purred.

She walked toward him, her hips swaying slowly. Her eyes and seductive grin said '*I'm coming to get you.*' With each step she took, she slid one strap of her dress down from one shoulder and then the other, gliding it down the length of her body, past each curve and sexy leg until it was a pile next to her high heel shoes and she stood before him in a black lace bra and panties.

"Patrick?"

A hand was waving in front of his face, trying to get his attention.

He pulled the recliner back into an upright position and hoped it hid his erection. He put the book in his lap just to be sure.

"Yeah," he muttered, embarrassed. *What the hell happened?*

"Are you okay?"

She'd obviously either tried to speak to him or ask a question. Gone was her sultry look, and in its place was the friendly but composed expression he was accustomed to. Her black dress, knee-length and sexy, was nothing compared to the dress he'd seen her in moments ago.

"Yes." His tone was more a question than an answer. "Why?" His eyes darted to her face.

Her eyebrows narrowed and her lips broke into a crooked grin. "I asked you the same question three times, and you didn't answer."

"Really? I was elsewhere."

"Where?"

He looked around the room to make sure another woman really wasn't there. *Was he going crazy?* "In the story." He gulped down the words *'you stripping to sexy lingerie',* and wiggled the book in his lap. It wasn't ready to be lifted.

"Must be some story."

"It was—is. What was your question?"

"Couldn't sleep?" She grinned.

He laughed. It was such a simple question and he'd missed it, lost in his illusion. She smiled and looked more tempting than she should. Having visions, or whatever it was he saw of her undressing, certainly didn't help. "Do you have a different black dress?" he asked tentatively.

Her eyebrows knotted tightly. "No, why?"

So much for that idea. "I must've dozed off, and thought I saw you in another dress," he commented offhandedly and hoped he didn't sound completely insane.

She moved to stand at the edge of the recliner. "You imagined me in different little black dress?"

"Imagined, no," he lied. "Dreamed is more likely."

"Do you think it was a ghost you saw?"

"What?"

She shrugged. "You said you might have dozed off, so maybe it was a ghost you saw."

"A ghost in black lace underwear who looked just like you?" He bit his lip to keep from saying more; he'd said enough.

Confusion, then intrigue, and finally embarrassment moved across her face.

"Black lace underwear, huh?" She shook her head. "Couldn't think of anything more original than that?"

He shrugged. "I'm a guy. Our imaginations aren't that complicated; not when it comes to things like that."

"Too bad."

Watching her head up the stairs, he longed to say he was willing to learn, but kept his mouth shut. He remembered her words 'hot yes, date no'. Was that her or part of his illusion?

Nothing like that had ever happened when he visited his uncle, so it must be her. From the moment she walked into the house, she'd turned things upside down. First interrupting his dreams when he was sleeping, and now when he was awake. Things were getting way more complicated than he liked.

• • •

Josie leaned against her bedroom door. Her hands ran along the wall to find the light switch. The warmth of the room welcomed her and she embraced it, still a little shaken by Patrick's questions. His confusion had mirrored the fear she felt when she saw the ghost. It wasn't the one she'd seen; she was certain his expression wouldn't be the open desire burning in his eyes if it had, but he'd seen something, and it wasn't just her in sexy lingerie.

A secret smile tugged at her lips. His inspection gave her a small measure of female pleasure, but not enough to do more, even after he admitted to imagining her half-naked. Tempting him would be like tempting a tiger with a giant steak, but instead of getting her arm ripped off, it would be her heart.

Behind this door, she could imagine anything she wanted, including what it felt like to have him run his hands and lips over her naked body. Outside her room, she'd be what everyone, including herself, expected: Josie, professional restoration architect, polite and in control. Without that control, things went awry.

She took a step toward the bed and her heel knocked against an envelope. Her heart raced as she picked it up. Was it from Patrick? Turning it over, she opened it slowly.

Inside were old photos. She brought the first faded photo closer. It was a face she knew well: serious eyes, laughing mouth, and stubborn chin. Her hands shook as she stared at herself in black and white.

Walking over to the bed, she sank onto the mattress. Someone knew she was staying in the house and which room was hers. Fear gripped her in a way it hadn't since the night the ghost appeared. She took a calming breath. *You're overreacting.*

Flipping to the other photo, she felt faint. It was a photo of her mother and the woman with her face. '*Lola and Mary Johnson before Lola left for Chicago*' was written on the back. Time stopped along with her heartbeat. Johnson was her mother's maiden name. *Who was Lola?*

Chapter 5

Josie ran a hand through her hair as she watched Patrick in Danny's makeshift kitchen—in a corner of the living room untouched by construction. Their morning meetings were usually spent discussing work for the day, but this morning she had difficulty concentrating.

It'd been three days since she found the envelope in her room. Her first thought was to ask Patrick if he'd left it there, especially given his look of recognition the first day they met, but the photo of her mother and Lola stopped her from asking him the next morning, and the morning after that. Her mother couldn't answer questions about Lola, like why she'd never mentioned her, ever. There was no one at home to question, but she did have a home to search.

Across the room, he whistled as his fingers tapped the top of the coffeepot. Before she went back to her mother's house, she had to be sure it wasn't him. Asking him once Danny and the crews arrived would be difficult. "Did you leave an envelope in my room?" Her breath hitched as she waited.

A single eyebrow rose in question. "No. What was in it?"

She flinched inwardly at his careful study of her. There were too many unanswered questions, and the last thing she wanted was her client to think she had problems that could interfere with his project. "Danny or one of the guys must have left it," she answered with a wave of her hand.

His skeptical gaze said he didn't believe her.

"Is coffee ready?"

"Yes." He poured out two cups. "Milk and two sugars, right?" he asked without turning around.

She smiled faintly as she took the steaming cup from his hand. It was perfect. That he remembered was a simple thing, but it struck a chord.

"What's the plan for today?" he asked, leaning casually against the wall.

"I'll be gone today," she said cautiously, "but Danny will be here to make sure the crew stays on track. I'll be back tonight."

Surprise and then disappointment crawled over his face before he prodded. "Where're you going?"

Taking off in the middle of the week this early in a project was an eyebrow raiser, but a bad explanation was foolish. "My mother's house. I have things to take care of." She held her breath and hoped he didn't ask why she couldn't wait until the weekend. She could, but didn't want to.

The turmoil in his eyes said he wrestled with wanting to ask more questions. Whether it was the politician or the lawyer in him, he didn't press her further, but softened his expression. "Do you need company?"

"Thanks, but no." He was offering to go with her?

He closed the distance between them and placed a hand on her shoulder. "A loved one's death is nothing to take lightly," he said softly.

Inquisitive green eyes made her heart melt like ice cream in the sun. Why couldn't he remain his arrogant, pain-in-the-ass-client self all the time? It made it difficult to keep him at a distance when he wasn't.

The problem wasn't just the client, it was the job. The connections she felt to the house and Patrick were strong. No matter how hard she tried to keep them both at a distance, they were quickly making their way under her skin, like a bad habit. "Thanks," she whispered and lowered her eyes from his probing gaze.

The hand on her shoulder moved to her neck and the pulse beating there quickened as it moved to her cheek. His thumb caressed the side of her face and her heart melted with each touch he made. She needed to step away from him and the exquisite touch of his skin against hers, but her body refused to cooperate.

"You can talk to me if you need to, Josie."

Her blood bubbled at the sound of her name so low and intimate on his lips. She swallowed hard. Words escaped her, the gentle caress of his hand silencing her words. She held her breath as he closed the already short distance between them so their bodies were inches away from touching. His head lowered toward hers and her breath stopped even as her mouth went dry.

The sound of the front door opening sliced through their intimate moment like a hot knife through butter. They stepped back from each other and she managed to compose herself just as Danny walked in.

"Morning all," he greeted cheerfully.

"Morning," they grumbled together.

He looked at her and then Patrick. "Did I miss something important?"

"No." Patrick moved farther away from her. "I need to go to the office for a few hours. I'll be back later to check on the progress."

"Sure." She gave him a small smile. "See you this evening."

He nodded and left her and Danny alone.

"What do you mean you'll see him this evening?" He grabbed one of the muffins in the jar on the makeshift table and took a big bite.

She shook her head. *So that's why the muffins are disappearing so quickly.* "I'm going to my mom's house today."

He stuffed the rest of the muffin in his mouth, chewed it quickly, and walked over to where she stood. "Are you going to be okay on your own?"

The concern in his voice made her heart lurch. Things would be a lot easier if she was attracted to Danny. He was funny and an all-around good guy. His unkempt blond hair, cute smile, and tall muscular frame made him easy on the eyes, but there was one problem. Other than friendship, there was no spark. Not the fireworks she felt with Patrick.

"You okay?"

She was staring at him and standing closer than she normally would. "I'm fine." She took a step back.

He studied her for a moment. "Josie, if you need someone to talk to..." He seemed to realize what he was offering.

She smiled at his struggle. "I know." Danny was not one to talk to her seriously about anything more than demolition and what was on the schedule for completion, despite being friends for over ten years.

"Go, do what you need to. I'll take care of things while you're gone."

"Thanks, Danny."

"Sure thing."

• • •

Eerie silence greeted Josie when she walked through the door of her childhood home. Her throat tightened when she remembered the day she'd entered her mother's room to find she'd stopped breathing.

The lemon curtains on the kitchen window were the only bright thing in the room. The countertops were fading white Formica with chipped edges and the floors dull brown linoleum. The rest of the house was the same—stuck in the past. A time when her father was alive and they were happy. She'd lost two parents the day he died. His death had devastated her mother and put her into a deep depression from which she'd never recovered. Josie never changed the house. The familiar spaces kept her mother grounded—sane—most of the time.

She made her way to the back of the three-bedroom house. Using the house as collateral to start her business was something she'd needed to do as badly as she needed leave the house and move to another town. It was the only thing her mother had done to help her. She swallowed the bitterness rising in her throat. She wouldn't let bad memories, or the mountain of debt her mother left behind, taint her memories.

Her hand hovered over the doorknob of her mother's room. The sight of her mother lying motionless in her bed, her eyes empty caverns of black, flashed before her and she squeezed them shut to block out the vision. Beads of sweat formed on her forehead as she turned the handle and stepped inside.

Death hung in the room—in the stale, moldy smell of the air, in the thick layer of dust on the surfaces of the dresser and nightstand. Teeth sat in a glass by the nightstand; a housedress was draped over a chair in the corner by the closet doors. This had been her mother's life, in this room that had remained unchanged, like the rest of the house.

The day her mother died was the last time she'd been in here, and when Patrick had accepted her offer, she'd walked away from the house and everything in it. She knew she'd have to come back one day, but did not imagine under these circumstances.

After searching the room for several minutes, she found a square decoupage box on a shelf at the back of the closet. Lifting the lid, she pulled out letters addressed to her mother from Lola Johnson. Her heart stopped in mid-beat. Hands trembling, she opened one of the letters and read.

My darling sister,

Her heart leaped. Lola was her mother's sister. She had a living relative?

> *It's been three months since I moved to Chicago. I found a job singing in a club called The Jazz Palace. I'm onstage every night and singing songs I love to crowds of people.*
>
> *I've met a man, William. He's a good and honest man.*
>
> *Here are a few dollars to help you and Mama. I wish it could be more. Take care, baby sister, and all my love to you.*
>
> *Lola*

She tore into the other letters, hoping to find out more about the woman—her aunt. It explained the emotional pull to go to Chicago; Lola was there. Each one told of Lola's success singing in the clubs and how her relationship was progressing. One of the letters confirmed she married the man she adored. The letters slid from Josie's fingers like a waterfall when she saw her aunt's married name—Pullman.

Chapter 6

Josie clicked the End button on her phone. Another dead end. It'd been two weeks since finding the photos, and she was still in shock. Her mother had a sister she'd never mentioned, and Josie was related to Patrick through marriage.

She picked up a photo lying on her bed of Lola and William's wedding. The resemblance of Lola and William to her and Patrick unnerved her each time she looked at it.

She'd gone home looking for answers, but only found more questions. The person who left the photos didn't want their identity known. Otherwise, they would've left a note to meet; something other than a nameless envelope that had caused her nothing but sleepless nights and dead-end days.

None of the Lola Johnsons in the phone book matched Lola's age and or ethnicity. Not that there were many. The only mention of Lola in the library archive newspapers was her success singing at the local jazz clubs. There were no listings for Lola Pullman and she certainly couldn't call any Pullmans.

Lola's letters hinted that William's family was adjusting to their sudden marriage, especially his brother, Myles. The words weren't said, but the message was there, between the lines. The Pullmans didn't want her in their family.

There were no records of their marriage, or mention of William getting married and having children, even in his later years. Lola was neither from his race or social background. Such a marriage would have been scandalous, especially for someone of his social status. Neither were there obituaries for anyone named Lola Johnson or Lola Pullman.

The letters from Lola to Josie's mother offered no answers, and stopped a few weeks after she and William married. Even if she and William divorced, why stop writing her sister? And why had her mother never mentioned Lola?

Josie twirled a lock of hair around her fingertip. Her family's connection to the Pullmans must be the reason for her strong emotions toward the house, and even Patrick. Was William the ghost she saw her first night at the house?

One thing she knew for certain; the answers were here at William Pullman's house. She couldn't ask Patrick about it—might never be able to ask him. It would complicate or possibly end their working relationship. This job was too important to the success of her business. She could kiss good-bye the high-end clients she wanted to attract. Who wanted to do business with someone who pissed off a Pullman?

She'd wanted to make her start in Chicago, like Lola had. Something had happened to her aunt. Whether it ended well or badly, she needed to find out. Someone felt it was important for her to discover the truth.

• • •

Josie walked to Mr. Roman's house first, and knocked on his door. When she had notified Patrick's neighbors of the renovations, he and Mrs. Anderson mentioned they'd been there since the fifties. They might remember Lola.

Moments later, Coke-bottle glasses and thin strips of gray hair peeked through the door, leaving the chain attached.

"Yes?"

"Hi, Mr. Roman. Do you remember me? I'm renovating the Pullman house."

He peered out and looked her up and down before she heard the chain being removed and the door opened. "Yes, I remember you."

"Could you help me?" she asked tentatively. Would he shout at her the way he did at the kids playing in the streets to keep the noise down? She wasn't shouting, but interrupting his day nonetheless. Everyone in the neighborhood seemed to prize their privacy and routines.

He glared at her before asking, "What do you want?"

"Do you remember seeing this woman in your neighborhood?"

He took the photo and looked at it, and then at her. "It's you."

"She's a relative of mine."

He adjusted his glasses.

"She would've been here in the late fifties, early sixties," she added, hoping it would help.

He lifted his head. "Young lady, I barely remember what I had for breakfast this morning, much less what happened that many years ago!"

She hid her disappointment. "Was anyone else living in the neighborhood then, besides yourself and Mrs. Anderson?"

He paused. "No, everyone else moved away years ago."

"Thanks for your time, Mr. Roman. If you remember anything, I'm right next door."

He didn't respond, but closed the door and put the chain back in place.

She headed to Mrs. Anderson's house, a weight the size of Texas on her shoulders. Foolishly, she'd believed someone would remember her aunt, which was ridiculous. It was nearly fifty years ago.

Knocking on Mrs. Anderson's door, she clutched the photo firmly in her hand.

Strawberry-blonde curls peeked at her from the side of the front door before baby blue eyes perused her from head to toe. "Well, hello there." They twinkled, making them appear younger than the lines on her face indicated.

"Hi, Mrs. Anderson," she said, shifting nervously from one foot to the next.

"Don't stand there dawdling in the doorway, child, come in," she chirped, opening the door wider.

She grinned. Only Mrs. Anderson would call her a child. That wasn't surprising. At her age, she was allowed to treat everyone like a child, and did. She'd dropped off two apple pies since the renovations started. The guys drew straws to see who'd get a slice— even Patrick.

"What can I do for you?" She stood in the entryway, not welcoming her fully inside the house and holding Josie's hand longer than necessary. Her grip was strong for a woman with delicate hands. It must be from working in the garden.

Josie handed her the photo.

She released her hand and brought the photo close to her face, studying it carefully. "Why are you showing me this photo?"

"Do you know her?" She brought the photo of Lola and her mother. William and Lola's wedding was kept a secret and, until she knew why, she intended to keep it that way too.

"Doesn't look familiar. Who is she?"

"My aunt. She stayed in this neighborhood fifty years ago."

"Here?" she asked in surprise.

The neighborhood was still predominately white, and would've been the same back then. "Well, not here, but at William Pullman's house."

"Oh...I see." The crinkles around her eyes lifted. "How scandalous," she said with a chuckle. "I always miss out on all the fun."

Josie smiled, despite the disappointment that gnawed at her that she'd reached another dead end. She'd hoped at least one of them would remember something, even a small clue. "Well, she didn't live there, but was there occasionally, helping Mr. Pullman," she mumbled, wishing she'd thought of a better reason for her aunt being there.

A penciled blonde eyebrow rose. "I see. Did you try Mr. Grump next door? He's as nosy a neighbor as they come."

"Yes. No luck there either." She smiled at Mrs. Anderson's choice of name for him.

"I'm not surprised; he can't remember to wear the same color socks," she clucked. "Didn't she leave a forwarding address?"

"No. I never knew her, but I'm trying to find her." Josie paused to nibble on her bottom lip. "She's the only family I have left."

Anguish crawled across Mrs. Anderson's face, distorting its normally cheerful appearance. The crimson polish on her fingers curled into her palms. "I'm sorry. I know what it's like to lose someone you love," she whispered, her voice heavy with sadness.

Josie looked over to the photos on the entry table and saw one of a handsome young man dressed in uniform, with his arm around a slim attractive woman. "Your husband?"

She nodded. "He died in the war…" Her eyes filled with tears, "…and I never got over it."

"I'm sorry."

With shaky hands, she reached out to caress his face through the picture frame. "No one could replace him, no matter how hard I tried," she said sadly.

Josie touched her lightly on the shoulder. Words stuck in her throat. She knew there were none that would bring her comfort, so she didn't try to fill the silence with empty ones.

"Oh my, I just remembered the apple pies I left in the oven." Her hands went to her rosy cheeks.

"We can't let them burn, now can we?" Josie said with a grin. "Thank you for your time, Mrs. Anderson." She turned to head out the still-open front door.

"Please, call me Sofia," she said with a motherly smile.

"Okay, Sofia." The warmth in her eyes sent a lump straight to her throat, making her wish her mother were still alive. Her mother never said much, but she always had a smile for her daughter, even if it was a sad one.

When her mother died, she'd felt alone. The photos were hope she had family, but if Lola was no longer living in Chicago, the chances of finding her were slim. She'd stopped writing her own sister—an indication she didn't want to be found—but why?

A note from Patrick was waiting for her on the counter when she got back to the house. He'd stepped out for a while. It was Sunday, and the guys had stopped working at twelve after finishing up the plumbing. The new kitchen cabinets were scheduled for installation first thing tomorrow. She had the house to herself.

Her heart raced as she stared at the foot of the stairs that'd been stripped down the bare oak flooring. She could check the attic. There could be treasures up there that might confirm Lola had lived here.

"No!" she said aloud. It would be crossing boundaries Patrick would not understand. *He wouldn't know. It'll only take a moment.* The words taunted her until she gave in and made her way to the attic.

Her hands shook as they gripped the railing of the staircase leading to the attic door. With each step she took, her shoulders felt heavy with the recognition that she was about to cross a line from which she couldn't return. She was about to go through a client's personal things without their knowledge, and not for the purpose for which she was hired.

She sneezed when she took her first breath. Her eyes took in all the furniture from the living room that'd been moved there, making it crowded and difficult to maneuver around. She pushed pieces of furniture aside so she could make her way to the back of the room. At the far corner of the room was a mahogany chest. She scrambled her way toward it, her palms sweating as she lifted the lid.

Inside were a scrapbook, clothes, small jewelry boxes, and posters. *Jackpot!* She grinned with excitement as she took out one item after another. She hadn't expected to find so many things. She opened the scrapbook and flipped through; it was filled with photos of Lola and Josie's mother as little girls, and at different ages growing up. The next pages were photos of Lola outside club entrances. Written underneath one of the photos were the words '*Me and Joe at the Jazz Palace*'.

Standing next to Lola was a young black man with a smile no one could forget. Was it the Joe she'd met days ago? He was certainly old enough, and in the right profession.

A noise from downstairs stopped her hands from flipping the next page. She listened intently. The front door closed.

She froze. "Crap!"

"Hello?"

It was Patrick and he was heading upstairs. She stood still, hoping he would go to his room and not continue looking for her. His footsteps stopped outside the attic door she'd left open. *Stupid!*

"Josie, are you up there?"

Now what? She scrambled to put the items back into the chest, her heartbeat thundering. The last item was placed in the chest just as Patrick's head became visible.

"Hi," she said casually, hoping she didn't sound as breathless as she felt.

He stood at the edge of the items packed closely in the space and his eyes glanced around the room before his eyes found her. He shook his head. "What are you doing in this dust infestation?"

She laughed nervously. "Looking for design ideas." It was more a question than an answer. *Think of something better than that. Nothing!*

He cocked his brow. "In the attic?"

She made her way through the furniture to where he stood. "You'd be surprised what design treasures you find in old houses."

His look said he wasn't convinced.

"Seriously!" she said with conviction.

He put his hands up in defeat. "If you say so; as long as you're not snooping through my uncle's things."

Her foot caught on a piece of furniture and she tripped, landing in a pile of dust bunnies. She coughed several times as she attempted to stand up. Was he serious or joking? Had he read the guilt on her face?

Patrick helped her up.

Her breath stopped when she noticed his eyes search the room behind her and settle on the open lid. She'd run out of time to put it down. She kept her expression as emotionless as she could muster, even as her heart raced out of control. His reference fluttered away on wings in front of her.

His gaze snapped to her. "Is there something you need to tell me?"

"What do you mean?"

"You've been searching my uncle's things?"

"I was merely admiring the designs on various items, she said with a wave of her hand, hoping he wouldn't notice it shaking.

He eyed her suspiciously and looked about the room again for good measure. He took a step closer to her. "You never did tell me what was in that envelope and if you found out who sent it to you."

Panic rose in her throat and she swallowed it back down. "I told you, it was from Danny," she lied. Would he ask Danny about it? She hoped not.

"What was in it?"

"Why?"

"I'm curious why you would ask me if I left it when you knew it was from Danny. Wasn't it obvious when you found it?" Green eyes studied her intently.

Her mind raced for an answer while her mouth opened and closed. "It was personal," she said finally.

"Personal? Too personal to tell me?" His tone was skeptical.

She nodded.

"Very well, Josie. Keep your secrets for now." Determination and danger lurked in his eyes and his words made her feel like a witness on the stand he planned to question again once he found out truth that couldn't be denied. She let out the breath she was holding after he left the attic. The line she crossed when she searched his attic wasn't just her professional ethics. It was into the realm of a man she knew nothing about.

The open chest called to her, but she knew she'd have to wait to get the items, or abandon them all together. Her search was riskier than she planned, but she'd gotten one clue—Joe. If he was the same man, it explained the emotional connection she'd felt to the club and him. The Jazz Joynt was a lead she hoped would have a better outcome than the others.

Chapter 7

A trumpet's tune is in the background, low and slow. The blare of a trombone and the frantic keys of the piano join in. The noise of each new instrument escalates as it joins the others. Their increasing volume is a signal to the crowd, and conversations simmer before halting. All eyes in the room focus on her, waiting. She doesn't see their faces, but the air crackles with excitement. The melody of the song "Lover Man" begins and joy pulses through her.

The excitement heightens when her eyes move to the door and the man who enters the smoky room. His face is clear, as though the spotlight on her has been moved to him. She knows his face, the sparkling, mischievous emerald eyes. Delight clenches her body when he smiles. He moves closer to the stage, his gaze never leaving her.

She closes her eyes when he takes his seat, and she continues to sing. His focus is on her every move. Her hand as it touches the stand of the microphone, and then her hips as they sway in time to the music.

Roguish eyes fill with desire and tingles creep through her every nerve.

With each word she sings, his gaze caresses her until she can feel his touch on her skin, softly at first, but as she nears the end of the song, stronger and more demanding until she is breathless.

She finishes the song and bows her head slightly to the applauding crowd. When she raises her head, the club is empty and she is standing by the bar. They're alone. He is behind her, his hands on either side, caging her.

"You were wonderful tonight," he whispers huskily in her ear.

His breath against her neck floods her mind with images of his mouth on her naked skin, and shivers travel across her. She turns and gives him an inviting smile. His fingers go under her chin and lift her lips to his mouth.

"Open your mouth for me," he whispers, his thumb caressing the side of her cheek.

She does, eagerly, and wraps her arms around his waist. With each soft caress of his tongue against hers, heat starts at the top of her head and works its way to the tips of her toes, spreading across each breast until they tighten, and setting a fire between her legs.

She moans and clings to him as his hands roam over the length of her body, seemingly everywhere at once. Delectable ripples run down the length of her back in anticipation of making love to him. It will be hot, delicious, toe curling.

• • •

Josie was startled awake at the feel of someone touching her shoulder. When her eyes opened, Patrick was leaning over her as she sat in the recliner, which she'd moved to her room the day before.

Her eyes narrowed as her mind struggled to awaken and adjust itself from the dream. Her body still tingled from being thoroughly kissed. If Patrick hadn't woken her, she would've made love to the man in her dreams. She'd felt every sensation Lola had. It should've scared her, but instead, thrilled her right to her toes and other parts of her body. It was supposed to be William in the dream, but because he looked so much like Patrick, she found herself pulled in as more than just an observer.

"Are you okay?" Concern-filled eyes raked over her.

Delicious shivers made a trail down her back as she remembered the seductive smile on the man in her dreams' lips, the sound of his whispers in her ears. The memory of his tongue caressing her own was still vivid in her mind and her pulse drummed in her ears as she looked into eyes that, moments earlier, had been dark with desire. Her gaze caressed his lips before returning to his eyes.

A playful smile tugged the corners of his mouth. She tried to shift her position, but he was too close and there was nowhere for her to go.

"Yes, I'm fine. Why?"

"You were moaning and making other strange noises," he said tentatively.

She blushed and averted her eyes. "It was just a dream."

"Some dream." He straightened up. "At first I thought you had someone in here with you, but your door was open so..." he finished cautiously.

Her eyes shot up and she took a deep swallow before professionalism shadowed her face. She was certain she'd closed—no, locked—her door when she came in earlier. Caution was her best friend since she'd found out about her connection to Patrick's family. Her eyes moved to her desk. Did she lock Lola's stuff away? She breathed in relief. It wasn't there.

"That would be unprofessional." *And wasn't going to happen with him in the next room.* Her calm gaze met his.

"And you're not seeing anyone," he said, matter of factly. "Why is that, Josie? You're an attractive woman. Men should be lined up at the door."

She shifted uncomfortably in the recliner. "That's none of your business." He thought she was attractive? That didn't matter.

He placed both hands on either side of the recliner and leaned closer to her. Her eyes widened and her heart beat loudly in her ears.

"What if I want to make it my business?" His eyes moved to her lips, licking his own before returning his gaze to her eyes.

"I...don't think that would be a good idea," she stammered.

"Why not?" His face moved closer to hers.

"Relationships under contracts only lead to disaster."

"You know this from experience?" The corner of his mouth twitched.

"No, but any sane professional knows that," she stated with more conviction.

"Really? Who?"

Her mouth opened and closed. "I can't think of any right now, but I'll get back to you."

He laughed and touched her nose playfully before he stood back. "Relax, Ms. Fagan. I was only teasing you."

"You're very convincing," she mumbled.

"I'm a lawyer."

"Yes, and that makes you a great liar." She smirked.

"I prefer the phrase 'eluding certain truths.'"

"That's putting it mildly, I'm sure."

"So, what was your dream about?" he asked, changing the subject.

She averted his gaze. "It was just a dream, nothing special."

"It sounded special and...hot." He finished with an arrogant grin.

Her eyes threw daggers at him.

Chuckling, he threw up his hands up in defeat. "Okay, I'll drop the subject."

Her pulse returned to normal when he put distance between them. When he found her in the attic two days ago, she was certain that their working relationship would be strained, but to her surprise, nothing had changed. She hoped it meant that he believed her lie about looking for designs and not that he was drawing her into a false sense of security before he pulled her secret from a file and threw her out the house—no job and no reference.

There was also the possibility he already knew and was toying with her. She pushed aside the fear and agitation.

•••

Patrick leaned against her dresser and realized this was the first time he'd been in her room since the day she moved in. The corners were stacked with design books, and large posters slanted against them. It was a virtual cornucopia of design samples, color palates, and everything to do with home designing. It was vacant of personal items, including clothing on the floor, the bed, or the simple wooden chair tucked under the desk.

A knowing smile tugged at his lips when he saw the surface of her desk. It was clear of paper. There were three stacked black metal trays with the papers piled neatly inside them with the labels 'Approved', 'In Progress', and 'Completed' posted on one side. A matching pencil holder held three pencils and nothing more. It was the complete opposite of the workspace around her, and he couldn't help but think the room was so much like her. Composed and organized on the outside, and piles of unknowns lurking beneath, waiting to trip you up.

He hadn't known what he'd find when he came into her room, but he certainly hadn't expected the residual desire in her eyes when she looked at him. It'd been unnerving, and delectable, making him wonder even more about her dream. Was it about him?

A small silver photo frame caught his attention. Beneath the glass was a photo of a woman, man, and young girl. It was Josie with her parents, both of whom were dead. He couldn't imagine being alone in the world, without family. With all the problems he had with his, they were there for him. He felt the sting of loss every day from his uncle's death and couldn't imagine the pain she felt from losing both parents.

He wanted to reach out and touch her, pull her into his arms and offer her some kind of comfort, but knew it'd be more dangerous than his earlier teasing. Flirting could be laughed off, but an intimate touch and embrace was something else entirely. Their near kiss had been a stupid gesture on his part and one he found himself unable to stop trying to repeat. Every time he was near her, he wanted to put his arms around her, kiss her, and do things to her body that made his mouth water in anticipation.

Shifting one foot over the other to keep his thoughts from drifting in a direction they shouldn't, he noticed for the first time that she sat in his uncle's recliner. "I didn't realize you were a fan of the recliner."

She ran her hands along the arms affectionately. "It grew on me."

"It suits you."

"A crumbling leather chair suits me?"

"I mean…"

"Don't worry, I thought so too." She grinned.

"It was his favorite chair."

"Really? I wonder why?"

He shrugged, although he remembered vividly his uncle's words: "Lola and I had many happy memories in it." It was one of the few things in his final days that made William smile.

"It's nice to have something that was special to him."

Patrick's eyes snapped to her face. It was the same expression she had the first time she saw it. He'd brushed aside any suspicions that arose when he found her in the attic, because he knew this job meant too much to her company to risk jeopardizing it. Was he wrong about that?

"I like to keep souvenirs of my renovations," she said quickly.

"I see," he said, but didn't. Why would she want something of his uncle's, a man she'd never met and didn't know? It didn't make sense, but neither did the visions he saw when they first touched, or the easy way he shared personal details with her.

"I'm going out of town for a few days." The disappointment on her face couldn't be hidden. Did it mean she'd miss him? "You and Danny will have five whole days without me underfoot."

A weak smile was her response. It was written on her face that she wanted to ask where he was going, but bit her lower lip instead. "When do you leave?"

"Tonight." He could tell her, but part of him delighted in her thinking he was doing something other than work. Would she care? Why did he?

"What are you working on while I'm gone?"

"We'll be finishing up the kitchen and working on the chimney in the living room."

"Good. I'll expect updates."

"Of course, Mr. Pullman," she said through gritted teeth.

"Mr. Pullman? Gonna miss me that much, huh?" he teased.

A grin tugged at the corner of her mouth. "No, but I know Danny and the guys will."

"I'm sure they will." He shook his head, certain they'd be celebrating when they heard.

Awkward silence hung in the air closing the room around them until it was small and too intimate for Patrick's liking. Would the day come when he was used to her presence and the way his heartbeat sped up each time she looked at him? God, he hoped so.

Chapter 8

Josie's hand grazed along the concrete wall leading into the club. Raw anticipation bubbled inside her. If Joe was the same man in the photo with her aunt, she would get answers to all the questions plaguing her for weeks. Was Lola still alive? Why had she stopped writing to her family? Was it voluntary, or was she coerced by William and his family? She took a deep breath and headed toward the bar.

"Hello there, young lady." Joe smiled with his perfect teeth.

"Hi, Joe." She took a seat in front of the chunky wooden bar counter.

"You remembered my name." He reached for one of the glass shelves behind him to take off a bottle of red wine.

"You remembered my drink," she replied, pleased, but somehow not surprised. From the moment she met him, he seemed to know more about her than he let on. He was seventy-five if a day and she wondered why he was still working. "Why aren't you retired?" She looked at him sheepishly for having asked such a personal question. They didn't know each other well, but it was a good place to start before easing into questions about Lola.

"I own this joint, and there's no one to leave it to." Sadness traveled over his face.

"You could sell it and retire to some tropical island," she suggested.

"You want to buy it?" he joked.

She shook her head.

"It was my dream to own it for many years. Why retire from your dream?"

She reached out to take a drink of the wine he placed before her. This was going to be easier than she thought. "Then you must have known Lola Johnson."

Darkness clouded his eyes and his head rose to capture her guarded eyes with his probing ones. "Yeah, I knew her," he replied carefully. "Do you?"

"No."

His conflicting comments didn't escape her. He implied she was dead, but then asked "do you" instead of "did you," giving the impression she was alive. The nervous shift of his body gave the game away the moment she mentioned Lola's name. He knew something. Would he tell her?

"Where are you from?"

"Detroit." She turned in her seat to face the band, mainly to avoid more personal questions he might ask. She turned back to the bar at the end of the song.

Both of his hands were braced on the edge of the bar and he was looking straight into her eyes. "Look, young lady, I'm seventy-five-years old—too old to be jerked around."

Heat filled her cheeks. She shifted her bottom on the barstool. "I'm Lola's niece. I didn't know about her until recently, and I'm looking for her."

"Why?"

"She's my only living relative," she mumbled, taking a drink from her glass of wine.

"I'm sorry." He gently touched her hand on the bar counter. "I know what it's like to lose someone you love." His gaze drifted to the stage for a moment before settling back on her. "How'd you know I knew her?"

"Your name is on an old photo, and I thought you might be able to tell me where I can find her."

Old eyes moved about the room before they settled back on her. "I'll talk...if you sing."

She laughed at his ridiculous suggestion, but his expression didn't change. "What? I told you, I don't sing!" Her words fell on deaf ears.

"It's in your blood." He gave her a reassuring smile and nodded toward the stage.

She shook her head, her eyes filled with fear. "I've never sung in front of people before. I'll just embarrass you." *And myself.*

"I saw you mouth the words the first time you were here, and the way you watched the stage. You want to be up there."

She didn't get the chance to argue and watched helplessly as he came from behind the bar and headed to the stage. He whispered in the ear of one of the band members just as the song ended. The music started again. She knew the song instantly. "Lover Man." It was her favorite. Had he played it because she looked like Lola?

Joe came to stand beside her and touched her shoulder reassuringly. "You can do this."

She shook her head again. "I can't."

"You don't sing, I don't talk."

His refusal was a punch in her stomach, or blackmail.

It's not. The words echoed in her mind as clear as if she had thought them. It was Lola. Josie didn't know how, but knew it was her. Her skin tingled as warmth passed over her, penetrating the pores of her skin like the steam of a sauna. Lola wanted in. Unlike the first time, Josie didn't fight her intrusion. To her surprise, calmness settled over her, steadying her rapid heartbeat. She strolled across the club to the stage.

"This is one of my favorites. I hope you enjoy it." The words tumbled confidently from her lips.

She closed her eyes and let the sound of the instruments flow over her skin and pull her into the song. Joy rose inside her, echoed in her voice, and the words flowed easily.

Joe's wide grin faltered for a moment and astonishment flickered in his eyes. At the end of the bar, Pearl's face was filled with pure hatred. Disbelief, as though he'd seen a ghost, was reflected in the eyes of a man seated at a corner table in the back of the room.

Applause flooded the room when she finished. She turned and beamed at the band, who watched her in amazement. Her gaze moved back to the crowd. People seated at the tables in front urged her to sing more. She found herself agreeing and asked the band to play "*Good Morning Heartache*." She sang three songs before the band stopped for a break.

Heaviness settled around her as she stepped off the stage and returned to the bar. Lola's presence was gone. She hadn't recognized it during her first visit to the club, but there was no mistaking Lola's voice in her mind. It could mean only one thing. She was dead. A person who was still alive couldn't speak to her the way Lola had, and their presence wouldn't be as strong, either.

All the hope she'd held onto tightly fell like crumbled dreams on the bar top. She took a big gulp of the wine she'd left while onstage, swallowing the pain lodged in her throat.

Even though she'd never met Lola, realizing she was dead was like losing her mother all over again, and reminding her she was alone.

"How did you know I'd sing?" She leaned forward on the bar toward Joe. To her disappointment, Pearl was nowhere in sight.

"I didn't, but figured you would if you wanted information about your aunt bad enough." Black eyes searched hers. "You sure you never sang before?"

Josie shook her head. "Only shower serenades."

"You sound like her."

She didn't need to ask whom he meant. "Thank you."

From the moment she stepped onto the stage, the thrill of being there had remained. What would Joe say if she told him Lola had helped her get onstage and her presence lingered in the club? The question was, why here, and not at the house? Was it because William was there?

She tapped her fingers on the bar in nervous anticipation.

"Your aunt came to work here in fifty-eight and became an instant success." His eyes lit up with open admiration. "She worked several clubs before the owner at the time convinced her to settle here."

"Did she have friends?"

He chuckled. "It depends on what you consider 'friends'. She had fans, and club owners who wanted to get their hands on her and the money she could make for them, and suitors—if they could be called that." He finished with a smirk.

"Men who were interested in her...romantically?"

"Yeah. There were slews of them every night, buying her drinks, flowers, gifts. She smiled and talked with them, but didn't see them outside the club."

"None of them?" she probed, hoping to find out if he knew about William.

His eyes narrowed. "She wasn't that kind of lady."

"I wasn't implying she was," she assured him. "I was just wondering if she had a special man in her life."

He visibly relaxed. "There was someone, but he's gone."

"What was his name?"

Black eyes studied her, gazed about the room, and settled back on her. "I don't recall." His bottom lip twitched.

He's lying, Lola whispered.

"You're lying, Joe. You always did when your bottom lip twitched."

His back straightened to his full height. "How'd you know that?" he asked, before realizing he confirmed her suspicions.

She shrugged. "I just do. What happened to her?" She changed the subject quickly.

Sadness clouded his eyes. "She disappeared one night, and no one saw or heard from her again."

"Disappeared?" It explained why her mother's letters from Lola stopped suddenly. "Did anyone look for her?"

"Her man did, for a while."

"The man whose name you don't remember but you know that he's dead?"

"Yeah," he mumbled and looked around the club again.

Why did he keep looking around the room? Was he looking for Pearl, or someone else? "Did anything unusual happen the night she disappeared that might explain why she left?"

He leaned closer. "Look, little lady. You're trying to uncover secrets that want to stay buried." It wasn't a threat, but ominous just the same.

Her mouth opened to ask more questions, but he interrupted. "Sing again and I'll tell you more about your aunt."

He stepped away from the countertop where she sat and went to organize the liquor bottles on the shelves. The conversation was over.

She longed to look in the direction he had earlier, but didn't risk it—not yet. The way he'd said "disappeared" reeked of malice. She hoped he'd tell her more, but someone in the club made him nervous.

The intense connections of Patrick's house, and then the club, fascinated rather than frightened her. She'd just entered a whole other realm of strangeness, as if ghosts and talking dead relatives weren't enough to throw a person off their game.

Casually, she turned in her seat to listen to the band and catch a glimpse of the person who made Joe anxious. She bit her lower lip in frustration, wishing she'd paid better attention to the people in the club when onstage. No faces had stood out except for Joe, Pearl, and...Her eyes rushed to the back corner of the club. The man, whose expression was the same as hers the night she saw William's ghost, was gone.

"Why're you here?"

She turned to find Pearl standing next to her. *Didn't she leave?* It was way creepy how she disappeared and reappeared. "Excuse me?"

She stepped closer. "You heard me. Hasn't your family caused him enough pain?"

"Who?"

"Joe."

"My family doesn't know Joe."

"I'm talking about Lola." Her muddy eyes narrowed.

"What makes you think I'm related to Lola?"

"A blind man could see that." She spat the words at her.

"You didn't like her, did you?"

"Everyone loved her, but she was selfish."

Did she love her, too? The poison in her voice said otherwise. "How was she selfish?" she prodded gently.

"Marrying the man she did, and then leaving without a word."

"What makes you think she left on her own?" She breathed deeply, the mixture of resentment and hurt flowing from Lola overwhelming her.

Surprise filled Pearl's eyes.

"How did Lola hurt Joe?" she asked quickly. If she didn't get away from Pearl, would Lola have her shake Pearl the way she felt the urge to?

"He never got over her leaving without saying good-bye," she said quietly, sadness creasing the already deep lines in her coffee skin.

"He must have. He has you."

"Not always." Her voice dropped to a whisper.

"What do you mean?"

"Joe loved Lola and I loved Joe, but I wasn't going to play second fiddle." Her tone rose with venom. "So I left him."

Josie remained quiet; Lola's distress bubbled below the surface.

"I made a mistake leaving him, but not again." Her fierce expression held Josie's. "I won't let you hurt him, bringing up the past."

"I don't plan to hurt him, just find the truth."

A wall went up around Pearl's eyes. "Finding out the truth will hurt him."

"What does that mean?"

"No one is going to hurt him again. I'll make sure of it," she said firmly. "Remember that!"

Pearl walked toward the stage before she could respond.

Lola's story was becoming more complicated with each person she encountered and every question she asked. She left before Pearl sang. Tonight's confessions were more than enough to digest, and Lola's emotions were starting to take a toll.

She headed upstairs, out of the past and into the busy crowded streets. The night air cooled her skin. People rushed past her on the sidewalk. The rich smells from the Italian restaurant across the street tickled her nose, reminding her she hadn't eaten dinner.

Blue and red lights from the stores flashed 'Open or Closed' from the store windows lining the street. Laughter and music from the restaurants floated in the air.

She hadn't given Joe an answer about singing again, but she would, and not just to find out about Lola. She'd enjoyed it. The freedom and exhilaration that pulsed through her far exceeded any shower performance. Would she have the courage to get onstage by herself, or would she need Lola again? She couldn't wait to find out.

Tonight she discovered Lola wasn't just dead, but had disappeared before she died. What she didn't find out was why. Was it voluntary or did someone make her disappear?

Was that why her spirit lingered at the club and not at the house with William? Did he change his mind about their marriage? William and his family had the most to gain from her disappearing and never mentioning the marriage, but was it something more sinister? The thought left a bitter taste in her mouth. Until Lola's reason for disappearing was discovered, there was no reason to suspect foul play.

When she read the letters between her mother and Lola, the secrets they'd shared and the love in their words said they were close. Her mother had lost a beloved sister, and then her husband, years later.

Growing up, she'd felt anger and embarrassment at her mother's weakness and neglect of her only child. Since finding out about Lola, Josie understood her mother for the first time.

She wanted—needed—to solve Lola's mystery. It was one way she could help her mother find peace, even if it was in her afterlife.

Half an hour later, Josie walked into the house. The lack of light under Patrick's door reminded her he was out of town for the next few days. When he first left, she'd wondered if it was to spend time with a woman—something he couldn't do with the renovations going on. She even had the urge to check the tabloids for news of his exploits, but resisted the temptation.

Jealousy had filled her to completion until he called, and continued to call her every night, not only to catch up with the renovations, but to tease her about missing him. It would be better if he was seeing someone else, but she didn't want to think about it.

Her hands ran along the wall of her room until she reached the lamp sitting on the nightstand. She eased her body onto the mattress and her head hit the pillow, hard; the fatigue of the long day had caught up with her. A muddle of color tickled the corner of her eye. A ledger-sized poster hung on the wall. One she hadn't put there.

A scream rose in her throat. *'Leave or die'* was splashed across it in blood-red ink.

Her hands shook as she pressed them against the bed to sit up. Beneath the menacing words, in turquoise and burgundy, was 'Showing for one night only, Lola Johnson.'

She thought the photos were left for her to find her aunt, but she was wrong. They were meant as a warning.

Whoever put the poster there wanted her to know they could get to her, and no locked door was going to stop them. Terror and excitement ran over her in rippling waves. She was getting closer to whatever they didn't want her to find out, if they would risk having their identity discovered by getting so close to her. It was one thing to slip an envelope under the door, another entirely to break into her room.

Josie paused. It could also mean they didn't care if she knew who they were. That scared her more.

Lola's file! She rushed to the closet and the box she kept Lola's things in. It was still locked. Looking around the room, Josie could see the culprit hadn't tried to search it. If they'd dug through her things, they left no signs; everything was in its place, from what she remembered.

If this was her house, she would file a report with the police, but this wasn't her house and these weren't normal circumstances. Making that call would mean telling Patrick. She could lose the job. They had a contract, but he was a lawyer and might break their contract to avoid scandal and protect his family's name.

There were rumors that Myles Pullman's campaigns were funded by members of the mob, and being a senator meant he had contacts in the police department. Panic swelled—someone from the mob might be after her. Nervous laughter escaped before she convinced herself she'd be at the bottom of a body of water sporting cement shoes if they were.

She was determined to solve the mystery of Lola's disappearance and scare tactics weren't going to stop her! She squeezed her hands into fists, and took a deep breath. Yanking the poster from the wall, she crumpled it into a tight ball.

She picked up her phone.

"Hello?" Danny's groggy voice greeted her.

"It's me. Did any new guys join the crew?"

"No, why?"

"What about visitors? Did anyone come to see Patrick while I was out?"

"Hmm, yeah. Some guy and a lady."

Josie's heart raced. "Did you get their names?"

"No, but I know Patrick wasn't happy to see either one of them. Why the sudden interest?"

"Just curious." She wished she could speak with Danny, but she didn't want to risk putting him in danger. "Can you pick up new internal door locks first thing tomorrow? No one gets copies of the keys but me, for now."

"Is everything okay, Josie?"

"Everything's fine."

"You're lying."

"It's none of your business!"

"He lays a hand on you, and it will be!"

She knew that tone. He meant every word, even if it meant the job. "This is not about him."

There was a moment of silence. "Then who?"

"That's not important right now, but when it is, I'll tell you."

"What the hell does that mean?"

"Good night, Danny."

"Josie, wai—"

She turned off her phone in case he tried to call her back. Tomorrow was a new day, and she would think about how to deal with everything that had happened then.

• • •

Patrick turned off his car. He got out and headed toward his house. His house. The words were starting to take meaning. In the past week, he'd been moving things from his apartment into storage so it would be move-in ready when it sold.

Once the house was finished, there would be no need to keep both places. His heartbeat raced as his hand reached for the front door. He missed his home. He missed Josie.

They'd kept in touch by phone, and she'd emailed him video of the changes at each phase to get his approvals on the look of the cabinets, with the backsplash and countertop. She was right about the red glass backsplash; he liked the combination. He was excited to see the changes.

He smiled as he remembered her sharing funny mishaps on the job, along with renovation updates, and managing to wiggle her way back into his good graces and farther under his skin.

The tension that'd hung between them before he left was gone, and any suspicions he had about Josie keeping secrets had long faded. She'd been nothing but professional since she arrived and had given him no reason to suspect her of anything more than being thorough. This job was important to her. Her passion for the house and her business were his assurances she wouldn't do anything stupid to jeopardize her chance for the reference they agreed on.

Jazz music wafted through the front door as he stepped inside. The sound of jazz in his home was a habit of hers he had grown used to and one that brought back happy memories of Uncle Will. Billie Holiday was the last artist he expected to hear from her room, but after a few weeks, he realized the dulcet, tortured tones suited her perfectly. Like Billie's unique voice, Josie was beautiful and mysterious.

The original style of the trim and wall framings remained the same. The new appliances fit together with the tiles and colors they'd picked out. A few details remained, but the majority of renovations were done. It looked better than the videos she'd sent him.

"Hi there."

She jumped at the sound of his voice. Her eyes widened at the sight of him. He was hours early.

"Hi," she said brightly.

Her eyes roamed over him, making him feel like a bowl of ice cream covered in caramel, ready for her to devour. A shiver ran down his back. Her eyes said she missed him—a lot. His heart thundered in his chest.

He shifted his weight from one foot to the other to stop himself from walking up to her, pulling her into his arms, and kissing her full on the mouth in welcome.

"You're cooking?"

She looked sexier than any woman should in the purple T-shirt and white sweat pants she was wearing, and more at home in his kitchen than she had before he left. He smiled at the thought of the anger that would flicker in her eyes if he told her.

He gazed over the black, curly hair that touched the base of her elegant neck and his lips twitched, wanting to kiss the delectable skin at the nape. He could easily turn her around and continue his kiss at the bottom of her throat while his hands worked to lift her shirt over her head. He could lift her up on the granite countertop while he took his time tasting her skin, one inch at a time...

"Yes, want to taste it?"

Did I ever! But it wasn't food he wanted, it was her.

"Which do you want?" she interrupted. "I made fettuccini Alfredo and tortellini carbonara."

Hearing the dinner menu was a dose of cold water on his wayward thoughts. That much food could mean only one thing. "Danny stopping by?"

She nodded. "We're celebrating finishing the kitchen."

He wanted to ask if she'd like to taste him, but instead took a seat at the new bar-style kitchen counter and watched her chop onions. "You're in a good mood." He observed the smile on her face as she tossed a handful of mushrooms into the skillet.

"The kitchen is done and my client will be off my back for a while." Her eyes twinkled with mischief. "It's nice to cook on a proper stove and not in a toaster oven. I was worried my cooking would get rusty."

"You like cooking that much?"

She gave him a sideways glance. "You know I do." She brushed a stray hair away from her face. "Like restorations, it's a passion."

"I cook out of necessity, and even then, I don't like it."

Throwing her head back, she laughed throatily. His stomach lurched. It was incredibly sexy. Everything about her was.

"I picked it up after my father died. He was the cook in the family." Her smile waned.

"Losing both parents must have been hard."

She turned her attention back to the stove before she responded. "So, what else do you have in that file?"

"What file?"

"The one in your nightstand drawer behind your locked bedroom door." A hand went on her hip. "I bet you have tons of stuff in there about me, a stranger, you asked to stay in your home."

He chuckled. "For your information, it's in my filing cabinet, not the nightstand."

Other than his family, no one could read him like Josie. He intimidated most people, but not her. It was that way from the day they met, and he admired her for it.

"It's only fair you share something about yourself…" She smiled over her shoulder, "…to even things up."

His mouth opened to speak.

"Something the local newspapers haven't printed and that I don't have in *my* file."

She had a file on him? Somehow that didn't surprise him. "That doesn't leave much." He usually didn't like discussing anything personal and was wary of anyone who wanted to know more, but that didn't seem to make a difference with her. He found he wanted to share things about his life that he didn't with others.

"What about your uncle? What was he like?"

He relaxed. "He was great! Funny. Loved baseball, easygoing, the kind of guy who'd give you the shirt off his back." What he didn't tell her was he meant more to him than his own father, or that he became so withdrawn in his later years, he only responded to Patrick's visits. She didn't need to know that.

"Did he ever get married, have kids?"

He opened his mouth to give her the answer drilled into him from childhood, but didn't, not wanting to lie. "The kitchen looks great." He looked around.

"I told you it would." She gave him a sideways glance.

"Yes, you did." He laughed. "Is this where you say I told you so?"

"Damn!"

"What?" Walking around the counter to stand behind her, he noticed she held her hand over the sink. Blood dripped from the small cut on her index finger.

"Here, let me help." He reached for her hand, but she pulled it out of his reach.

"Thanks, but I have a first aid kit in my room; comes with the trade." She wrapped a paper towel around it.

"There's one in the bathroom." He took her hand and led her up the stairs and down the hall.

"I can do it myself," she declared when they reached the bathroom.

"I know you can." He motioned her to sit on the closed seat of the toilet and removed the blood-soaked paper towel.

"This isn't right," she mumbled.

He raised a dark eyebrow. "What, me bandaging your finger?" Was that nervousness in her voice? A thrill shot through him that his presence made her nervous.

"You're my client."

"That's ridiculous."

She bit her lower lip. "Thanks."

He looked down at her hand as it rested in his own, and then at her. She looked nothing like the confident restoration architect he saw every day, or the stubborn woman who challenged him on designs ideas for his house. She gazed up at him through dark lashes, with open vulnerability, surprising him. It was a side of her he'd never seen before. As quickly as it appeared, it was gone. He secretly hoped it would return.

She stood up, ready to bolt like a frightened rabbit, but his body blocked her path. He reached out to touch her hair. It tormented him as much as the nape of her neck. He twirled its softness between his fingertips and watched her mouth open in shock. With his other hand, he ran his thumb along her bottom lip.

"Patrick." Her voice was strained. Was it fear or lust? He hoped it was the latter.

His head lowered to kiss her, not wanting to give her time to move away or him time to change his mind. He was tired of being tormented by her lips when they moved to smile, laugh, and even smirk when Danny made a joke. One quick kiss. That's all he needed, he told himself as his lips touched hers, and she'd be out of his system.

They were soft and warm against his. His hand went around her waist, and he drew her against him and slipped his tongue into her mouth. A moan escaped between them and he wondered if it was hers or his. It didn't matter.

Her hands moved up his neck and her fingers raked through his hair. That motion and the softening of her previously stiff frame against him told him what he wanted to know. She wanted him as badly he wanted her.

Her tongue became bold, moving against his, deepening the kiss. Her hands moved down his back, her fingers digging through the thin fabric of his shirt. Shivers raced down his spine. Her soft yielding to his kiss, along with her tongue against his, was driving him crazy and he grew painfully hard. He pressed her against the wall of the small bathroom and ground his hips between her legs, moaning when her hands gripped his shoulders and she rocked against him.

His mind flooded with visions of her naked beneath him as he plunged himself into her welcoming body. Her face was clear in his mind and he could feel her naked flesh beneath his hands and the warmth of her breath against his ear as she moaned his name.

The problem was, the vision wasn't his. It was a memory from another time they'd made love, which didn't make sense. But he knew it was true as clearly as he knew Josie wouldn't resist if he took her right there in the bathroom. *End the kiss, now!*

He pulled his lips from hers and took a step back. His hands went behind his back to hide their shaking. *Did she see and feel what I did?*

"I shouldn't have done that," he said when her eyes searched his. He wouldn't apologize for something he wanted, only state the obvious.

The rejection in her eyes stung, making him feel guilty for ending their kiss so abruptly.

She stared back at him, her lips swollen from their kiss, lingering desire in her eyes. Walking to the door, she paused at the entryway. "No, you shouldn't have."

He cursed under his breath and ran a hand through his hair in frustration. He didn't want to stop, but take her to his room and reenact the scenes that flashed before his eyes like a slideshow. He wanted to keep her in his bed until she didn't torment him and say to hell with their working relationship, but he wouldn't.

The connection he felt with Josie was strange enough, but got weirder when he kissed her. Their kiss had heightened it to a level that scared him. He'd never felt that way when he kissed a woman before, not even Sharon. He was a fool to think one kiss would be enough. The feel of her mouth and body molded against him was going to haunt him for days to come.

• • •

Josie longed to slam her bedroom door and let it echo through the house for Patrick to hear, but she closed it quietly instead, not wanting to give him the satisfaction of knowing she was upset by his abrupt end to their kiss, or what he said after. *"I shouldn't have done that."* The words were like salt in a raw wound. He wanted her. She'd felt the evidence of it pressed between her legs, but he ended it even as she clung to him.

Damn him for dismissing their kiss so casually! Did he think she did that with all her clients? Her hands trembled when she touched her lips and remembered. It was nothing like the kisses she'd shared with her college boyfriend. Patrick's kiss was toe curling, hot, and deep. He'd made love to her with his mouth. She would have let him take whatever he wanted from her.

Heat flowed to her cheeks at the thought of him touching her, intimately, with his hands and mouth. Sex with Patrick would be nothing like it was with her college sweetheart. That'd been rushed and clumsy, with an overwhelming awkwardness afterwards that left her regretting her rash decision to get the loss of her virginity over with out of embarrassment at being twenty-two.

Things would be different with Patrick. She knew that from the way she reacted to him, and not just physically. When he was in the same room, her eyes devoured him when no one was looking. The strong lines of his jaw, his childlike smile that made her stomach flutter and his laugh that caused goose bumps to inch over her arms.

She wished she could be happy about it. A relationship between them wasn't possible, for more reasons than their contract.

His file told him who her parents were and where she attended school. What he didn't know was their connection through marriage. Neither did he know that someone had made threats against her. Ripples of fear ran over her skin as she looked at the wall where the poster hung days earlier. She'd covered the spot with a photo of a previous job, but the words written on the poster still haunted her when she closed her eyes at night.

She had two tasks to do and when they were done, she'd be gone and Patrick would be out of her life. Waves of regret tried to make their way up her throat, but she swallowed them.

The sting of anger she felt earlier left. He was right. They shouldn't have kissed. It didn't matter if the force of their attraction crackled in the air every time they were alone. Since finding out about Lola, all hope of anything between them had gone out of the window like the garbage from the demolition.

He was the first man in years she was physically and emotionally attracted to, and she wasn't even going to get a chance to ruin it. She punched the flowered print on her pillowcase, hoping to vent her frustration; it didn't help.

Chapter 9

The new smoke alarms installed downstairs were silent, but there was definitely a smell coming into her room. Having a house burned down after she'd put her heart and soul into its renovations didn't sit well with her. She headed downstairs to check it out.

She had the urge to laugh and scream at the sight that greeted her. Patrick was standing by the stove, gray smoke hovering above him. His hands were working overtime to keep up with the pots on the stove, without success. All three were bubbling over, making a mess and leaving bits of food under the burner covers. Partially cut pieces of veggies were neglected on the counter and small containers of spices littered the black granite countertop.

"Trying to burn down the kitchen I worked so hard to finish ahead of schedule?"

He jumped, so engrossed in whatever he was attempting to cook that he hadn't heard her come downstairs.

"You scared the hell out of me." He turned to face her. "I'm trying to cook dinner for my family."

Her heartbeat stopped. Myles Pullman, here? The knowledge made her shudder in apprehension. If she saw him, or maybe even touched him, there might be a reaction, like the other connections she felt. Whatever emotions his eyes, or Lola, revealed, might give her a clue—something. "It doesn't look successful."

"Yeah, but my mother insisted on seeing the house. What Mother wants, Mother gets." Patrick looked down grimly at the liquid in the pot. "I should have ordered take out." His head snapped up when he realized the personal information he'd let slip.

"I won't tell, promise." She sat at one of the stools, leaned her elbow on a clean part of the counter, and held up two fingers to show Scout's honor. "What time do they get here?"

"One hour," he said grimly. "Just enough time to clean the kitchen and order take out." He put the metal spoon down in defeat.

His attempt to make things perfect for his parents tugged at her heart and her told more than he knew. After her father died, nothing she did got her mother's attention. Not straight A's at school, not getting a full scholarship to design school—nothing. She knew what he was feeling. It was also an opportunity.

"Maybe not." She stood up and walked to the refrigerator.

He watched as she pulled out a number of ingredients and set them on the clean side of the counter. She gave him a gentle shove from behind the counter and began pulling out pots, pans, and bowls. He rushed to clean up the mess he'd made.

The heat of his eyes on her while she cooked and from their bodies nearly touching as they worked side by side in the kitchen sent shivers down her back. Their casual conversation died a slow death and was replaced with the vivid memory of their kiss days ago. Her nipples tightened, remembering his tongue against hers and his erection pressed between her legs. His hot gaze met hers when she looked up. *Is he thinking the same thing?*

"I'm sorry for what I said after we kissed." His voice was low.

Her breath caught in her throat. He hadn't regretted their kiss. She nodded, unable to find her voice. Their conversations the past few days were forced and awkward. At the end of the day, they went to their rooms with only a polite good night.

"I've wanted to kiss you for a long time," he said with sexy grin, "but kissing with our working relationship is a bad idea. That's what I was trying to say...badly." He paused as his gaze moved slowly over her face to her lips. "If things were different..."

She wished she could agree with him about things being different and suggest they wait until the end of the job, but she couldn't. Things needed to be more different than he could imagine for them to have any kind of relationship.

When he found out about their family connection and the threats to her under his roof, he wouldn't want to see her again. She cleared her throat, finding her voice. "There's an attraction—we'd be fools to deny it—but I agree, it would only complicate things."

His disappointment was obvious. "Friends only, then," he said, his hand outstretched.

It was more a question than a statement. Desire lingered in his green eyes. Her hands itched to touch his face, to take his hand and pull him to her instead of just shaking it, but that was not an option. Not without risks she wasn't willing to take. She reached her hand out tentatively.

The warmth of his hand engulfed hers and an electric charge coursed through their clasped hands. Their gazes locked and Patrick took a step, closing the already short distance between them. Her heart thundered in her ears when his other hand reached out to touch her face. Delicious tingles raced across her skin as his fingers stroked her cheek, and her stomach lurched when his head lowered.

The blaring noise of the smoke alarm pierced the moment like a tightly blown balloon being popped. They released their hands quickly and took a step back, the interruption reminding them of his '*friends only*' comment.

"It should've gone off when you were trying to cook. I'll get Danny to look at them tomorrow."

"I'll get it," he said, raising his hand when she moved toward the living room.

She reached above the stove and pressed a button. "It helps if you turn on the vent."

He grinned as he returned from living room. "Now why didn't I think of that?"

Her raised eyebrow asked if he really wanted an answer.

Leaning against the kitchen counter, he watched her cook. "I'm going to take a shower. Will you be okay?" He'd cleaned the kitchen spotlessly, except for the space she worked in. "I feel a little guilty leaving you here cooking for my family."

"Only a little guilty?" she teased.

He answered with a smirk. His mouth opened to say something more, but he stopped and headed upstairs.

• • •

Patrick rubbed shampoo into his hair vigorously, remembering her sidestepping his open invitation—if things were different. She hadn't denied their attraction, but she hadn't agreed or suggested a date—something, anything—at the end of the job. Her rejection left a bad taste in his mouth and he wondered if all she wanted was his reference. Sharon's face and words before their engagement ended flared, unwelcomed, in his mind.

He pushed her image aside. Josie was nothing like her. Sharon gave the impression she was warm and caring, but her insides were ice. Josie was reserved, but beneath the surface was a caring and compassionate person. That was evident in her relationship with Danny and the crew. When it was time to work, she was an avid professional, but not to the point of being rigid and distant. But what did he know? He'd known Sharon most of his life and she'd managed to deceive him. Was his judgment of Josie going to end the same way? He hoped to God it wouldn't.

Other than Uncle Will, there were few people in his life he could comfortably be himself with. Josie was one of them. He didn't need to walk around on eggshells with her, as he sometimes had to do with his family. When they had words, he didn't have to worry that she would crumble into tears. She told him exactly what was on her mind and didn't care if he liked it or not. He admired that about her and hoped his family would, too. He stopped in the middle of pulling a shirt over his head. *Where did that come from?*

He tucked his shirt into black pants. Who was he kidding? It mattered to him what they thought. He wanted them to meet and like her as much as he did. If he didn't, he would've asked her to leave the house tonight.

From the moment his mother called, he knew their visit tonight wasn't to see the renovations. They were coming to see the woman he'd asked to live with him. He took a long hard look at himself in the mirror. Tonight wasn't going to be easy.

Billie Holiday's voice filled the hallway when he stepped out of his room. He walked towards the stairs to the kitchen. It reminded him of the records Uncle Will played and the weekends he'd spent with him at this house as a child, and then an adult. They were happy and sad memories. He'd watched him slowly die of a broken heart.

He stopped when he reached the kitchen. Behind the counter was Josie, singing as she held a wooden spoon in her hand like a microphone. When the lyrics stopped, she stirred the steaming pots on the stove. He leaned against one of the walls in the living room and watched in fascination at the gestures her hands made and the sway of her hips. He remained silent and still, knowing the spell would be broken if she knew he was there.

Even with red sauce splattered on the front of her shirt, he couldn't remember seeing a more beautiful sight. He shouldn't be watching her; she'd be horribly embarrassed, but, for the moment, he didn't care. It was rare to see her with her guard completely down, and he wanted to savor it. After dinner with his parents, he'd need it.

"Are we interrupting?"

Patrick jumped.

Behind him were his parents and brother, Noah. The smirk on Noah's face said '*we caught you watching the help*'. His father's eyes were narrowed and his mother, as always, wore a composed air that made you wonder what wheels turned in her mind.

"I didn't hear the doorbell." Patrick reverted to the self-control he maintained in his family's presence. 'A Pullman never reveals more than they should' was the family motto he hated but adhered to—mostly out of bitter experience.

"It's not working," his father retorted. "We knocked, but there was no answer, so we let ourselves in."

"I'll get Danny to look at it tomorrow. Come in. Excuse the mess; the living room is still not finished." His hand gestured in a wide sweep, including the scaffolding in the corners of the living room.

"That's why we're here." His mother took a step forward and kissed him on the cheek.

"I thought we were here to see the woman he's shacking up with," Noah stated nonchalantly, ignoring the disapproving look from both parents.

"We're not shacking up, she's renovating the house," Patrick said simply, although a part of him balked at the thought of people thinking they were shacking up.

"Sure she is." Noah's sarcastic tone said he didn't believe him.

"That *is* all I'm doing here," Josie said from the kitchen entrance.

Patrick cringed at Josie hearing his brother's words.

His father's face lit up briefly with surprise and, then, polite control. His mother's remained the same. Noah's was curiosity.

"No one is implying otherwise, my dear." His mother gave his brother a look he knew meant 'watch your words always'.

"I'm Elsa, Patrick's mother." She took a step toward Josie and extended her hand.

Josie shook it. "Josie Fagan."

"It's a pleasure to meet you." His brother stepped forward. "I'm Noah, Patrick's brother."

"Nice to meet you," she said politely, extending her hand, although she eyed him warily. That was no surprise, given his earlier comment.

"The solemn faced man next to me is my husband, Myles."

Josie extended her hand to him.

He hesitated for a moment, his expression showing cold disdain. He took her hand and shook it quickly.

Her hand dropped to her side and her friendly smile waned. "Enjoy your dinner."

"Please, join us." Elsa stepped forward. "After all, you cooked it."

Patrick shrugged at being caught. What did he care? His parents knew he didn't cook. "Yes, join us."

"Thanks, but I don't want to impose."

"You won't be," Noah declared. "Join us."

Patrick rolled his eyes, knowing his brother wasn't just being polite. He wanted her to join them, like his mother, so they could grill her with questions. The strain in his father's face told Patrick what he suspected; he didn't want Josie joining them.

Josie looked at his family and then down at her clothing.

"Why don't you clean up first?" Patrick suggested, and smiled at the relief in her eyes.

"I won't be long."

He turned to face his family when Josie was safely upstairs.

"I see now why you invited her to stay at the house." Noah wiggled his eyebrows, then flinched when Patrick punched his arm.

Patrick turned to his father. "Please don't give her a hard time."

"Why?"

"She's a nice lady and doesn't deserve hostility from you."

His father raised an eyebrow. "Hostile, me?"

Everyone looked at him.

"You don't know what you've done, inviting her into this house—our lives," his father said cryptically.

"She's here to renovate the house, nothing more." His father was suspicious of everyone.

His mother came to stand next to his father and put her hand on his shoulder. "Your father's just being cautious," she said tentatively.

Patrick's jaw twitched, but he held his words at his mother's stern look. He nodded curtly.

• • •

Josie shook her hands to stop them from trembling. *Get a grip!* In a few minutes, she was going to sit down to dinner with the powerful Pullmans. She could hardly contain her excitement, or the trickle of fear that ran down the base of her neck. She couldn't come right out and ask, "Did you bribe my aunt to leave William? Or did you leave that threatening poster in my room?" It wasn't exactly dinner conversation. To her disappointment, there'd been no connection or hints from Lola, but she had to take advantage of this situation, she wasn't likely to get another one.

Lola's letters mentioned that William's family was unhappy about their marriage, but she didn't say who. It could mean Myles or the father, who died in the 1970s.

The truth was, she wanted to question them for more reasons than to find out if they knew about Lola's disappearance. William and Lola were married, which meant they were family—her only family—and she wanted them to like her. Would they welcome her if they knew who she was? Not likely. It would mean admitting their family covered up the secret of William and Lola's marriage, which would lead to other questions.

It wasn't going to be easy. They were wary because she was living at the house, despite assurances it was purely professional. Patrick's mother and brother seemed nice enough, but his father's cool disdain had been blaring.

After one last look in the mirror, she headed out to face Patrick's family and the questions she was certain they'd ask. She wore a pair of black slacks and a striped silk blouse, and ran a hand over her smoothed hair. It wasn't styled like Lola's, but the trap was set to get a reaction from Myles. It might be futile—after all, fifty years had passed—and he might not even remember what Lola looked like.

Her heart thundered in her ears with each step she took downstairs, her mind filled with questions and how she would drop them into the conversation.

Patrick's parents and brother sat in the living room, laughing. Her heart hurt with the raw emotion that she didn't have a family, but more surprising was that she seemed to be nothing more to Patrick than his restoration architect. But she'd made that choice, and wouldn't change her mind.

Surprise and something that resembled anger flared in Myles' cold eyes, but she couldn't be certain because as quickly as it arrived, it disappeared. An eyebrow on his wife's face rose slightly. Noah's expression didn't change.

She touched her hair. "I look different, don't I?" she said calmly, and hoped they didn't notice her hand shaking.

"You certainly do." His mother smiled coolly. "Very pretty."

"Is everyone ready for a treat?" Patrick interjected. "Josie's not only an amazing restoration architect, but a fantastic cook!"

"He's only saying that because he doesn't like to cook," Josie joked.

"She's right!" he chuckled.

Tension filled the room to capacity when everyone remained silent. Everyone's eyes were on her, but she kept her gaze on the clear plastic sheets that blocked the living room area still under renovations.

"Could you help me in the kitchen, Josie?" Patrick asked.

"Sure." She stood up and followed closely behind him. The laughter between them had quickly evaporated when she entered the room. "Is everything okay?" She took the serving dishes from the cupboard.

"What do you mean?" he asked as he busied himself with spooning her cooking into the dishes she had set on the counter.

"Your parent's reaction when I came back into the room was... strange," she probed.

"Really? I didn't notice."

A blind man could have seen his parents' reaction, but she didn't push him. When they first met, Patrick's reaction was similar, as if he knew her, but she was certain it wasn't for the same reasons as his parent's. He wouldn't have hired her if he suspected she was related to Lola. One thing she knew about him was that he didn't like complicated relationships.

They walked into the dining room and placed the dishes filled with food in the middle of the table.

"What made you choose restoration architecture as a career?" Elsa asked, spooning ziti pasta onto her plate.

"My father loved architecture, especially old buildings. His passion became mine when he died."

"I'm sorry for your loss," she said quietly.

"Thanks. It was a long time ago."

"You lost your mother, too, just recently," Myles added.

Josie nodded.

"The changes you've made to the house are amazing." Elsa complimented her, changing the subject.

Josie smiled. "There's a lot more to come. Upstairs still has to be done. A new bathroom to add, and I'm still trying to talk Patrick into changing the attic into an office," she said excitedly.

"I already have an office, I don't need another one."

"Well, you won't consider a man cave, so I have to think of something."

"A man cave with no friends," Patrick said quickly before he turned red.

"Maybe if you had one, your brother might visit." Josie looked to Noah.

Noah just stared at her. Elsa and Myles looked from Patrick to Josie, watching their banter like tennis fans watching a game.

"How about a study? Somewhere quiet for you to read."

"That's what the living room is for."

"What about a sunroom? A skylight up there would add so much light and life to that dull space."

Patrick laughed. "What would I do with a sunroom?"

"You see what I have to put up with?" She pointed her hand toward Patrick in exasperation.

"The feeling is mutual." Patrick grinned. "You won't consider my designs or ideas. It's my house!"

"I consider the good ones," she countered with a fake pout.

"Ha! Those are far and few between," he answered before realizing he'd insulted himself.

They burst into laughter and turned to find Patrick's family watching them strangely. Their laughter trickled away. Awkward silence hung in the air as everyone ate their food.

"So, Josie, did you always live in Chicago?" Noah asked.

His question was a reminder of who she was and what she was there to do.

"No, I just moved."

"Where did you live before?" Myles asked.

"Detroit."

"Do you have family here in Chicago?" Elsa asked.

"Yes, I have an aunt, but I'm having trouble finding her."

"Really?" Patrick's parents asked in unison.

Josie nodded, her mouth full.

"What's her name? Perhaps we know her," Myles pointed out. "Elsa knows many people in the community through her charities."

Elsa nodded.

Josie's gaze cruised over Patrick and his family. Once she spoke Lola's name, there'd be no turning back. It might be the end of Patrick's reference, as well as ruin any chance of their wanting to get to know her, but there was the minuscule chance of finding out more about Lola. The vein at her neck pulsed with excitement and dread.

"Lola Johnson."

Everyone but Elsa choked on their food. The clatter of silverware against china echoed through the room.

Chapter 10

"Do you know her?"

Their reactions told her what she wanted to know. She was careful to say "do" and not "did". She knew Lola was dead, but did they? Was their reaction because someone knew about the marriage their family tried to hide, or something more sinister?

They looked at each other, then back at her. No one answered.

When the silence dragged on, she changed the subject. "How is the food?" She spoke calmly, as if she hadn't just dropped an atomic bomb into their dinner conversation.

"It's good," Elsa replied, the first to recover. "You're the great cook Patrick said you are."

"Thank you." She felt Patrick's eyes boring into her, but she didn't dare look at him, scared of what she would see there. Anger, betrayal—both?

"Dessert, anyone?" she offered.

"No, thanks, you've done enough." Myles' voice was filled with distaste.

She stood up to leave. "It was a pleasure meeting you all." Halfway up the stairs, she turned around. "I'm going to the Jazz Joynt, Patrick, so I'll be late."

Angry gasps came from Myles, confirming her suspicions that he knew more about Lola and William than he was letting on. Steeling herself, she looked at Patrick. Accusations and anger shot back at her. Looking away quickly, she continued upstairs. Regret pressed in around her at the way she'd handled the confrontation with his family. Perhaps she should've approached them with honest questions instead. It was too late to go back now.

When she walked out the front door five minutes later, she felt worse, knowing she wouldn't get the opportunity to question them about Lola now. She hoped to God she had a job when she returned.

• • •

"She's here to blackmail us!" Myles roared.

Josie's polite smile and nervous chatter gave no indication that she dropped Lola's name on purpose, but Patrick knew better. She'd used the same calculating methods on him when she wanted him to choose her designs instead of his. She knew damn well what she was doing.

Patrick sighed deeply in frustration. His father hadn't been this angry since he told him he'd never run for office.

"Then why didn't she use it to get the job?" Patrick offered.

Silence and his father's angry gaze bored into him.

"Why come to me when she could go directly to you and demand money, and a lot more?" He tried to convince his father, although he wasn't sure why. She'd lied to him. "She didn't admit she knew about Lola and Uncle Will, merely said she was looking for her aunt."

His father wasn't convinced. "She threw Lola's name out there to intimidate us; let us know she suspects something."

"It's been three months. If she wanted to blackmail us, why wait?" Patrick asked.

"We could just pay her off," Noah cut in.

"No!" Myles insisted. "It would admit guilt, and we're guilty of nothing!"

Patrick and Noah looked at each other, but remained silent. Uncle Will's marriage to Lola was a dirty secret his parents had kept quiet for as long as the brothers could remember.

"It's been years. Would anyone still care if they found out? This isn't the fifties," Patrick said, his tone heavy with disgust.

His father's narrowed gaze caught his. "She destroyed my brother's life, and you think people won't care if they find out about her sudden disappearance?"

"I thought she left on her own," Patrick said. Did his father know what really happened, or was there something else he wasn't telling them?

Elsa gently touched her husband's shoulder. She was the only one who could calm him down when he got this upset, which wasn't very often. Like their mother, he was usually in control.

"She needs to be fired!" Myles said adamantly. "Get her out of William's house and away from us."

"No," Patrick said a little too quickly. "This is my house now." He knew his parents would need better excuses. "We have a contract and breaking it would cause suspicion, especially since Josie has fulfilled her part of the contract. This business means everything to her and she wouldn't take canceling our contract lightly."

"She doesn't have the money or the resources to fight it in court," Myles insisted.

"I'm not going to have my name dragged through the newspapers," Patrick countered.

"Why are you protecting her? Your family is more important than some person you hired!"

"I'm not protecting her!"

"You are!" His father stood up from the table and started pacing. "If you weren't, you'd find a way to get rid of her before she causes trouble. I saw the way you looked at her during dinner. You're falling for her, just like William did with Lola."

"Don't be ridiculous!" He changed his tone at his father's stern stare. "I'm just being careful. Josie's a smart woman and won't be easily dismissed."

His mother spoke for the first time since Josie left. "Patrick's right, Myles. I seriously doubt she knows anything more than that William and Lola were together, if she even knows that much. There's nothing to do but wait and find out what she wants."

Myles moved away from his wife and her attempt to calm him. "Find a way to get rid of her, Patrick, or I will!" he promised.

He stunned everyone with his malicious tone. When he made a promise, he kept it.

An hour later, Patrick walked back into the kitchen and sat on a barstool. If he hadn't contacted Josie himself, he would've assumed she came to him under false pretenses. He clenched his fists, remembering her offer the day he interviewed her. He hired her of his own accord, but she clearly had another agenda that didn't just include renovating his home. His own thoughts—*Josie is nothing like Sharon*—came back to mock him.

He took a deep breath. His family had differing opinions of what to do with her. Personally, he wanted to shake her senseless. Besides that, he didn't know what to do with her.

His father's reaction when she mentioned the Jazz Joynt was significant, but he didn't dare ask. His father was angry enough. After calling the directory for the address, he headed out the door.

Patrick knew in his heart his family was not responsible for Lola's disappearance, but if Josie had evidence Lola and William were married, it could complicate matters. There was one option no one had suggested—asking Josie what she wanted.

• • •

The faint smell of stale smoke welcomed Josie like an old friend as she made her way down the stone staircase. Her pulse quickened at the thought of singing in just a short while. If someone told her months ago she'd be singing in an underground jazz nightclub, she would've laughed in their face; but she was here twice a week, singing her heart out and enjoying every minute of it.

The sounds from the street ended and the noises of muffled instruments and staggered talking and laughter started softly at first, then became louder as the stairs came to an end and opened up in the club.

Vibrations resonated through the floor from the force of the instruments playing and people who stomped their feet in time to the music. The music was real, uncensored and unplugged jazz that shook her core. The happiness and sadness of the words reached into her soul and brought awareness of intense emotions she didn't know existed inside her. It was that way every time she came.

With each day that passed, she was more drawn to Lola and the home she shared with Patrick, much to her dismay. The connection to the club was one she welcomed. It was her escape from the emotions Patrick stirred, the threatening poster that loomed even though she took it off the wall, and the frustration of not finding out who had made Lola disappear and why. Each time she sang, Lola took over a little more and her friendship with Joe deepened. Or was that because of Lola? When she was here, she didn't care.

Behind the bar, Joe waved. "Hello young lady." He greeted her warmly.

"Hi, Joe."

"The usual?"

She nodded and turned her attention back to the band onstage.

"How are things, Joe? Meet any nice ladies?" She picked up the glass of red wine he set before her. They both knew he was with Pearl, but she hoped the question would make him talk about their relationship. She was certain there was more to the story than Pearl had told her. Maybe Joe would share something.

"I'm saving myself for you," he teased.

She laughed. "You're out of luck, Joe; I'm already taken."

"A man can dream."

That he was romantically attracted to her was laughable. He'd treated her like a baby sister from the moment she stepped into the bar.

When the band ended their song, she emptied her glass and headed onstage. There was no need to tell the musicians which song to start with—they knew. When it was time for her last song, "Lover Man," she smiled as the dancers left the floor and the regulars shifted to the edge of their seats in anticipation.

The blare of a trombone and the frantic keys of the piano filled the room. The noise of each new instrument escalated when coupled with the others.

She closed her eyes and started to sing, letting Lola's warmth spread over her body from the top of her head to the tips of her toes. That warmth turned to tingles and the hair on her arms felt like tiny daggers against the smooth fabric of her dress. Her mind drifted. Her body was weightless.

When she opened her eyes, she stumbled over the words of the song. Her surroundings had changed. She looked about the room frantically.

What the heck happened? Where am I?

The room was not the dingy club she knew and loved. She was still in the Jazz Joynt, but it was different—very different. The tables looked new, not cracked and warped as they were when she had closed her eyes. So were the people who watched her sing. Their clothes and hairstyles were from a different era. The club was busier than she'd ever seen it—people filled every space and more smoke hovered in the air, if that was possible.

Now what?

Behind the bar stood a strikingly handsome young man who winked mischievously at her as if she'd suddenly discovered something he'd known all along. *It was Joe!* She knew that smile.

Lola had gone too far this time! It was one thing to experience an emotional connection to the club, but a hallucination this intense was another matter. Her heart stopped. *Did she take me back in time?*

Fear coiled in her stomach at the thought. Had she given her aunt too much control? How the hell was she going to get back?

Her hand brushed nervously against her clothing, but instead of the soft black cotton dress she'd put on earlier, gritty sequins scratched her fingers. The silver dress was so tacky she would have laughed if she didn't feel like crying instead.

Play it out, Lola whispered. Josie took a deep breath and prayed to God that playing it out meant the end of the song and not the entire story Lola wanted her to know.

Awareness ran like an ice cube up her back, spreading chills to every hair on her body. Her eyes searched the club until she found the upper platform close to the stage. Staring back at her within the sea of faces was Patrick. Like everyone else in the room, his clothing and hairstyle were different. Was he really there with her, or just another figment of Lola's illusion? He looked like the photo she'd seen of William.

Whether it was Lola's love for William or her own attraction to Patrick, every emotion she'd experienced from the moment they'd met poured out as she watched him.

His eyes mirrored the passion and love that churned within her from the tips of her toes all the way to her lips, and she smiled ecstatically. Before it ended, he stood up and stumbled down the stairs of the second level, out through the crush of people around him.

As quickly as the vision started, it ended abruptly when the song finished. She gripped the microphone stand to keep from losing her footing as the crowd clapped. She was back.

• • •

Patrick took big gulps of air when he got outside. He leaned against the side of the jazz club, hoping to stop the pounding in his head and heart. His skin tingled and felt like it'd been dragged over tiny needles. His heart ached in a way it hadn't since Sharon told him she only wanted his name and the prestige that came with it.

Getting into his car, he started the engine. The need and love in Josie's eyes haunted him even as he tried to block the memory out. It'd felt good, damn good, but it, and the whole incident, had freaked him out! One minute he was watching her sing, and the next he was somewhere else. He needed to get out. Away from her and the emotions she'd provoked in him.

He'd come to the club hoping to ask Josie what she wanted from him and his family. He'd discreetly searched the crowded for her, but he hadn't expected to see her onstage, singing.

Her voice was soft and haunting, reminding him of Billie Holiday. She had on more makeup than he'd seen her wear and she shone brightly, blindingly. Her dress was sexy and hugged her curves in a way that made him wish his hands were the fabric.

He'd made his way to a staircase close to the stage, up to the second level of the club. The force to go there was powerful and deliciously inviting; something amazing waited for him.

When he leaned against the chair, a shock went through his body, jolting him upright and blurring his vision. His eyes refocused, but his stomach lurched, and he thought he'd lose his dinner. He'd settled his stomach with deep breaths, but when his eyes moved about the room, he realized the people around him were different—their hair and clothes from another time.

Josie had changed, too, but it wasn't just her clothing and hairstyle. The movement of her body caught his attention. It was the woman he'd had visions of. Josie's movements were sexy in their own way, but this woman was different: softer, sexier. He watched one hand touch her provocatively swaying hips, while the other touched her cheek, then her neck, as she sang the seductive words.

Need had shot through him and he'd wanted her more in that moment than he'd ever wanted another woman. He sensed she sung just for him while she imagined he was making love to her, her hands touching her face and neck. Her gaze found his, and he was right. She wanted him, too, but also loved him passionately. He felt it, fed on it, and returned it to her for just a moment. Once he remembered who and where he was, he tore his eyes from her and got away from her as quickly as his legs could take him.

He came to the club looking for answers, but all he found were more questions and a tangle of emotions he couldn't explain. In just a few hours, his relationship with Josie had gone from complicated to problematic. He didn't like it one bit.

...

Josie's knees gave out and she slid slowly to the floor after she closed the door of the room behind the stage. She hadn't trusted her legs to make it to the bar, and she was right.

There was a soft knock on the door. *Now what?* Was Billie Holiday going to be standing behind the door when she opened it? As exciting as that would be, she didn't think she could handle it right now.

It was Joe, his eyes wide with worry. "Is everything okay?"

"Yes, everything's fine."

"You were...different...onstage tonight, and when Patrick rushed out, I didn't know what to think."

"Different how?" she asked quickly; then his entire comment sunk in. "Wait...you know Patrick?"

"Everyone knows Patrick Pullman, son of Myles and Elsa, William's favorite nephew and successful lawyer."

"That sounds like something you read from a magazine."

"Some of it," he said with a toothy grin.

"How was I different tonight?"

"You were more like Lola," he said tentatively.

His answer surprised her. He'd never told her that before. She studied him for a moment before she asked, "Did you see anything else unusual while I was onstage?"

"Unusual?" He wrinkled face creased deeper.

"When I was up there, everything, everyone was different, including you."

"How was I different?"

Please don't let him think I'm crazy. "You were younger."

Joe's ageless eyes studied her for a moment before he burst into laughter. That wasn't the response she expected, but at least he didn't call her crazy. Not yet.

"Younger, huh? What else did you see?"

She took a deep breath. "It wasn't what I saw," she said softly, "it's what Lola showed me."

His eyebrows knotted. "What kind of game are you playing, missy?"

"No game." She paused, searching for the right words. "Since I was a young girl, I've felt connections to people and places. The first night I came here, I felt a connection to you, to this place."

His expression said he knew what she meant. She pressed on. "I sensed...Lola."

His eyes widened to saucers. "Lola?"

"Yes, she's here, waiting...For what, I didn't know at first, but tonight she revealed it to me—part of it, anyway."

"What was it?"

"She wants me to find out why she disappeared—for you and Pearl, so you can be happy again." That wasn't a complete lie. She was waiting for William, but Josie kept that to herself. The sensations that coursed through her when Lola saw Patrick, William, were powerful. She felt Lola's, and her own, heart breaking when he left suddenly.

"Is that what she said?"

"Not exactly, but I can sense it."

His expression was perplexed, as if trying to decide if she was telling the truth or if she would break into a smile and claim he was on *Candid Camera*.

"You felt the connection the first day I came here, didn't you?" she asked softly.

"Yeah, I felt it."

"Then you know I'm not lying."

"That don't make what you said easier!" He shuffled toward Pearl's space and sat on the stool.

She looked around the room for the first time. She'd never been back here before; there was no need. When she sang, she stayed close to the bar and came ready to sing.

The petite cherry wooden table implied it was once a changing room, but the cases of wine and beer said it'd morphed into a storeroom over the years. Pearl had notched out a little spot for herself in one of the corners, complete with a mirror and fresh flowers. To her surprise, there was a photo of Lola and an attractive young woman next to her on the wall. She walked closer. "Who's that with Lola?"

"Pearl."

"She keeps a photo of her and Lola?" She remembered Pearl's words when she spoke about Lola, and Lola's conflicting emotions.

"That's my photo. She knows better than to touch it." His tone implied he'd told her so. "Pearl was a looker—still is," he said with a grin.

She looked closer at the photo. Both women were smiling, with their arms around each other.

"They were best of friends."

She turned to face him. "What happened?"

"She was jealous of Lola." His gaze moved to the ground and pain etched his face. "That's why Pearl left me," he mumbled.

Lola's pain reflected Joe's and Josie bit her lip to keep from asking more questions about Pearl. Instead, she changed the direction of her questions. "Did you know about Lola and William?"

"Yeah. I didn't realize you did." He lowered his voice. "Just how much do you know about Lola and her connection to the Pullman family?"

She shifted from one foot to the other. She knew Joe could be trusted, but she didn't want to put him in danger if things came to that. "All of it. You?"

"Same." He looked about the room, as if he expected someone to walk through the door at his confession. No one did. "If you're involved with Patrick, be careful. His family has dangerous connections."

"So I've heard." She sidestepped his comment about her relationship with Patrick. "Did anything special happen the night Lola disappeared?"

His wrinkled face creased with pain. "No."

She touched his shoulder. "Are you certain, Joe? It was a long time ago."

Sad black eyes looked up at her. "I relived that night over and over in my head the first thirty years she disappeared. I memorized everything she said, who she spoke to, and what songs she sang. There was nothing that explained why she just disappeared. She was happy."

"Does the man in the corner of the room the first night I sang fit into this?"

He looked pensive before answering. "Gary?"

"Yes. He made you nervous."

"He's been connected to the Pullmans for many years," he said casually, sidestepping her real question. Was he afraid of Gary?

"Really? How?"

He hesitated for a moment, as if trying to decide what and how much information to share. "He and William were best friends.

He was the one that introduced William to Lola, although it was William who won her heart."

That comment got her attention. "What do you mean?"

"Gary was crazy about Lola and brought William to see her sing. Sparks flew between them, and that was the end of Gary."

That explained his reaction when he saw her onstage.

He continued. "That's no surprise. We were all in love with her. She was sunshine on and off the stage."

"It didn't bother him that William won Lola's heart?"

He shrugged. "No. He knew they loved each other."

"What about you, Joe?"

"I only wanted Lola to be happy, and it worked out for the best."

"What do you mean?"

He eyes twinkled. "When my infatuation for Lola was gone, I realized I was in love with Pearl."

She looked at Joe in confusion. "If you were in love with Pearl, why doesn't she like Lola?"

"She didn't believe me when I told her I wasn't in love with Lola anymore. She's the jealous type."

Was that reason enough for Pearl to get rid of Lola? She didn't know Pearl very well, but she'd seen the hate in Pearl's eyes when she sang onstage.

"So you and Pearl got married?" she asked, although she knew the answer. Both he and Pearl told her she'd left him.

He shook his head. "No, she returned to her hometown just before Lola disappeared. She came back to me this year." His eyes lit up. "I'm not letting her go this time."

Her smile didn't waver even as alarms went off in her head. Was it merely coincidence that she left before Lola disappeared, or too convenient? Was Lola trying to tell her something through her reactions to Pearl?

She said good-bye to Joe and headed out the back entrance, not wanting to face Pearl, whom she knew lay in wait to swoop down on her when she walked out the door.

Despite the shadows cascading against the dumpsters lined against the buildings, it wasn't frightening. There was enough light for her to reach the main street quickly and head back to the house.

What would happen now that Patrick knew that she knew about Lola? Her mind played out scenes of what probably occurred during dinner and after she left. Compounded with what happened between them in the club tonight, she wouldn't be surprised to find herself in court fighting the terms of their contract. God, she hoped it didn't come to that. She'd dropped Lola's name, but had said nothing about her relationship with William or her suspicions. Leaving out those crucial details were what she hoped would make it possible for her to keep her job.

With every corner she turned, she was plagued with more questions and suspects. Finding out what happened to Lola was proving to be more difficult than she imagined. She wished she could just ask Lola, but it wasn't that simple. Their connection was strong, but it was more emotional than anything else. When Lola spoke to her, it wasn't like someone whispering in her ear. Instead, it was a swell of feelings: love, anger, sadness. If Lola could speak, she would tell her everything.

She looked down the street, saw the house in the distance, and suddenly felt weary. Her talk with Patrick would have to wait until tomorrow; she didn't have the strength tonight.

The revving of an engine behind her caught her attention. She turned to see a car heading in her direction. The high beams flashed on, blinding her. The car accelerated as it moved closer, then turned toward the sidewalk.

Her heart stopped. She stood frozen as the car came nearer, faster and closer to the curb—and her. She couldn't see what kind of car it was, or read the license plate. She wanted to run, but her legs wouldn't move. Her mind screamed at her, urging to get out of the way before the car hit her, but her body wouldn't listen.

The car lurched up unto the curb and veered toward her. She heard the car accelerate even more. When it was a few feet away, her legs finally decided to move her out of the way. The car whizzed by so closely, she felt the breeze of its passing against her skin.

Damp grass wet her clothes, her breath was ragged, and her body was shaking from the tension it held moments earlier. The sound of the car engine grew distant as it raced down the road and away from her. Hot tears spilled down her face. She half-expected the person to get out of the car and attack her, or for bullets to come flying at her out the window.

Her declaration of not being intimidated came back to mock her. She'd said the words confidently, part of her believing the poster was an idle threat. The driver's attempt to run her over proved they meant every word they'd written.

They didn't want her finding out what they'd tried to hide fifty years ago. It was becoming easier to believe that maybe her aunt didn't leave of her own accord, but was forced to—permanently.

Was finding out why her aunt disappeared worth her life?

Chapter 11

As soon as the sun rose the next morning, she stood outside Patrick's room. Her mind raced with questions, and fears of his possible demands, like "get out now." Then there was their shared experience. What did you say to someone you'd exposed everything in your heart to?

The door opened after she knocked twice and Patrick stood in the doorway, his hair ruffled, gorgeous eyes filled with sleep, naked from the waist up, and pajamas hanging loosely on his hips.

Her mouth went dry.

"Don't you own a decent pair of pajamas? You're a wealthy lawyer, for crying out loud. Surely you can afford a pair or two," she blistered.

He looked confused before looking down at his apparel. "I sleep in the nude."

Oh God! "We need to talk," she spit out.

Conflicting expressions contorted his face, as if he was torn between talking and shutting the door in her face. "Yeah, give me a minute." He closed the door.

She headed to the kitchen, sat at the counter, and waited, chastising herself for the tone she used. Not a good way to start with someone who held the future of her business in his hands. Between the emotions he stirred up and nearly being run over last night, her nerves were on edge. After five minutes passed, she got up and started making pancakes.

She was about to put a skillet on the stove when he walked into the kitchen. To her relief, he was properly dressed in a pair of dark green linen shorts and a white polo shirt. His wet hair flopped in his face and her mind filled with mental pictures of him in the shower with streams of water falling over his broad shoulders and muscled naked body.

"Damn!" she hissed.

"Excuse me?"

"Nothing," she mumbled. Her life was threatened, she could be losing the job supporting her company, and all she could think about was his naked wet body. She needed therapy. Lots of it.

He headed to the coffee machine and started a pot. She turned her attention back to the stove.

"You're making pancakes?" he asked as he watched her stir a bowl filled with white batter.

"Yes, but you don't have to eat them." She sprayed the skillet with cooking oil.

He didn't answer.

"I thought we could talk before the guys started work today."

"I told Danny to give them the day off," he said quietly.

Her heart skipped a beat. He stopped them from painting the living room? He'd been pushing for them to complete it for days. Not a good sign. "Okay."

He put a fresh cup of brewed coffee on the counter next to her. "Let's talk about your aunt."

She nodded slowly. Boy, he didn't waste any time. Not that she blamed him. She did wake him at the crack of dawn to talk.

"How long have you been looking for her?"

"Not long."

"Before you moved to Chicago?"

He held a coffee cup in his hand and was leaning against the kitchen counter mere feet away. Shaking her head, she replied, "I found out about her after I moved to Chicago."

He visibly relaxed.

"How could you not know about an aunt?" he asked, obviously not fully convinced.

"My mother never mentioned her. She didn't like to talk about the past."

"I see." His tone said he didn't see.

Annoyance rose inside her. "Look, my mother suffered from depression, among other things, and barely said two words to me after my father died. I thought you of all people would understand, or wasn't that in my file?" She spat the words at him.

His hard gaze softened. "I'm sorry. Tell me how you found out."

She took a deep, calming breath. "Someone left photos in my room."

"Was that the envelope you asked me about?"

She nodded.

His jaw clenched. "Why didn't you tell me?"

"I just started the job, and I didn't want you to have doubts about hiring me, and things got weird when I found out about William. I know you don't like complications."

She placed three pancakes on a plate and put them before him. She'd lost her appetite. He must have, too, because he didn't move to eat them, and pancakes were his favorite.

"I thought someone just wanted me to know about her, but when the poster showed up in my room a few weeks later, I knew—"

"What poster?" he cut in.

"A poster announcing Lola performing for one night," she said quietly, avoiding his gaze.

"What aren't you telling me?"

She poked at the pancakes on her plate before raising her eyes to meet his. "The words 'leave or die' were written on the poster," she muttered.

"What?" He pushed himself away from the counter. "Someone threatened you in my home and you didn't tell me?" he roared.

Her eyes widened. She'd never seen him so angry. Annoyed, but never verbally angry. "It happened while you were away. I didn't want to worry you," she said softly.

"Didn't want to worry me?" He paced before her, his eyes saying he wanted to strangle her. "No, instead you dropped Lola's name into dinner conversation with my parents," he said snidely.

"I'm sorry."

"Why didn't you talk to me about it instead of bringing it up the way you did?" He pulled his hand through his hair in frustration.

Her eyes dropped to the floor. "I said I was sorry. I didn't think you'd look at it objectively, since your family could be suspects," she countered. The anger in his eyes didn't subside. "It seemed like a good idea at the time," she mumbled.

"Bringing my family in made matters worse in ways you can't imagine."

He was right. "I'm sorry. I should have spoken to you instead of handling it the way I did."

He sighed deeply and moved to sit on the stool next to her. "Tell me everything that happened since the poster. Is there anything else I should know?"

She quickly told him about the photos she found at her mother's house of Lola and William's wedding. She didn't miss the surprise in his eyes, or his guarded gaze that followed.

"Is that everything?"

"No," she whispered.

"I'm not going to like this, am I?"

She shook her head. "Someone tried to run me over last night."

His jaw tightened and his hand on the counter fisted, as if struggling to stop another outburst. "Why didn't you wake me, call the police, something!" His voice was low, but deadly.

"You want me to call the police?"

He stood up and paced the room. "The last thing I want is to have my name in the papers, but it shouldn't be at the expense of your safety. We could file a report, something." His face searched hers and ran over the length of her, as if looking for signs of damage. "Were you hurt?"

"No, but it really shook me up." Her legs and back were still sore, but she didn't tell him. Neither did she tell him her she saw the blinding headlights racing toward her when she closed her eyes.

"Jeez, Josie! Why didn't you wake me?"

"The car was already gone. There was nothing you could do. Besides, I didn't see what kind of car it was, the license plate number—nothing. So I had nothing useful."

He opened his mouth to argue, but changed his mind and closed it. "Do you want to file a report with the police so there is a record of the threat?"

She ignored the swell of her heart at his concern. "No, the police might make things worse, especially given our family connections." If the police stepped in, she wouldn't be able to casually question anyone. People might clam up if uniformed officers were asking the questions.

He raked a hand through his hair so roughly that she imagined a lock or two coming loose. His intense eyes held hers. "If another threat is made, you tell me right away and we contact the police." It wasn't a question.

She nodded.

After taking her half-eaten plate of pancakes to the sink, she turned to face him. "How much do you know about Lola and her disappearance?" she asked.

His sharp eyes met hers. "You know about her disappearing?"

"Yes. I'd hoped she was still alive, but after speaking with Joe..." She neglected to mention how she knew Lola was dead.

"Who's Joe?"

"He owns the Jazz Joynt. He was a friend of Lola's."

"What did he say about her?"

She brought him up to speed on what she learned from Joe, including her suspicions of Pearl, but she didn't mention Gary. Until she knew who she could trust, there were things she planned to keep to herself.

He took a bite of the pancakes before him. "I know as much as you do about Lola's disappearance. She left my uncle one night and didn't return."

"What about your family?"

He eyed her warily. "What about them?"

"Do they know anything?" She met his gaze boldly. "They didn't like her, after all."

"Why do you say that?"

"Lola said as much in her letters to my mother."

"My parents don't like a lot of people. What does that have to with her disappearance?"

"Your family had the most to gain from Lola...disappearing." She chose cautiously. "Wasn't your father running for office for the first time?"

"My family was not responsible for Lola's disappearance!" he insisted.

"Are you sure? Were you there fifty years ago?" The angry intensity of his gaze sent a ripple of apprehension up her back, but she pressed on. "It's not a coincidence someone tried to run me over after my confession to your family."

Green eyes narrowed to slits. "What are you implying?"

"Well, your parents came by the house when I wasn't home. They could've placed the photos, and the poster, in my room. They also knew I was going to the club last night."

"What?" he bellowed. "You think someone in my family tried to kill you?" He took a calming breath. "They weren't the only ones to stop by the house. So did Gary and the neighbor with the awful colored wig."

"Mrs. Anderson?" she chortled. "Yes, she delivers dangerous apple pies." She gave him a sideway glance and shook her head. Wait. Gary was at the house? Why? The hairs at the back of her neck stood up when she remembered his shocked gaze at the club.

"What about your suspicions of Pearl?"

She shrugged. "Pearl is also on the list, but she didn't have access to the house, so that puts your family at the top. There are no records of Lola and William's marriage, other than my mother's photo. They could be trying to hide what happened, especially since Lola disappeared."

His mouth tightened. "My family wouldn't go to those extremes. If anything, they would pay you off."

"Is that what they talked about last night?"

"That was one of the choices."

"What were the others?"

"To fire you," he said plainly.

Her pulse stuttered. "Was that your father?"

He nodded.

"Have you decided?" she asked, her heart in her throat. He did stop the crew working today.

His intense gaze moved over her. "We should try and solve this together."

"What?" That wasn't the answer she expected. "Why?"

"You're living under my roof, working for me—"

"I didn't ask to live under your roof. You insisted!" she interrupted.

He crossed his arms over his chest. "You're suspecting my family of a lot of...hostile acts, and I plan to prove you're wrong." His lips pursed arrogantly.

She longed to throw the words 'what if you're wrong?' at him, but kept quiet. She didn't want them to be guilty, either; technically, they were the only family she had left.

"Agreed?"

She looked down at his extended hand, not wanting to touch him after what happened last night, fearful of what she'd see or feel.

"Yes," she answered, but ignored his hand. He was right. Working together was the fastest way to find out what happened to Lola. He'd have access to information from his family that she wouldn't.

Stillness settled around them as he finished eating.

"Is there anything else I need to know?" he asked as he leaned farther across the kitchen counter.

"What did you see last night?"

Apprehension moved across his face. "You, singing onstage."

"Anything else?"

"Like what?" he asked a little too quickly.

She needed to know if he saw what she did, or if he only felt the emotional connection. She took a deep breath and hoped he didn't think her crazy. "I saw something. Something I can't explain."

"What?"

"The people and things around me changed. I think I flashed back in time." Her eyes watched him as she said the words, but to her disappointment, the wall behind his eyes remained in place.

"Back in time? Seriously?" His tone said she was crazy for thinking it.

She nodded. "The club was newer, the people were different: their clothing and hairstyles, among other things."

Silence hung in the air as he contemplated her words, as if trying to decide if he agreed. "I saw the same thing, but I don't think we traveled through time. I think it was a hallucination."

She visibly relaxed, thankful he didn't continue to deny it. "You're probably right. I'm just glad I wasn't the only one who saw it."

His searching glance found her. "What else did you experience?"

She remembered the hurt she felt when he rushed out the door. He didn't feel the same. The emotions were William's, not his. "It's obvious we were caught up in an experience Lola and William shared," she said with a wave of her hand. Even if he did feel what she did, keeping him at a distance was more important now than before. For all she knew, what they experienced from the moment they met could be from Lola and William.

The mood in the room changed when she said the words. The weight of what happened between them in the club and the emotions they shared hung in the air like an unpleasant smell of something burnt in the kitchen.

Disappointment filled his eyes. "I hadn't thought about it that way."

"It's the only logical explanation." She avoided his gaze. "Lola wanted me to see what I did."

"What do you mean?"

She took a deep breath. She'd wrestled with whether she would tell him about her emotional connections, especially those to the house, and then the club. If he hadn't shared her experience last night, she might have second thoughts; but he had, and that meant something. "I know this sounds strange, but I know Lola is dead and she's been trying to tell me what happened to her."

Skeptical green eyes held hers for several moments, as if trying to decide if she was telling the truth or off her rocker.

"I've had emotional connections to people and things for as long as I can remember, but nothing like I have with this house, the club, or you." Her eyes rose to meet his. "I think it's because of Lola."

•••

Patrick leaned back in the barstool, digesting what she said and recalling his own experience. Strangely enough, it made him feel better that there was a reason behind their hallucinations, even if it was a crazy one.

"Well, that certainly explains a lot," he said solemnly. "Since we're being honest, I saw something the first time we met when I shook your hand. Then there was the vision of you in your underwear."

"That's doesn't make sense." Her brows knotted. "I've never felt Lola here at the house, unless..."

"Unless what?"

"The first night I moved in, I saw a ghost. I think it was your uncle."

"What? Why would he have shown himself to you and not me?" he asked, but quickly found the answer. "Your connection to Lola."

"Maybe William's showing you his experiences with Lola."

He ran a hand through his hair. This wasn't going to be as simple a solution as he hoped. Nothing ever was with Josie. "That explains the intense sexual attraction," he mumbled.

"What?"

"Nothing."

"Now what?" she asked, her eyes wide and expectant, as if he had the answers to finding Lola. He wished he did.

He should be relieved that every unsettling emotion Josie had stirred in him was because of William and Lola; it gave him an out. An out was the least complicated, but did he want one?

"We'll take things one day at a time and gather all the information we can about Lola that might help find out why she disappeared, and what happened to her after she did."

Her taut frame visibly relaxed as she breathed deeply in relief, and for the first time he realized she'd been doing this on her own and was happy to share it with him, even though his family were suspects. Her mother died months ago, but from how Josie spoke about her, she wasn't a strong presence in her life. As irritating and interfering as his family was, at least they were there for him.

"Why are you doing this?" Knowing the reason would tell him more about her. He suspected it was something other than blackmail, as his family assumed.

"For my mother."

Her reason surprised him. He suspected it was to find family, since she had none. He reached across the countertop to take her hand. It was dangerous for them to touch, with everything that passed between them since she moved in, and especially after last night. Right now, he didn't care.

"I couldn't help her when she was alive, but maybe finding Lola will bring her peace," she said softly.

His thumb caressed her hand. "And you, too," he added.

Soft curls bobbed against her temple as she nodded. Lifting her chin, he watched pools of water swim in her eyes, ready to fall down her cheeks.

"I'm sorry," she whispered. "I'm not normally this..."

"Vulnerable?"

She gave him a weak smile. "Must be Lola."

If Lola was making her vulnerable, that was a good thing. He liked her this way. He wanted to tell her everything would be okay, that he'd make it right, but he didn't want to make a promise he couldn't keep. Finding out what happened to Lola was not going to be easy.

She took a hesitant step forward, and he pulled her against him, wrapped his arms around her, and stroked her hair. Lavender, and the scent of her skin, swirled around him. His heart tightened painfully.

"Josie, I..."

"I know," she answered, even though he hadn't said anything coherent. "It's only Lola and William's emotions, but right now, I don't care," she whispered against his chest.

Those weren't the words he expected, but he couldn't agree more. "They're really going to complicate things, aren't they?"

Her shoulders began shaking, and for a moment, he thought she started crying. He heard giggling.

Glorious caramel eyes looked up at him, their edges crinkled with laughter. Her chuckling quickly escalated to boisterous laughter and he looked down at her in fascination. It transformed her face, making her girlish and incredibly sexy, which didn't take much. His heart swelled as he thought how magnificent she looked, but was it his feelings or his uncle's?

"Oh, Patrick," she said between chuckles. "Only you would say that."

He didn't answer, but gave her a brief smile. Only she would find humor in what others considered an annoyance. It was yet another way she captivated him. He cleared his throat and took a step back, putting distance between them. "You mentioned letters from Lola. Do you have them here?" Talking about Lola was safer.

"Yes," she said hesitantly.

"If we're going to be working together, then we'll need to be honest with each other. That means you share what you have and I'll share what I have. Agreed?"

Apprehension-filled eyes raked across his face. "I'll be right back."

He watched her go upstairs and took a deep breath. The sooner he found out what she had, the sooner she would be safe, and his family's name cleared.

The venom in his father's words, "Get rid of her or I will," and his insistence that they wouldn't pay her off nagged him to the point of sleeplessness, making him wonder how his father planned to make her leave.

He raked a hand through his hair in frustration. Someone had tried to hurt her, and it turned his stomach that he hadn't been there to protect her. He would be there from now on, even if it meant contacting the police. What good were contacts if you couldn't use them? His father wouldn't like it, but that didn't matter. What mattered was that Josie was safe. So what if the strength of his need to keep her safe was due to his uncle? An ache squeezed his heart when he thought of her being hurt—or worse, killed—because of something that happened fifty years ago.

He'd moved back into the house to make it his home, and meet someone special who he could share his life with and start the family he wanted. The sooner she was out of his life, the faster things would return to normal and he could move on with his life. But the thought of not having her in his life didn't give him the satisfaction he felt it should.

His expression was solemn when she came back downstairs. "Do you know for certain Lola's your aunt? Is there any chance it's a mistake?"

She gave him a harsh, sideways glance. "I have the photos from my mother's house and the letters from Lola calling my mother 'sister'."

"Maybe they were high school friends who considered each other sisters," he offered.

Her face crinkled in doubt. "I hadn't thought about that. It might explain why neither of my parents told me about Lola." Her hands covered her mouth. "Oh my God, Patrick, what if she isn't my aunt? The things I said to your parents, and to you..."

Guilt nailed his gut. It wasn't his intention to make her feel bad; he had only wanted her to start thinking in another direction.

"I'll make inquiries."

She put her file on the countertop. "Start with Lola's letters." She pushed them toward him. "They begin with her moving to Chicago and how she met and married William. The letters also show the close relationship she had with my mother."

He shuffled them into date order before reading them.

"You're right. The letters do state Lola and your mother were not only sisters, but very close."

She shot him an 'I told you so' glance.

"Is this everything?"

She tapped her finger against her cheek. "There's the chest in the attic."

"You could finish looking at whatever you found the day I caught you." He grinned.

"It could provide clues to what happened to Lola," she said excitedly.

"Agreed." He stood up and headed upstairs, Josie close behind him.

• • •

Josie carefully pulled out the items she'd shoved back in place when he walked in on her suddenly. Nothing appeared damaged when she took them out.

"Why would she leave personal things behind, or such expensive jewelry?" she asked, caressing a stunning diamond necklace and wondering if it was real or just part of her costume when she sang onstage.

"She could afford to with the pieces that supposedly went missing," Patrick said.

Her eyes shot daggers at him for implying Lola had stolen the jewelry. "That still doesn't explain why she'd leave behind childhood photos and end all communication with my mother. They were very close."

"Who says they didn't keep in touch? Your mother could've hidden or thrown away the other letters. It might also explain why she never told you about her."

She opened her mouth to argue, but he did have a point. It was something she hadn't considered. Was it guilt for her sister's sins that sent her mother down the path she took? "What about the photos and the poster left in my room?"

"It doesn't make any sense," he argued. "Why would my family bring up a past they tried to hide all these years?"

"Maybe I remind them of what they did, and the threats were made to keep what happened to Lola in the past."

"What do you mean by 'what happened to Lola?'" His eyes narrowed. "You don't think she just disappeared, do you?"

Her silence gave him her answer. "And you think my family… killed her, and are trying to get rid of you to keep the truth from coming out?" he asked incredulously, even though it wasn't the first time she'd made the accusation.

Contempt laced her voice. "It's not an unreasonable assumption. Your father had questionable connections at the time, so he wouldn't have had to sully his hands."

His eyes grew dangerous. "It's just as possible someone else could be the suspect!" he yelled. "You yourself suspect Pearl, and there's also Joe." He took a menacing step toward her.

She placed her hand on her hip. "I know that! Heck, it could even be Gary, for all we know. He's been cleaning up your family's messes for years!" she shouted, meeting his ominous glare with one of her own.

"How the hell did you know that?" Fervent eyes raked over her in a way that made her wish she'd kept her mouth shut instead of starting an argument with him.

"I just do," she murmured.

He was close enough for his cologne to tickle her nose. She didn't dare look into his accusing eyes. The tension between them was a rollercoaster on most days; since last night, it was a joy ride any amusement park would kill to have.

"That's not good enough," he said putting, his forefinger under her chin so her eyes met his.

To her astonishment, there was no anger in them. They were on fire with the sexual tension that'd burned between them each time they were within inches of each other.

"I...I have more letters," she stammered, the heat of his hand on her skin causing havoc to her senses.

His thumb moved to caress her cheek, and the vein in her neck pulsed wildly against his fingers. The dusty attic faded around her until there was nothing but Patrick, his large frame narrowing the small space where they stood, surrounded by pieces of furniture. A sharp gasp escaped her when his hands moved to grip her firmly by the shoulders.

"I told you, I want to know everything," he insisted, his face moving closer to hers.

Her heart hammered in her ears. "You don't need to know everything."

"I want everything." His voice was thick.

Of their own accord, her hands moved up to grasp the collar of his shirt. She knew what was coming and she didn't want to stop it, even though she knew it wasn't a good idea. *Yes, take it, take everything,* her mind and body screamed. No words left her lips as she pulled his mouth down to hers.

Their lips crashed into each other and their mouths opened, hot and eager as their tongues stroked and sucked. Desire came at her in crashing waves and moans echoed in the room. She didn't know or care whether they came from him or her.

His lips moved to her neck, making a heated path with his tongue to her collarbone as his hands pulled at the collar of her sweatshirt, but settled instead on her breast, stroking it through the layers of material.

She clawed at his clothes, pulling him closer until she felt his erection pressed between her legs, and she ground her hips against his, gyrating to his rhythm.

Her fingers worked to pull his shirt of out of his linen shorts and over his head, and she groaned when her fingers met his naked flesh. She ran her hands down the length of his back, clutching his shoulders—partly for support—as he pushed her shirt up to her elbows and pulled her bra down. His mouth found her bare breasts and it was heaven when his tongue licked her already hard nipples. Urgent need swirled in her stomach and burned a trail between her legs until she pulsed and yearned for more.

Her hands ran like claws along the skin on his back and made their way to his shorts. Her hand searched until it found his erection, and she smiled with feminine gratification that it was there because of her, and she caressed and teased him. Patrick groaned, his breath hot against her ear.

Downstairs, the noise of the front door opening drifted through the attic floor, along with the rumble of footsteps and Danny's loud voice. "Hello?"

Patrick went still beside her. She closed her eyes to clear her head from the fog of desire. When she opened them, she found his once emerald eyes a pale aqua, searching hers.

"I told him to come alone." He spoke so calmly that she wanted to smack him. How could he dismiss what happened between them so easily when her legs felt like Jell-O?

She gave him a tight-lipped smile. "I see," she said coolly, sidestepping his outstretched hand and adjusting her clothes.

He caught her by the elbow. His gaze raked over her face and mouth before he planted a swift kiss on her lips. "Later," he whispered hotly.

The word hung in the air long after they left the attic, leaving her wondering what was coming later.

• • •

"Where were you guys?" Danny asked. His eyes narrowed when they reached the bottom of the stairs.

Despite their efforts, their clothes were slightly out of order and her cheeks were flushed.

"Taking a nap," Patrick mumbled.

She avoided Danny's piercing stare and looked down at her shoes.

"What were you up to?" Danny's tone was dangerous.

"In the attic, getting a visual feel of the choices we're going to make," she said, knowing she was going to get a lecture. It wouldn't be the first and she doubted it would be the last.

"You two are terrible liars." Josie and Patrick looked at Danny to find him shaking his head at them.

They opened their mouths to protest, but he stopped them with a raised hand. "Save it!" His gaze moved to Josie. "We'll talk later." His eyes found Patrick. "Don't waste my time. I could use a Saturday off."

Patrick cleared his throat. "I called you in so we could discuss the design for the attic without interruptions." He looked to Josie to agree with him.

"Yes." She nodded eagerly. It wasn't a complete lie. Patrick had asked Danny to come alone. "I want to split the space and put skylights in the ceiling, so we need to check out the roof to make sure it'll work."

Danny crossed his arms over his chest. "I thought we were starting on the new bathroom first."

Josie and Patrick looked at each other. "We are," she insisted, "I—"

"I'll be in court next week, so I won't be available to discuss the design then," Patrick cut in.

Josie did a poor job of hiding her relief. "Yes, that's it."

Danny shook his head, implying he didn't believe them. "Okay, let's get started then." He pushed past them. "We'll start taking out the walls in the third bedroom to make space for the bathroom, along with removing the necessary walls in each bedroom to update the electrical and plumbing. Have you two thought about where you'll be staying?" he asked when they reached the attic.

They looked at each other. "Josie can stay with me at my apartment," Patrick said a little too quickly.

She gave him a stern look. "If we paint the living room tomorrow, I can sleep on the couch until you finish my room."

"I don't want you staying here by yourself after what happened." Her gaze cut him in half.

"What happened?" Danny blurted. No doubt, he remembered her unusual call a few weeks back.

"Someone tried to break in," she offered and ignored the guilty knot in her stomach at her lie.

"What?!"

"They didn't succeed," Patrick declared, "but I want you to put in a security system right away."

"I'll take care of it." Danny turned to Josie. "You can stay with me until then."

"She stays here with me," Patrick said with too much possession in his voice.

She rolled her eyes. "I need to be here, but you can stay at your apartment until your room is finished. You're the client; you should be comfortable."

"I'll be comfortable right here."

"With guys going in and out to work on the electrical and plumbing? You'll only be in the way," she insisted.

"This is my house."

"You're the one with the tight schedule."

His jaw tightened. "I know that, but I won't risk leaving you here alone."

"I'm not a child, Patrick, nor am I your responsibility." Her tone rose in annoyance.

"Enough!" Danny shouted, moving to stand between them. "Jeez, you two sound like an old married couple."

A hint of color rose on both their cheeks.

"We'll finish painting the living room and working on the spare bathroom. We'll work on Josie's room first. Patrick, you'll sleep on the couch, and Josie will stay in your room. I'll feel more comfortable with her sleeping behind closed doors." He shot Patrick a sideways glance, daring him to disagree.

He didn't. Warmth spread across Josie's body when she thought about sleeping in his bed.

Chapter 12

Smoke fills her eyes and nose as she steps onto the wooden stage from the backroom of the club and turns to face the crowd. The roar of laughter, conversations, and the clinking of glasses become a low hum in the background when the single white light appears where she stands. "Lover Man," she says to the band behind her.

A trumpet plays the first bars of the song and the noise in the club diminishes to silence. A smile creases her face as the piano joins in, and then the clarinet. She closes her eyes as her skin is bathed in the smooth combination of the instruments' sound, and she loses herself in the atmosphere they create, and begins singing.

She senses someone watching her and looks up to the second level of the club. The figure of a man is there in the distance, but the dimmed lights of the club shadows his face. She feels the intensity of his gaze, on her face, neck, and the shape of her body outlined in the tightly fitting blue-sequined dress. She blushes, and quickly starts to sing the next song.

Her heart beats faster as she watches him get up from his seat, and walk towards the stage. Her voice cracks over the words she is singing, growing weaker as he draws nearer. With each step closer, the faster her heart beats, until it's a drum beating in her head, drowning out the sound of the band.

The shadow cast over him moves higher up his body as he get nearer, first highlighting his black shoes, his chestnut slacks, the ebony belt around his waist, then the snowy shirt across broad shoulders, moving up to his neck, and strong square jaw line. There is a flash of silver and black. The man moves closer and she realizes he's pointing a gun at her.

Josie woke up screaming and clutched her throat as sweat streamed down the valley between her naked breasts. She reached over to the nightstand and turned on the light. As she looked around the room—whose corners were piled high with tile samples, designing books, and other familiar items—she remembered where she was. She took deep breaths until her pulse returned to normal, and a drink from the glass of water on her nightstand. She jumped at the sound of sharp, urgent knocks on the door and cursed when the water spilled on the sheets.

"Are you okay?" came from the other side of the door.

"Yes, just a bad dream."

"Should I come in?"

"No! I'm not dressed!" The words escaped before she could stop them. The table fan didn't cut the summer heat, and she'd resolved to do what was necessary for a good night's sleep, even if it meant sleeping in the nude.

There was a faint curse from the other side of the door before she heard a pained, "I don't mind...if you need help."

"Thanks, but I'm fine," she assured him.

There was only silence. She grumbled as she got out of bed and wrapped the sheet carefully around her body. She made sure every part of her was covered before she headed to the door. He obviously wasn't going to leave until he saw she was okay. The gesture would be sweet if it weren't so annoying.

When she opened the door, Patrick stood in the doorway with only a pair of pajama bottoms hanging loosely on his hips. It was her turn to be speechless as his broad shoulders and sleepy, concerned green eyes flooded her senses, along with the masculine scent of him that was a combination of lingering cologne and his heavenly skin. She pulled the sheet tighter around her small frame and ran a quick hand through her hair, hoping it smoothed down the locks instead of making them a bigger mess.

"You sure you're okay?"

She hated the reaction his presence had on her. His fathomless eyes saw places she hid from others. Her fingers ached to burrow themselves in the thickness of his hair, and his lips—those damned gorgeous lips—taunted her every time she saw them. She remembered them pressed against hers. He'd been coming home late in the evenings due to his latest case. She tried to convince him to stay at his apartment downtown without success.

She tore her eyes from his lips to find his frowning forehead. "I'm fine!" Her voice held more agitation than she intended.

He gave her a blank stare before answering, "Okay, good night, Josie." He said it quietly and turned to leave.

Goosebumps formed on her skin at the sound of her name in his deep baritone voice. "'Night," she said and closed her door.

Leaning against the door, she breathed a sigh of relief, then felt a pang of guilt at her rudeness. As she looked around, the room began slowly closing in around her and the fragments of the dream and the fear she thought had passed flooded her senses.

"Damn!" She yanked her door open and rushed after him.

"Patrick, wait." She reached him at the edge of the staircase. "I'm sorry," she said simply. She looked up at him with fearful eyes and hoped he would take the hint without her having to tell him she was scared by a dream after she'd been adamant she was fine.

He ran a hand through his rumpled hair and nodded.

The smell of his hair wafted around her. She peeked up at him to find him watching her hotly and she realized the bedsheet contained a huge wet spot from the water she'd spilled. The outline of her breasts and nipples were very clear and he was taking in every inch. Heat flooded her cheeks. "I didn't realize I was...so visible."

"Don't worry... I was enjoying the view," he said huskily. His glance moved from her face to her breasts and to her face again. His eyes turned to emeralds.

To her utter embarrassment, her nipples tightened as she remembered his mouth and tongue tormenting them. "Thanks for telling me," she muttered.

He gave her a wicked grin. "I thought you were trying to make up for being rude."

"I'm sure I could think of something less personal." She hit his arm playfully.

"How about breakfast? It's almost morning."

She laughed. *How about inviting me to your room for a different kind of breakfast? Shut it!* "Okay, breakfast it is." She swallowed deeply, hoping to control the butterflies in her stomach at his winking dimple.

"I'll make the coffee," he offered.

"Deal. Let me change first," she said, gripping the sheet closer to her frame.

"Don't change on my account." His eyes grazed over her wickedly and he took a step closer.

"Go! I will meet you downstairs." She pointed toward the stairs. "And put on a shirt!"

She dressed quickly and walked past the plastic sheets covering the entrance to the third bedroom. Patrick had decided to convert it to a bathroom since it was the smallest.

Part of the attic was being kept for storage and the remaining space changed into the sunroom she suggested, but could double as a spare bedroom with the fold-out couch she recommended he purchase. The renovations were the only thing about this job going according to plan.

Since he worked late the last few nights, there was no chance to talk about what happened in the attic. During the day, they kept their distance and tone professional. Josie suspected it was more for Danny, who was still wary of Patrick.

Part of her was relieved to avoid talking about what had happened between them. Lola and William's emotions were trickling into their lives; not just the sexual attraction, but in how they related to each other, clouding what could've been a natural attraction. She'd never know if her thoughts of or feelings for Patrick were her own or Lola's.

When she reached the kitchen, he stood next to the coffee machine and turned when he heard her.

"You don't have the ingredients ready for me?" she teased. Humor was easier to handle than sexual tension.

"I had to leave something for you to do."

"Making breakfast isn't enough?"

"I can't do everything around here."

She gave him a sideways glance. He didn't do anything around the house since it was being renovated. "Okay, boss." She saluted him.

"Good. You know your place around here," he taunted.

"I'm suddenly having second thoughts about breakfast," she warned.

He threw his hands up in defeat. "All right, I give. You do all the work around here."

"Get cracking on that coffee," she ordered playfully.

She turned on the stove while he moved to where she stood and poured out two cups of coffee. Thankfully, the tension after her suspicion of his family was no longer in the forefront. It was as if discovering her secret made him feel better than not knowing.

"What was your dream about?"

Her shoulders tensed as she remembered the fear she felt when the man in her dream pointed the gun at her. Since they'd agreed to work together, telling him wasn't a bad idea. He might see something in it that she hadn't.

"I've been having..." She chose the words carefully. "...strange dreams."

He took a sip of coffee. "It sounded more like a nightmare."

She placed the plates of scrambled eggs on the counter in front of the barstools. "They aren't, usually." She walked to the other side and took a seat. He joined her.

"How are they usually?"

"Pleasant." She smiled sheepishly.

He raised an eyebrow. "Like the day I came into your room and you were moaning?"

"It's not X-rated or anything, just someone special."

"Who?" he asked a little too quickly.

"I know him, I just can't see his face." It wasn't a complete lie. She didn't always see his face.

"That makes total sense," he said with a quirky grin and a raised brow.

"I know the feel of his eyes on me, how his hands feel against my skin, and how he kisses." She looked at him from beneath lowered eyes. "Sounds like I'm ready for a white jacket, right?"

He shook his head. "Not after everything you've already told me. If I didn't call the nuthouse then, I'm not likely to now."

There was a long pause before she continued. "I think it's William," she said quietly.

"Really? Wow. Sounds like Uncle Will's having better luck getting into your bed than me," he said with a wicked grin.

She rolled her eyes. "I haven't felt Lola's presence at the house, so it must be him."

"I guess that makes sense." His eyes narrowed. "But you said your dream was different this time."

"It started the same—with the scene in the club and Lola singing for William—but this time, William was pointing a gun at me...Lola."

His eyes widened before his gaze moved away from hers so she couldn't see his face while he digested her words.

"What do you think it means?" he asked moments later.

"I know what your uncle means to you, Patrick, but is it possible he got rid of Lola?"

"What? Never!" Fiery emeralds blazed at her. "He died of a broken heart."

"Maybe it was guilt." she said quietly. The heat of his anger filled the room to capacity. She shifted in the stool.

"It wasn't guilt!" he insisted. "Uncle Will loved Lola, and she abandoned him."

"She didn't abandon him," she blistered. "She loved him!"

"How do you know? You weren't there fifty years ago." He threw her words back at her. "Maybe she just wanted his money."

"Maybe he didn't want a black wife anymore, or maybe your father didn't want her ruining his political career!" she shot back.

His menacing gaze found and held hers, warning her to stop the direction of her comments. She took a deep breath. "You know as well as I do that she didn't want William for his money. You felt the love coming from her at the club," she insisted.

"And so did you," he shot back. "Your accusing my father is getting really old." Standing up, he walked behind the kitchen counter.

She watched him pour another cup of coffee. "You're right," she said quietly.

"What?" He turned and stared at her, stunned.

"I said you're right. Us arguing over what could've happened and making accusations about Lola and William isn't helping to find the truth." She met his gaze squarely.

"Truce?"

She nodded. Their gazes locked and silence dragged out.

"Josie, I..." He leaned toward her, his eyes as dark as they'd been in the attic.

The doorbell rang.

"Damn!" Patrick shouted. Josie couldn't agree with him more as she watched him walk out the kitchen.

• • •

"What the hell are you doing here, Gary?" Patrick asked when he opened the front door. "This is really *not* a good time!"

Gary waved his hand in a casual gesture and walked past him. "I'm here to make an inspection, something within my obligations." He ignored Patrick's comment. "It looks good," he observed after circling the living room.

"Of course it does!" Patrick said defensively.

Gary studied him for a moment before a smile tugged at the corner of his lips. "I see."

"What does that mean?"

"Nothing."

He walked through the living room and stopped at the dining area. He nodded his head on occasion as if to say he approved of the selection and changes made.

"She's a talented young lady," he regarded. "She'll have no trouble making a name for herself."

"Thank you!" Josie stepped out of the kitchen.

"Oh!" he exclaimed as his eyes glanced over her face. "You're welcome."

She extended her hand for him to shake and Patrick watched in disgust as Gary kissed it.

"A pleasure to meet you," Gary said with more enthusiasm than Patrick ever remembered him displaying.

Gary moved to stand closer to her, his lean frame towering over her petite one.

Her friendly smile wavered for a moment. "I've seen you at Joe's club."

"Yes, I go there once in a while." He turned to Patrick. "This lady has an amazing voice and is more beautiful up close."

Patrick nodded, his eyes raking over Josie as he remembered what passed between them. Her gaze remained fixed on Gary.

They'd agreed the experience was from William and Lola, but that didn't stop Patrick from thinking about her. Had Gary been there that night and seen what happened between him and Josie? Was that why he was here?

"I'm Josie Fagan, but I'm guessing you already know that."

"How right and smart you are. I'm Gary Williams," he said quietly, watching her in a way that made Patrick uncomfortable.

She blinked in surprise. "The family lawyer?"

"It seems I'm not the only one who knows the other," he grinned, but it left his face when her face turned gray. "Is something wrong?"

"No," she stammered before regaining her composure. "You must know Joe, then." She gave him a charming smile that made Patrick roll his eyes.

"I helped him with the paperwork when he bought the club."

"I didn't think he could afford someone like you." She took a step closer to Gary.

She was interrogating him. Days earlier, Patrick would've stopped her, but after recent events, he also wanted to know the answers.

"I've known Joe for years."

"Really? I didn't realize you were friends."

"'Friend' isn't the word I'd use, but we know each other. He asked me to help him out."

His cryptic answer got both their attentions, and Patrick could see the wheels turning in Josie's mind as she digested his words, preparing to attack him again with more questions. She didn't get a chance.

"Please excuse us, Josie; we have business to discuss. I look forward to seeing you again." Gary bowed graciously.

Patrick almost felt sorry for her. She didn't stand a chance against a master of elusion like Gary.

"Of course." Her pursed lips told another story before she smiled and headed upstairs.

"What's this really about, Gary?" he asked when he was certain she was out of earshot. "I know you didn't come all this way to see the renovations."

Gary didn't answer, merely removed imaginary fluff from the arm of the couch he stood next to.

Patrick looked at him sharply. "My father called you."

He should've known. He was not only the family lawyer, but their watchdog, getting him and Noah out of any trouble they got into growing up, and, no doubt, their father and Uncle Will before them. His father was pulling out the big guns to get rid of Josie. It must be bad; he didn't like using Gary unless he absolutely had to.

"He did," he confessed, "but that's not the reason I came."

Patrick crossed his arms over his chest, waiting for his answer. Gary pulled an envelope from a pocket in his jacket and handed it to him.

"What's this?"

"Open it."

When he did, he wished he hadn't. "Who is she?" he asked, although he already knew.

"That's Lola. You've never seen a picture of her?"

"No," he whispered, his legs suddenly heavy. "Uncle Will packed them away years ago, said it was too painful to see them and remember her."

He walked over to the couch and sat down—and was glad he did, because he was shocked to find a photo of himself in black and white. "I didn't realize I looked so much like him." *Or that Josie looks just like Lola.* It's no wonder she felt the connection she did. She could be Lola's twin.

"Yes, you do," he said sadly.

"Why are you showing me these photos now?"

Gary went to sit in the only other available chair in the room. Patrick knew he wasn't going to like what he had to say. Contrition etched lines on Gary face.

"A condition of your uncle's will was that any family of Lola's be entitled to part of the inheritance," he said tentatively.

"Yeah, so?"

The moment the words left his mouth, he understood Gary's meaning. Josie would be entitled to part of his inheritance. "How much?"

"Eighty percent of the money, along with ownership of the house—if they want it."

"What? You can't be serious?" he roared, but lowered his voice when he remembered she was upstairs.

"Very serious."

"Why would he do that?" His tone was heavy with the weight of his uncle's decision. Uncle Will knew how much this house meant to him. Despite asking him to restore it for Lola, he never dreamed he'd have to give it up. "She abandoned him!"

"She did no such thing! She loved your uncle...very much!"

He'd long suspected that Lola deserted his uncle; his father and mother had said as much. But after the emotions from his and Josie's shared experience, Lola's love for Uncle Will couldn't be denied.

Gary gave him a sympathetic smile. "He figured no one from his family would need that much money. You and Noah will get your parents' money. Even after you split it, it's still a substantial sum."

Gary was right. What he didn't know was that Patrick had promised a large portion of Uncle Will's money to Noah for campaigning. He had no desire to go into politics himself, but it was his brother's dream. Noah didn't want to rely on supporters for large portions of the funding and be accountable to anyone. That was a mistake their father had made at the beginning of his political career.

Beyond his promise to Noah, he didn't care much about the money, but he didn't want to lose the house. It was to be his salvation—his chance at a home, and family. Josie loved it as much as he did and wouldn't give it up. But was that love her own or Lola's?

Thoughts of him and Josie living at the house with their children filled his mind. Were those his thoughts or his uncle's? He pushed them aside. "I don't want to wait to get my hands on it. Father's as strong as an ox and will likely outlive the cockroaches if there's a nuclear war."

Gary's eyes widened, stunned at the venom in his voice. Especially since he knew Patrick didn't care if he got his father's money, as he had said so on several occasions.

"What options do I have?"

"You could dig further into her background and find out if she really is Lola's niece, or you could come right out and ask her for the proof," he suggested. Gary leaned forward in the chair. "This option is only open for a year after his death, which is four months away. You could avoid saying anything and hope she doesn't find out."

Gary's last suggestion shocked him. He'd steered him in the direction of doing the right thing for as long as he could remember, whether he liked it or not.

The real question he wanted answered was how would it affect their relationship if she found out? He didn't suspect her of anything unscrupulous, especially after what she told him about Lola, but he didn't trust her completely, either.

"It's a lot to take in one day. You have time to think about it. The deadline is still months away."

He nodded as Gary stood up and walked toward the door. He stopped in the foyer.

"Ask yourself what your uncle would want you to do."

He gritted his teeth in frustration when the front door closed. That's the last thing he wanted to hear. He was tired of people telling him what he should and shouldn't do all his life. For once, he'd felt the freedom to make his own choices, but now it seemed that was being taken away from him again. "Shit!" he shouted to the empty room. Things were getting more complicated by the minute.

...

Josie sat on the bed and opened one of Lola's letters. She wanted to make sure she remembered the words correctly.

Gary came by the house today to offer his support and convince me William's family needs time to accept our marriage. I know he cares, but I couldn't help wondering if he's smoothing the way to an offer of money to get me out of William's life. He is the family lawyer and always cleaning up their messes. I'm starting to feel like I'm a mess William made. I hope I'm wrong.

She jumped at a knock on her door. When she opened it, Patrick stood in the doorway.

He took her gruffly by the hand and headed toward the stairs.

"What's going on, Patrick?" she asked, a little scared by his roughness. Whatever Gary had said had upset him.

He stopped on the stairs to look back at her. He loosened his grip when he saw her pained expression. "I'm sorry. I didn't mean to hurt you."

"Is something wrong?"

"No, everything is fine." He continued down the stairs. He was lying, and doing a bad job of it.

She pulled on his arm to stop him when they reached to bottom of the stairs. "I know what it's like not having someone to talk to. I'm here if you need me," she said softly.

The warmth of his hand in hers felt righter than it should. The connection she felt to him and his home intensified with each intimate moment they shared. The harder she fought, the stronger and quicker it came.

"Why did you come here?" His eyes searched hers more than usual.

She gave him a puzzled look. "I came here to renovate your house—the job you hired me to do." Guilt clenched her. That was the truth in the beginning, but it wasn't the only one now. "I'm sorry for accusing your uncle of Lola's disappearance," she said quietly.

"Thanks." His soft gaze moved from her face to her lips.

She pulled her hand out of his. If they stood there any longer, William and Lola would have their way—they'd be kissing, and who knew what else. Her heart raced at the idea of Patrick's naked skin beneath her fingertips. *Stop it!*

She headed into the kitchen and took a seat at the counter. He stood at the end, watching her with an expression she'd never seen before. Anxiety, if she had to name it. "What's wrong?"

He remained silent, his gaze intense.

"Gary told you to fire me, didn't he?" she said quietly.

"What? No. He wouldn't."

That made her more curious about what the lawyer had said to unnerve him. She longed to ask, but patted the seat next to her instead and gave him a warm smile.

"Danny and I are having a party for the guys this weekend to celebrate finishing the downstairs renovations. We'd like you to come."

"We?"

She grinned. "Okay, me, but it would be nice for the guys to see you in a different light."

His eyebrows knotted. "A different light?"

"Relaxed." She chose carefully. With his family connections, she knew it wasn't easy for him to relax, especially around people he didn't know.

He shifted uncomfortably in his chair and Josie knew the conversation was over. She decided not to push her luck.

"It's no big deal," she said with smile. "Why don't we talk about Lola and how we'll go about finding out what happened to her?"

He took her hand. "I'll be there."

Her heart flipped-flopped at his warm smile.

"So, what did you have in mind?" he asked, releasing her hand.

She cleared her throat. "Let's look at my suspects and my reasons. We'll compare our suspects and decide how they can be crossed off the list."

"Okay, shoot."

"Well, the photos led me to Joe and Pearl, but I'm certain Joe's not a suspect."

"Why?"

"Lola's response to him. It was...different from her reaction to Pearl."

"Ah, right," he said with a skeptical grin. "So Pearl was suspect number one?"

She bit her lip nervously. "Actually, your family was. They had the most to gain."

"Agreed, but that doesn't mean they had anything to do with it."

"Then, earlier, it was Gary," she said cautiously as she handed him the wedding photos.

"I didn't realize Gary was at their wedding, but it makes sense. He was Uncle Will's best friend and the only one who continued to help him look for Lola after she disappeared."

"Hmm," Josie said, tapping her finger against her cheek.

He knew from her tone and the look on her face that he was about to be interrogated.

"Are you and Gary close?"

That question surprised him. "Not so close," he said, wondering at the direction of her thoughts. "Why?"

"Is it possible he saw Lola as a mess he needed to clean up?"

His eyes snapped to her. "Are you saying Gary...got rid of her?" he said warily.

Although they both suspected she was murdered, neither wanted to admit any of the suspects was responsible for such a cruel ending.

She shrugged. "Why not? He's friends with your father, and could've seen it as a favor. It's possible he did it for your uncle."

His sharp gaze was a warning.

"Maybe he found out something about Lola and was trying to protect your uncle from her?" she offered.

"Gary may clean up our family's messes," he said with disgust, "but he wouldn't go to such extremes. He's always made sure my brother and I did the right thing."

"I wasn't implying he'd get rid of her by hurting her. I meant maybe he bribed her to leave after finding something in her past?"

"Now you're just grabbing at straws," he insisted. "Who else is a suspect?"

"That's it."

He raked a hand through his hair. "No wonder you thought my family were suspects. There are only three other people."

"Three? You mean two. Pearl and Gary."

"I mean three. Add Joe to that list."

"But Lola..."

"Lola is dead," he cut in, "so maybe her signals are off."

"No they're not!" she insisted.

"What did Lola say about my parents?"

Her mouth became in thin line. "Lola's not here at the house, only William."

"Maybe she's wrong about Joe," he offered.

Her look said she didn't agree, but she stayed silent. His eyes held the same expression they had the day he kissed her. Heat flooded her cheeks and she looked away.

She could feel him watching her, and was thankful she wore her gray sweats and purple shirt that was covered in stains. Not that it made a different to him. He could undress her down to her underwear no matter what she wore.

"I'm going to make you one of my favorite lunch dishes," she said, changing the subject to one thing she knew he wouldn't mind discussing. Food.

"Oh? What?"

"I make a mean lasagna."

He laughed. "You've been holding out on me."

"It was my mother's favorite. It was the only thing she cooked really well. I haven't been in the right frame of mind to make it."

"I'm sorry, Josie." His hand reached out for hers.

She knew she should pull her hand away before he touched her—their relationship was already complicated enough—but she didn't want to. It felt right. He felt right, as though being with him was where she belonged, just as she felt she belonged in the house. If only she knew whether it was her own feelings or Lola's.

The warmth of his hand engulfed hers, making her feel safe and scared at the same time. His thumb stroked her fingers, and the heat of his touch spread across her entire body. He leaned closer until their lips touched lightly.

She smiled beneath his lips at the screeching sound of her stool being pulled closer to his. He put his lips to hers again. Unlike the first time he'd kissed her, it was soft and undemanding—until he slipped his tongue into her mouth. Heat spread quickly throughout her body and the flames flickered stronger with each caress of his tongue against hers.

His hands moved from her shoulders to the side of her face and he deepened his kiss, but it remained slow, and her knees melted as thoughts of his body pressed against hers flashed before her in slow motion. Each slow stroke of his tongue against hers was the feel of him inside her body. He was making love to her with his mouth.

It was Patrick who pulled away.

She groaned in disappointment and he laughed.

"As much as I want to keep kissing you, a guy can only take so much torture without satisfaction."

She looked at him, confused, before she realized what he meant. Heat rushed to her cheeks and she avoided his very hot gaze, which was a mistake as her eyes came in contact with the very evidence of his discomfort.

"Sorry," she mumbled, although she wanted to ask, 'what's stopping you?' There were more reasons than she could count.

His hand went under her chin and lifted it. "Don't be. I'll live."

I might not. She wished it was a different time and place. Her attraction to him was bordering on dangerous, and sleeping with him would only make it worse.

Chapter 13

Smoke swirled above the BBQ grill, and with a flick of her wrist, Josie turned over another burger. They were celebrating the completion of the downstairs. She'd never admit it to anyone, but she'd had doubts whether they'd be able to finish it within the deadline. They had.

"To finishing the ground floor!" Danny shouted over the loud crew.

"Yeah!" Voices rippled through the crowd and the guys laughed and clinked their beer bottles. They were happy to have the milestone behind them.

"Only three months to go," Danny added playfully.

A round of groans answered him.

"Got room for one more?"

Everyone turned and found Patrick standing at the edge of the sidewalk. He was met by silence, and she almost felt bad for him. Dressed in khaki shorts and a soft blue long- sleeved shirt, he looked out of place among the paint-stained shirts and faded jeans.

"I brought beer."

Awkward silence erupted into cheers and some of the men patted him on the back in welcome. He led a couple of them to his car, where he popped the trunk and had them unload case after case of beer.

"Looks like we're going to need another cooler," Danny observed.

"There's one in the attic."

He gave her a sideways glance.

"What? I have to keep an eye on the burgers." She quickly flipped one to prove her point, only to realize it was the same one she'd turned over moments earlier.

He shook his head and headed into the house. It'd been almost two weeks since he'd given her the lecture about Patrick.

Her eyes searched the crowd for him the moment Danny was out of view. He stood within a small circle of the crew, laughing and drinking beer. There was no sign of the uptight, serious, and annoying man they'd seen every day since the project started. Gone was Patrick Pullman, son of a senator; he was merely one of the guys. She knew how difficult being here was for him, being the private person he was. Part of her secretly wished he had come for her benefit.

Watching him was a bad habit she couldn't seem to break. Whenever he was in the room, her eyes were drawn to him: the artful movements of his body when he walked or sat down, his beautiful soul-searching eyes that caught and held her own. As she thought the words, they came to fruition and he found her. She turned her gaze back to the burgers and decided to go inside the house to help Danny—anything to avoid his gaze and remember the heated kisses they'd shared.

She headed inside the house and her eyes settled on the kitchen counter. On top sat a stylish cream envelope with her name printed in elegant script. Her hands shook as she picked it up. She turned it over with trepidation. It was not left in her bedroom, but that didn't stop the fear growing in the pit of her stomach as her fingers broke the seal and she pulled out the paper inside.

Please join the Pullmans for their annual fundraiser
Saturday, March 21st at 6:30 P.M.
Pullman Manor

There was no address; there was no need. Anyone invited knew the manor's location. She was certain even those who weren't invited knew its location, which brought about the question of why she was invited.

"Going?"

She shrieked and jumped. Standing behind her was Patrick, grinning the way he always did when he scared her. "You seriously need to stop doing that!"

"I'm having too much fun." His dimple winked.

"At my expense, no less." She shook her head.

He moved closer to her, taking the envelope from her hand. "Planning on going?" he asked again.

She bit her lower lip nervously. "I'm thinking about it."

"But?"

"I'm just curious why your parents would invite me when they clearly don't like me."

He raised a cynical eyebrow. "Why would you think that?"

She gave him a sideways glance.

He put his hands up in mock defeat. "Okay, they aren't crazy about you, but my family believes in keeping their enemies closer than friends."

"They think I'm their enemy?" she gasped, daunted by the thought of being an enemy of the Pullmans.

He rolled his eyes. "It's an expression, Josie."

She let out the breath she was holding in. "The last thing I want is for your parents to hate me."

"Then you probably shouldn't have said what you did to them."

"Maybe it's just an interrogation: what I know and what I want," she said, her voice filled with hope.

He chuckled. "Only you would be relieved that my family wanted to interrogate you."

She tapped a finger against her chin. "Maybe I can ask them some questions."

His expression turned pensive, as if remembering what happened the last time she spoke with his parents. The party could be the chance she needed to make up for the blunder she made at their first meeting. If she redeemed herself in their eyes, they might be more open to questions about Lola. Although Patrick agreed to find out what they knew, she wasn't completely certain he would tell her what he found out, especially if it was incriminating.

"Don't go near them without me." He interrupted her thoughts.

She pouted. "I only want to apologize for how I handled our first meeting."

He gaze moved over her face. "That would be a start."

She put her hands on her hips. "I have no intention of kissing their asses."

He chortled. "That won't be necessary. An apology will be sufficient, but don't question them about Lola," he warned.

"I wouldn't think of it," she said innocently.

"I mean it, Josie. Leave the questions about Lola to me. I assured them blackmail was never your intention and that we're working together, but they're still wary."

"Okay, fine. I'll leave it to you, but remember the promise we made to tell each other everything, no matter what it is." She wagged her finger at him.

"Same applies to you."

"Here's the second cooler," Danny said from the bottom of the stairs, interrupting them.

She took a step back from him at the sound of Danny's voice. Had he heard them?

Danny eyed Patrick suspiciously.

"Thanks," Patrick said, taking the cooler from his hand. "We'll finish our talk later," he said to Josie before he headed toward the front door.

"What's that about?" Danny asked.

She said a silent thank you that he didn't hear them. He didn't need to know about Lola—not yet. "The Pullmans invited me to their fundraising event. He wanted to know if I'm going." It wasn't a complete lie.

He slapped her on the back. "That's great, Josie. That'll open doors to high-end clients."

"Want to go with me?"

He chuckled. "They won't let me through the door in what I wear."

She gave him a sideways glance, but knew he was right. He wouldn't dress in anything more than a T-shirt.

"Looks like your business will be taking off."

He didn't need to know it wasn't a good turn, but a way for the Pullman family to find out more about her, and, as Patrick had said, keep an "enemy" close. "Yeah, it won't hurt you, either."

He grabbed her by the arm as she headed to the front door.

"Josie, that's not what I meant," he said gently. "I want you to be successful and happy."

His hand moved from her arm to her shoulder, took a step closer, and his other hand reached out to touch her hair. "You deserve to be happy." His thumb stroked the side of her cheek.

She looked up at him in surprise. He'd never touched her so intimately before. "Danny, I..."

He lowered his head and pressed his lips to hers. It was surprisingly gentle and undemanding. She didn't pull away when he pulled her into his arms, and even opened her mouth when she felt his tongue run along her bottom lip. Part of her wanted to know how she would react to a man's touch other than Patrick. Lola's connection to William unlocked passions in her she didn't know or think she had, but was what she felt for Patrick her own emotions or Lola's?

Someone clearing their throat broke them apart. It was Patrick.

"Burgers are ready."

Danny stepped away from Josie first. "Thanks. You coming, Josie?"

She managed a nod, her heart racing. Patrick's gaze was as dark as midnight when it rested on her. Was the one he gave Danny as menacing? It couldn't be, since Danny was grinning at her when he left. Maybe that was his intention. She gritted her teeth.

"Is there something you want to tell me about you and Danny?" His tone was low and dangerous.

A flutter of fear gripped her as she searched for the right answer. There was no disguising the anger directed at her. "No." Her voice squeaked.

"I see." He studied her intently for a moment. The darkness on his face lifted and returned to the composed one she was used to. "I guess I'm not the only one you have a connection to."

She sighed in relief when the door closed behind him. If his cool demeanor hadn't returned, she might have thought he was jealous. Did she want him to be jealous? She shook her head and headed back outside, wishing the end of the party wasn't hours away.

Danny's kiss had answered one question. It hadn't stirred the same emotions. She felt more of a reaction from Patrick's anger than she did from Danny's kiss.

Her eyes betrayed her by searching for Patrick the moment she stepped outside. They found him, but his back was turned to her and the BBQ area. The crew was lined up at the long plastic picnic table they had set out earlier for the potato salad, baked beans, and corn on the cob.

Danny was standing by the grill, waiting for her and still grinning. She groaned. She had enough complications in her life right now. The last thing she needed was a strain between her and her contractor and only friend.

She suddenly saw the mistake of letting Danny kiss her, as she pictured Patrick shaking his head no when she went for her reference because she hadn't finished the job. Her contractor had quit when she let him down easily that she wasn't romantically interested. She cursed under her breath. When had she ever been so careless with her decisions? Never!

Across the yard, Mrs. Anderson walked toward them. Josie handed Danny the spatula and went to meet her halfway. She hoped the older woman remembered something about Lola.

"Nice to see you again, Mrs. Anderson." She greeted warmly.

The plump woman waved her hand, motioning that such niceties weren't necessary. "I told you to call me Sofia." She straightened her strawberry-blond wig and took Josie's arm.

"Having a party?" Her tone asked why she wasn't invited.

"Yes, we're celebrating a milestone in the renovations. It's just for the crew," Josie added.

She appeared pacified by the response. "Walk me back to my house. We have a lot to talk about."

Josie's heart raced in excitement with every step she took to the house. Did Sofia remember something important? Was this the clue she was looking for?

They reached the edge of Sofia's front porch and Josie helped her up the white wooden steps to the bright blue door. She was about to jump out of her skin as Sofia opened her front door and led her past the entryway.

She scampered across the room, with as much energy as Joe, to sit at a gaudy flowered print high-backed chair. The mint green and chocolate striped ottoman clashed with her pink pants and burgundy polo shirt. She motioned for Josie to take a seat on the hibiscus-print loveseat.

Every corner of the sunny living room was covered with knickknacks, ranging from brightly colored roosters and chickens to Indian-styled elephants and lamps that sat on the tables, mantle, and beside oak furniture pieces scattered about the room.

The walls were lime green with lemon yellow and pink striped wallpaper on the bottom half of the wall. Bunches of strange, rusty keys hung on various sections of the wall behind her seat, along with framed black-and-white photos of people Josie assumed were family. The glimpse of items on the wall around the corners to the next rooms told Josie the décor must be the same as this one: eclectic.

"I didn't remember Lola, but I do remember William coming by and asking me if I'd seen anything unusual one night."

"Did you?" Josie held her breath in anticipation.

"Yes, a woman leaving the house late."

"Was she carrying anything? A bag, suitcase—anything like that?"

Mrs. Anderson looked at her strangely. "Why would she be carrying luggage?" She placed a wrinkled hand over her mouth. "You don't think she stole something, do you?"

"No, I just wanted to know if she left empty-handed."

"Yes, I believe she did, but it was a long time ago." The skin around her eyes crinkled with disappointment.

"Do you remember anything before or after William came to see you?"

She tapped a finger against her rosy cheek. "Why, yes I do. William was arguing with his brother outside the house. I have a clear view of his front door from my sunroom. I couldn't hear everything they said, but I do recall one thing: 'She's going to ruin our lives.'"

Josie hid her reaction by looking toward the window and took a breath to calm the racing of her heart. If Myles were a suspect, she certainly didn't want to let on she was doing anything more than looking for her aunt. Until she and Patrick got down to the bottom of what happened, it was better this way. She hoped she wouldn't regret keeping it all a secret.

"I'm sorry I wasn't more help."

"You've been a great help, Mrs. Ander—Sofia." She corrected herself and got up to leave, patting the woman's delicate hand.

"Will you continue looking for her?"

"Yes," she said without hesitation. "I need to know." She didn't say what she needed to know and hoped Sofia wouldn't ask.

Mrs. Anderson's eyes drifted outside to the lawn, where the crew continued their celebration before they settled back onto Josie again. "Pursuing something doesn't always give you what you want."

Her words hit Josie right to her core. They were spoken like someone who had been unable to find the solution to her own dilemma. She remembered the sadness when Sofia talked about her husband.

As she walked back along the stone pathway and got closer to the house, she saw Danny at one end of the table and Patrick at the other end. Danny winked knowingly and Patrick's brow wrinkled in question at her.

It was going to be a long three months.

Chapter 14

A warm touch woke her up. Patrick stood over her, a strange expression on his face. She sat up in surprise. She'd agreed to stay in his room while he slept on the couch until her room was renovated, but only with the understanding he wouldn't come in without her permission. She yanked the covers up to her neck, thankful she was wearing pajamas tonight.

"I knew you'd return." His hand reached out to move a stray curl from her face.

What the heck was he talking about? He'd seen her earlier that evening. She held her breath as his hand grazed across her cheek. It was warm and gentle, but didn't cause the butterflies in her stomach to run rampant the way his touch usually did. The face and body before her was Patrick, but something wasn't right.

"I missed you. Where did you go?"

Shock ran through her as she realized who was in his body. But that wasn't possible, was it?

"William?"

He nodded. "I knew you'd come back." His lips curved into a brilliant smile.

She stilled, stunned that William was able to possess Patrick's body. If Lola hadn't done the same to her, she'd be terrified. Instead, she wondered if Patrick was still in there and if he'd remember anything. Her lips curved, thinking of the fun she could have with him. Not a good idea, she reminded herself. Things were already tense since he saw Danny kiss her.

But then she had an idea. She could question him. This was Lola's husband. From the emotions Patrick exuded that night in

Joe's club, she knew he loved Lola, but was it a crime of passion? Several men had been in love with her. Did one of them get her attention as much as William?

"Was that you the first night I came to the house?"

"I didn't mean to scare you. I just wanted to touch you again."

"Why did I leave?" she probed.

He shook his head. "I don't know. You left one night and didn't return." His eyes filled with tears and he pulled her into his arms. "God, how I missed you, Lola," he whispered in her ear.

"I missed you too." He didn't kill Lola. She knew that, despite her dreams and her doubts. Safe and loved was the only way to describe the comforting warmth that surrounded her. There was no animosity between Lola and William that night at the club. Surely there would've been if another man or woman had come between them. "Did someone ask me to leave?"

"No, but..." His jaw tightened. "Myles and Elsa didn't want me to marry you, and after I did, they tried to change my mind about the marriage, and you."

"Why?" she asked, although she had a pretty good idea.

"He didn't think you were good enough for me."

It wasn't the answer she expected. "No other reason?"

He shook his head.

So much for the idea that Myles didn't want their relationship to ruin his political career. Maybe he didn't say it to William, but thought it. No, somehow she couldn't see Myles not speaking his mind, especially to his brother.

"Did Lo—Did I say where I was going the night I left?"

"To meet a friend."

"What friend?"

"I don't know, you didn't say. But it was late at night. I thought it was strange, but you said it was important. I should have gone with you. Maybe if I did...I'm sorry." His voice cracked with pain.

"Shh." She reached up to touch his face. "It's not your fault."

"Stay with me. Be with me." He eyes pleaded.

Her heart lurched at the longing in his eyes—Patrick's eyes. A part of her wished it was him asking the question, but another part of her was thankful it wasn't. It might not be so easy to say no.

Would he remember if they spent the night together? She pushed the thoughts aside. It was Patrick, not William, she wanted to be with.

"I can't," she said weakly. When had she decided she wanted to sleep with him? *From the moment you set eyes on him.*

He smiled sadly. "I know." He touched her cheek softly. "Let me hold you."

It was a simple request and one that tugged at her heart. She leaned into his embrace, happy to enjoy an unguarded touch with Patrick. She'd worry tomorrow whether he remembered it or not. Her eyes closed and she imagined it really was Patrick who held her safely in his arms and loved her as William had Lola. Before she realized it, she drifted back to sleep.

•••

Patrick opened his eyes and found himself in his bed, his arms around Josie, who was fast asleep. The last thing he remembered was going to sleep on the couch, although sleeping had proved difficult with pictures of her in his bed filling his mind each time he closed his eyes. How did he end up here?

Daylight streamed in through the windows, giving him a view of her personal items scattered about his room. Warmth filled him that her things hung in the closet next to his.

She was curled up very close to his body, their legs entwined. Her face held a peaceful smile and she looked more like a young girl than a woman in her thirties. He reached out and touched her hair; her soft curls in his hand told him she was real and he wasn't dreaming.

He touched the smoothness of her cheek and she smiled. His heart reeled and he knew he was in trouble. *You want her badly, and not just her body. That's* not possible, I barely know her. *You know her.*

It was true. He did know her. He had felt the recognition from the moment he'd laid eyes on her. The connection deepened with every minute he spent with her. She'd slowly scraped away the wall he'd built after Sharon.

If only she hadn't confessed to being related to Lola. He could get past getting involved with someone who worked for him for a short while, but her connection to Lola complicated the situation in more ways than he could overlook.

Their physical attraction was strained to uncomfortable each day, but for him, it was slowly becoming more. She was warm, compassionate, and funny, and intoxicated him to the point of pain from wanting to touch and kiss her, make love to her. A vision of Danny kissing her slammed into him, taking his breath away. It was a blow not only to his gut, but his pride. He thought he meant something to her, even if it was the result of their aunt and uncle's connection. He knew Danny liked her, but up to when he saw them kiss, she'd only shown him friendship. Was he so blinded by his own attraction that he hadn't seen there was something between her and Danny?

She stirred and stretched her body across him like a lazy cat. Her hands wrapped around his neck and he felt himself growing hard as he watched her breasts strain against her tight-fitting T-shirt. Beads of sweat formed above his top lip and heat rushed to the back of his neck as he remembered the feel of them in his mouth.

To hell with it!

He pressed his lips against hers and pulled her closer to his body.

She moaned and opened her mouth under his, and he slipped his tongue into her mouth and gently wrestled with hers. He released her mouth and his lips made their way to her neck.

"William?" she whispered, half asleep.

Patrick's blood that had started to boil ran cold. "Who's William?" he asked gruffly. Jeez, first Danny, now some guy named William? How many men were there?

"What?" She rubbed her eyes and looked up to find she was lying across his body. She scrambled to move off him and stand up, but failed miserably and landed on the floor beside the bed.

He offered her his hand, but she ignored it.

"What happened?"

"I woke up with you laying on me," he said simply. Why didn't she ask why he was in the room?

She blushed.

"So how did I end up in here with you?"

"You don't remember?" A mischievous smile cracked her face before quickly disappearing.

"Who's William?"

"What?"

"You said 'William' when I kissed you."

"I did?"

He studied her. "I thought we'd moved past keeping secrets."

"It's not a secret," she said quietly.

"Then tell me who William is."

"You know him," she offered.

His eyebrows knotted in confusion at her words. His mind searched through the faces of people he knew—who she knew—that could be William. Wait, his uncle's name was William! His eyes widened when it became obvious from her expression that his uncle was exactly whom she was referring to. "You were dreaming about my uncle again?" That didn't explain how they ended up in bed together. Not that he minded.

"Not exactly." She bit her lower lip nervously.

"Then what? Don't dance around the answer, Josie."

She avoided his gaze as she sat down next to him on the bed. "He...you showed up in my room," she said quietly.

"What?!" He shot off the bed. He looked down at Josie, trying to decide if she was really was crazy, or had she just lost her mind after she came to work for him?

She swallowed nervously. "I know it sounds crazy, but it's true. I was sleeping and you—your uncle—woke me up. He thought I was Lola."

He crossed his arms across his chest to hide his own nervousness. First his uncle was giving him visions of Lola, now he was taking control of his body. What next? Would he wake up and find himself married to Josie? His insides warmed at the thought of seeing her in the kitchen every morning—her hair mussed and dressed in flannel pajamas he could remove for real, not just in his mind. He grew hard at the vision of her in his bed every night. He raked a hand through his hair in frustration, then paused when a thought occurred to him. "You knew you were with my uncle instead of me?"

"Yes...no," she mumbled.

"Which one is it, Josie?" he demanded. Talk about an ego buster.

"Why would I want to kiss your uncle, someone I don't even know?" she shot back.

"How did you know it was me and not him?" he countered.

She gritted her teeth. "It just didn't feel the same, okay."

"What does that mean?"

Her eyes threw daggers at him. "When he touched me, I felt nothing; but when you touch me, I feel different."

"Different how?"

She stared at him long and hard. "Hot," she mumbled, embarrassed.

Damn! How did he respond to that?

He chose the coward's way out and switched the subject, ignoring the urge to drag her back into his bed, and keep her there until they uncovered whether their attraction was real or just a result of Lola and William.

"What did my uncle say?" He leaned against the dresser.

"He doesn't know why Lola disappeared and doesn't suspect anyone."

"I could've told you that. Nothing else?"

She bit her lips nervously. "Your parents didn't think Lola was good enough for him."

"He said that?" he asked, although his uncle had said as much to him on more than one occasion.

She nodded. "Nothing about them bribing her to save my father's career?" Surprise filled her eyes. "What? I just want to make sure I'm right." His lips curled into an arrogant grin.

Thick curls bobbed as she shook her head. "But I did find out one important clue."

He held his breath for her answer.

"She told William she was meeting a friend, and it was late at night. That confirms Mrs. Anderson's memory of seeing her leave late the night she disappeared," she blurted out.

His eyes narrowed. "Mrs. Anderson said that? Why didn't you tell me?"

She lowered her head. "You didn't ask," she mumbled.

He gritted his teeth and walked closer to the bed. So much for them telling each other everything. "What else did she say?" he asked, not pushing the point. He had yet to tell her about the conditions of the will.

"Just that she was fairly certain she left empty-handed and..."

"And what?" he asked, dread creeping in around him. He knew that look and knew he wasn't going to like what she had to say.

"She remembered hearing William and Myles arguing outside the house the day she disappeared."

"Did she hear what it was about?"

Her brown eyes searched his. "Yes. Lola was going to ruin their lives," she said quietly, as if saying it softer would make it less menacing.

The meaning of the words hung like a pungent smell in the air. He recalled his father's threatening words about Josie: "Get rid of her or I will." He suddenly wondered if his father meant to remove her from their lives in a more final way. What if his father hadn't been able to bribe Lola? Would he have taken more drastic action to get rid of her? The confidence he'd felt that his family were not responsible for Lola's disappearance and the threats made on Josie's life were quickly slipping from his grasp.

Chapter 15

Josie handed her keys to the valet after she stepped out of her car. Cool night air nipped at her skin and she wrapped her shawl closer to her frame as she walked up the bricked driveway to the Pullman Manor. She was purposefully late. She wanted to speak with Patrick's parents, but knew she had to wait until he did first, no matter how strong her urge to ask her questions without waiting.

A two-story gray brick building stood at the end, its width spreading across more rooms than she could count. The beauty of it in the glow of the outside lights embracing it from all sides caught her by surprise. It belonged in a vast English countryside, not ten minutes away from downtown Chicago. Lights along the walkway leading up to the house not only welcomed guests, but also highlighted the lush landscape of trees and shrubs bursting with their final bloom before frost forced them into hibernation.

She handed the man at the door her invitation when she made it to the top of the stairs and ran her hand nervously over her violet silk gown. Excitement pricked the back of her neck like a porcupine.

Two weeks of renovations had passed peacefully. Danny, thankfully, made no attempts to further their relationship, which she suspected he didn't want to display in front of the crew, and she'd be moving back into her room once they finished plastering and painting the bedroom walls. Only the lack of clues to Lola's disappearance plagued her. She and Patrick spent hours going over photos and retracing Lola's steps from Joe's and Sofia's comments.

The next step was to speak with his parents, but she didn't want to push. Trying to find answers to someone's murder, knowing your family were the main suspects, was nothing to jump into.

Once a week, she awoke in cold sweats from dreaming about William trying to kill her in the club or someone trying to run over her. On the nights she sang at the club, she drove her car, instead of walking, and made sure she parked in well-lit areas.

She'd managed to rule out William as a suspect, but still hadn't found out who made the threats. If she did, she'd find Lola's killer. Only she, Danny, and Patrick had keys to the house. No one but her had keys to her room, and the documents she'd compiled were kept under lock and key in her desk. She was relieved no further threats were made, but it brought them no closer to their goal. Time was running out. The end of the project was fast approaching and she'd be out of Patrick's house, and his life. Her heart tightened with an unwanted twinge. Pushing it aside, she walked into the party.

A hundred people or more were crushed into the drawing room. It reminded her of an old ballroom from the 1800s: large, with high ceilings, an enormous crystal chandelier, and marble as far as the eye could see.

Just a few feet inside, she found herself standing next to Elsa and Myles. She turned to head in another direction before they saw her. The last thing she wanted was for Patrick to think she'd approached them.

"Josie," Elsa called out.

"Mrs. Pullman." She turned and smiled. She'd agreed to keep her distance, at least in questioning them, but she certainly couldn't ignore them.

"Please, call me Elsa." She gestured for her to join the circle of people around them.

Josie avoided Myles' penetrating gaze, certain he wouldn't be as civil as Elsa. Her head still spun that she'd been invited. After what happened the first time they'd met, she didn't think they'd trust her in a crowd of their friends and colleagues.

"This is Josie Fagan, the talented restoration architect who's working on Patrick's house."

She hid her surprise at his mother's compliment.

"Really?" a bald-headed man in the crowd asked as he looked past her.

"Yes."

Turning, she forced a smile as Patrick joined them. Since she told him about her conversation with Sofia, he'd been distant. She didn't allow herself to think it was because he saw her kissing Danny.

William taking over his body had shaken him up, and she couldn't blame him. She'd had years to adjust to her connections, but Lola taking over her body shook her in ways her other connections never had.

"Good to know," the hairless man said with a nod.

She was about to give him her business card when Patrick moved to stand beside her and placed his hand on her back. He ran his fingertips along the patch of bare skin not covered by her shawl for one second too long.

She froze and resisted the urge to give him a cutting look as she watched a possible client being taken away by Myles. Patrick's mother remained, her inspecting gaze taking in their interaction, making her feel like a suspect in a lineup, before Elsa's attention was captured by a guest.

Patrick's gaze raked over her face and the length of her entire frame to the hem of her dress that brushed the floor before they settled back on her eyes. "Nice dress," he whispered warmly.

Her expression remained polite and she nodded as if he'd said something about their project. The goose bumps on her arms began to protest profusely, and she wished she'd worn a dress that covered her arms. "Thank you."

"You smell amazing." His husky voice rumbled in her ear.

Shifting uncomfortably, her eyes moved to the people standing around them to see if anyone noticed he was standing closer than necessary. Only one person noticed.

"Patrick." Elsa spoke before Josie could respond to his comment. "Why don't you dance with Josie? Perhaps you'll inspire others to do the same."

After nodding like a dutiful son, he held out his arm.

She took it and followed him to the dance floor, even though she wanted to walk away. What the heck was the matter with him? He was flirting with her, and in front of his mother at his parents' fundraiser that was filled with important people. It wasn't just inappropriate; it was a really bad idea.

He put his arm around her and pulled her into his arms, and his scent. Her senses and body came alive as he moved her easily across the dance floor to the instrumental strains of "The Shadow of Your Smile."

The crowd on the edges of the dance floor paused for a moment, and, to her relief, some joined them on the floor. More people drew the attention from them; however, it also provided them with privacy that Patrick took advantage of, pulling her even closer to him.

"I didn't know you danced." For every step back she took in an attempt to put distance between them, he took one forward.

"Like you, I also have secret talents," his whispered huskily.

She ignored the ripple of pleasure that traveled up her spine, especially when she noticed Myles a few feet away, watching them. His face passed by quickly, but she was certain he was frowning.

"What's up with you tonight?"

"What do you mean?" His eyes twinkled mischievously.

"You're flirting!" His feigned ignorance irritated her. "This isn't the time or place." He'd kept a professional distance between them the last couple of weeks and his sudden change in attitude didn't make sense. It certainly wouldn't help her get on his parents' good side.

"You're incredibly sexy when you're mad." He chuckled and pulled her closer.

She wanted to smack him, but as she looked closer at his eyes, it hit her why he was different. "You're drunk!"

"Not drunk, just really relaxed." Patrick put his index finger to his lips. "Shh, don't tell anyone," he said with a sideways grin.

If it was under difference circumstances, she would've laughed and enjoyed him in this condition, but with his parents and God-knew-who-else watching their every move, it was far from funny.

He laughed out loud at her disapproving look. It caught the attention of several people close to them, who stared.

Smiling politely, she said through gritted teeth, "Would you behave already? Your parents aren't crazy about me as it is, and you're not helping." He'd promised to talk to them about Lola, but he certainly couldn't do it in this condition.

His hand traced a line down the length of her neck. "You'll charm them," he whispered.

The man was incorrigible! "Stop before we end up on the evening news." She seriously doubted the questions she planned to ask would charm them.

His eyes twinkled. "It wouldn't be the first time."

"You're chasing away all my clients," she mumbled in a final attempt for him to see reason.

"I knew we'd move nicely together, but this is better than I imagined." His emerald eyes darkened. "It makes me wonder where else we'd move nicely together."

She shivered under his intimate gaze and images of his lips against hers flickered before her. She became more aware of his hand holding hers, and the other around her waist. To her relief, the song ended, and from the corner of her eye she saw Elsa walking toward them. Her expression gave no hint of annoyance, unlike Myles, who watched her through narrowed eyes.

"Your mommy's coming to get you," she threatened. He still hadn't removed his hand from around her waist, even though she'd taken a step away from him as a hint.

"Nice try."

"Josie, there are more people I want you to meet," Elsa said when she reached them.

Josie nodded and grinned when Patrick straightened up and removed his hands from her waist. To her, Elsa's expression gave nothing away, but it must've meant something to him because he immediately took a step back to put more space between them. Served him right!

"Excuse me, Patrick," Josie said graciously.

"Hurry back," he teased before he greeted Elsa. "Mother."

Josie gave him an I-can't-believe-you-said-that look before she was led away. Apparently his mother's arrival wasn't enough to remind him to behave.

Elsa led her through the crowd, nodding and greeting people who addressed her.

"I'm sorry for making everyone uncomfortable when I mentioned my aunt a few weeks ago," she said when there was a break in the crowd. "It was..."

"Inappropriate," Elsa offered, indicating she was familiar with the word.

It wasn't the word she was looking for, but she wasn't about to argue with the hostess at her party. She was already on thin ice with Patrick's family as it was, and her mother always said you catch more flies with honey than vinegar.

"Apology accepted," Elsa said graciously.

Josie gave her polite smile, surprised she accepted so easily. It was probably because of their surroundings. It might not have come so easy if they were alone, which raised another question. "Why did you invite me tonight?"

Elsa slowed her pace when they reached a secluded spot in the crowd. "I believe in getting to know people before passing judgment, even when they make...foolish decisions."

Did she feel that way about Lola and William? Was Elsa giving her the chance she hadn't given Lola? They weren't in the same situation, but she was thankful for the chance. She wanted to ask more questions, but the surrounding sea of people descended around them.

The beads of sweat in her armpits had dissolved. She'd get the opportunity to meet prospective clients that could help her business if things between her and Patrick went sour. She was Elsa's pet for the night, but she didn't mind. If it got her on Elsa's good side and smoothed over relations with the rest of his family, she'd jump through hoops tonight if asked to. She wanted the Pullmans to like her. Whether it was to help solve Lola's mystery or her growing affection for Patrick, it didn't matter. Growing affection? That was an understatement.

•••

Patrick felt someone's eyes on him and turned to find Sharon watching him. He'd seen her the moment he arrived and had avoided her. Their families were old friends, so he knew she'd be here. She gave him one of her fake smiles—one he used to think was real, at least for him. His body tensed as she closed the distance between them.

"Nice to see you, Patrick," she purred, her hand stroking the shoulder of his tuxedo.

Sex had been the one good thing in their relationship, one that was enough for her, not for him. "I can't say the same," he said coolly, stepping out of her reach.

"I see you have a new plaything. How clever to hire her to avoid suspicions. I'm sure your parents love it."

"She's only working for me," he lied. He had yet to define their relationship. He wasn't about to share it with Sharon.

She chuckled, something he used to love. Now it seemed cold and calculated, just like her.

"Why did you agree to marry me?" His question surprised them both.

"We were good together."

"No other reason?"

Her cool eyes held his for a moment. "What? Like love?"

He nodded.

"Did you love me, Paddy?" she asked, using his childhood nickname.

"I thought I did, but you didn't, did you?"

Silence was his answer. He expected the pain of her coolness, but it was only a distant throb.

"I saw the marriage your parents had, like mine, and I thought you understood."

"I was just another merger for you, wasn't I?" His voice cracked as he remembered how distant she was while planning their wedding. No excitement, or the closeness he'd expected, wanted. It was just another job to her. That's when he realized he wanted the passion and love his uncle had for Lola; even though it left him brokenhearted, Uncle Will had loved her deeply right to the end of his life. "That wasn't enough for me."

"I know." She reached out to touch his face.

"You could be happy in a loveless marriage?"

"I loved you in my way," she said quietly.

"What about kids? Building a future, growing old together?" She'd known he wanted those things with her, but had continued to keep her love at arm's length.

"I planned to do all the things."

"Did you?"

"I thought I'd grow to love you the same way, in time."

"And if you didn't?" His gaze held hers. "You could just move on. Is that it?"

Her eyes met his steadily. "I hoped our friendship would sustain us."

Glancing at her from head to toe, nothing was out of place. A perfect package, or so he'd once thought. Her baby blue eyes were nothing but colored ice. Pink pert lips he'd kissed many times were vessels of lies, spilling nothing but fake smiles and laughter. They'd been childhood friends, and he'd foolishly thought she would care for him more than the other men that'd come and gone from her life, casually dismissed.

Josie's dark purple dress caught his attention. Standing in a circle of people with his mother, with a real smile on her face as she laughed and talked. He was an idiot to ever think she was anything like Sharon. His chest tightened when she laughed again; her entire face lit up.

"I feel sorry for you," he said, turning his attention back to Sharon.

She snorted, but managed to make it ladylike. "Why?"

"You'll never know the joy of real love by keeping it at a distance."

A line on her forehead twitched, seemingly in pain, but it disappeared faster than it arrived.

"Bye, Sharon."

"Paddy, wait." She tugged at his arm. "I'm sorry," she said softly. "I didn't mean to hurt you. I truly hope you find the love you're looking for."

He studied her face and knew she meant it. His eyes widened in surprise when she smiled at him and it reached her eyes, melting them from ice blue to a darker shade.

"You too," he said in earnest.

He watched her leave, then turned to find Josie watching him. She looked away when he found her gaze. His heart swelled as he remembered the love shining in them that night in the club. William and Lola may have been responsible for the strong emotions that night, but was it them before and after then?

"What was that about?" Noah asked as he came to stand next to Patrick.

"Nothing, just clearing the air."

"About time," Noah mumbled. "You two have been tap-dancing around each other for almost a year."

He laughed. Only his brother would think clearing the air was a good thing. Noah was more like their mother, where he was like their father—hold it all in and let it fester.

"I'm glad you approve." He pulled his brother into a neck hold and rubbed his head.

"Hey, there are future voters here," he grumbled, smoothing his hair back into place when Patrick let him up.

Patrick grinned in a way only a big brother can after torturing his little brother.

"So, how are things with Josie? Mother said you're working together now, that she's not out to blackmail us."

"Yeah, that's right."

"So how's it going?"

He eyed a passing waiter and contemplated reaching for another glass of champagne, but changed his mind. He'd started drinking to drown his sorrows, remembering Danny and Josie's kiss and having to see Sharon tonight. After speaking with her, however, he realized the pain was more for their lost friendship.

"Not so good." He watched Sharon approach Josie and contemplated interrupting them, but decided against it. He was certain Josie could handle her. After her confession, he doubted Sharon's intention was to make a scene.

"I'm not surprised. Lola left a long time ago. Are you certain she's even alive?"

"We're certain she's dead."

"Oh, how do you know that?" His brother's voice filled with interest.

"You don't want to know."

"You know that only makes me want to know more."

He gave his brother a sideways glance. "You wouldn't believe me if I told you." He released the breath he didn't realize he was holding when he saw Sharon leave Josie to circulate through the crowd.

Moments later, his mother pulled Josie into another group of people, most of whom were men. He watched them move closer to her than he liked. He gritted his teeth when one of them seemed inches away from putting his hand on her bare back. "Excuse, I have business to take care of."

"Is that what they're calling jealousy these days?" his brother taunted.

"Shut up," he growled before walking away, his brother's laughter following him.

• • •

Josie watched the couples on the dance floor, thankful for a moment of peace from the crowds of people Elsa had paraded her past. She'd managed to hand out several business cards, some of which were requested.

"He likes you."

She turned to the voice behind her. It was the woman who was talking to Patrick earlier. The way she touched him said they were more than friends, or she wanted them to be. "Who?" she asked, feigning ignorance.

"Patrick."

She lifted a glass of champagne to her lips. "He's my client," she said nonchalantly, even as her pulse raced at the woman's confession. Was she telling the truth or just looking for a response?

The woman laughed, but it didn't reach her eyes. "You almost have me convinced."

Josie didn't answer, taking in her perfectly styled blonde hair. She was beautiful—the classic kind. She wouldn't be caught dead in sweatpants or anything that wasn't designer. This was the type of woman Patrick's parents dreamed of him being married to, who'd fit in with them and the other wives.

"He didn't tell you about me, did he?"

Josie moved the glass to her other hand. "Mr. Pullman doesn't share personal details about himself," she lied.

Her ice-blue eyes assessed Josie, a predator about to attack its prey. "You're good." A smile made a crease in her perfect expression. "I'm Sharon, Patrick's ex-fiancée."

"I know who you are," she said casually, as though her confession meant nothing to her. "I read about you two somewhere." She skipped that it was in a tabloid magazine. Was she there to rub her relationship with Patrick in her face, or merely to snoop?

"Did it say why we broke it off?"

She shrugged. "I didn't read the whole article."

"He broke it off." Icy eyes watched her intently.

Josie kept silent, despite the strong urge to ask why.

"He wanted more than I could give him," she said quietly, giving her the answer Josie wanted.

"Why are you telling me this?" What she really wanted to ask was 'what couldn't you give him?' She certainly fit the bill, not only for Patrick, but his family.

"I've seen the way he looks at you. Regardless of what happened between us, I care about him and I don't want to see him hurt again."

She met Sharon's gaze with indifference, even as her heart drummed in her chest.

Sharon sighed deeply. "If you don't care about him, then tell him now. If you do, the same advice applies. He deserves to have the happiness he wants."

"We all do," she said quietly.

Sharon's sharp gaze studied her. "His family will not take it easily, and not just because of your race or social background," she warned.

"I'm more aware of the Pullmans' expectations than you can possibly imagine." She didn't elaborate. Neither did she argue that a relationship between her and Patrick was impossible.

Laughter spilled from Sharon's peach colored lips, surprising them both. "It seems Patrick's family will have their hands full with you. Good. A shake-up is long overdue." She said it in a way that made Josie wonder if she didn't wish she was the one doing it.

"Are you in need of a contractor?" she asked, thinking of Danny. "Not me," she said quickly, swallowing a wicked grin as she envisioned Sharon distracting him from their kiss, and any hopes he had of a relationship. He had a thing for blondes.

"My bathroom could use remodeling."

"I'll send him over next week."

"Patrick didn't stand a chance, did he?" Sharon shook her head.

Josie grinned, thinking she was the one who didn't stand a chance.

• • •

Patrick watched in dismay as Josie laughed with another man his mother had introduced her to. It'd been like that all night, one person after another, so that he couldn't get her to himself for even a minute. That was probably his parents' plan. Every attempt he made to approach her was sabotaged by one of them.

"Things progressing well?"

He turned to find Gary standing behind him. Figures he'd be involved with interfering.

"The renovations are coming along fine."

"That, too," Gary answered cryptically.

Patrick started to ask what he meant, but changed his mind. He was in no mood to deal with Gary. He put off speaking with his parents about Lola. It wasn't the ideal time, but he knew he was safer from his father's fiery responses in a crowd of people than in a less public place. He was still deliberating how to question them in a way that didn't imply they were suspects, despite the mounting motives.

His parents were relieved, although not entirely convinced, that Josie only wanted to find Lola and had no intention of trying to blackmail them. She gained further sympathy when they found out she had no living relatives. Family was something they valued, but the wrong question might put her back on their bad side, so he had to tread carefully.

"She's certainly the social butterfly, isn't she?" Gary taunted, rubbing salt into his already open wound from her attentions being on other men instead of him.

Patrick ignored his comment, but turned to catch Gary watching Josie as though she was the most beautiful woman in the room. The longer he studied Gary, the more Patrick realized he was attracted—or, at the very least, fascinated—by her. Or was it her resemblance to Lola?

Uncle Will mentioned that Gary had introduced him to Lola. Was there more to the story than his uncle told him? "How well did you know Lola?"

Gray eyes grazed over him, searching, trying to figure him out. Both he and Noah had been scrutinized by that look more than once over the years.

"I knew her well enough," he whispered, his gaze moving to Josie.

"How did you meet?"

"At a club where she sang." He turned his gaze back to Patrick. "Why the twenty questions, Patrick?"

His parents hadn't told Gary about he and Josie working together. Not that he was surprised. They didn't like Gary despite his being their lawyer.

"Just curious," he said, shrugging. It wasn't a complete lie.

Gary turned and glared at him with steel gray eyes. Not a good sign.

"What is it you really want to know, Patrick? Did I ask Lola to leave William? Did your father ask me to get her to leave? Did I get rid of her myself?" His voice filled with amusement.

Gary knew him too well. He tried a different direction.

"Did you love her?" It worked. Gary's eyes became white saucers before despair moved across his face, making the wrinkles around his eyes crease deeper.

"Yes, very much."

"Did Uncle Will know?"

"Of course he did. It was never a secret."

Honest. That was Gary, whether it hurt your feelings or not. "What did Uncle Will think of it?"

Gary shrugged. "It didn't bother him. He knew Lola loved him."

"What about you? Didn't it bother you she was in love with your best friend instead of you?"

A smile tugged at his mouth. "She dazzled me when I saw her onstage, and with her bubbly personality in person, but I knew the moment she and Will locked gazes that she wouldn't be mine." He shrugged. "I got over it."

"Do you know why she disappeared?"

Gray eyes burned into him. "No."

"Do you think it had anything to do with my father's connections?" he asked in a hushed tone, his breath held. The possibility had weighed heavily on him since Josie's run-in with his parents and the nosy neighbor's observations. His stomach turned each time it entered his mind, so he chose to push it aside.

"I honestly don't know." He raked a hand over his face. "If it did, she won't be found," he said quietly, pain filling his eyes. "I know. Will and I couldn't find her these fifty years."

He pictured Josie's eyes filled with sadness at not finding the peace she wanted for herself and her mother. It unnerved him that he might not be able to make her happy. Would she let him try?

"You care for her, don't you?" Gary said, putting a hand on his shoulder.

He nodded, not bothering to deny it. Gary knew him too well to lie.

"I was never able to find out why she disappeared," he said carefully. "Your parents thought she abandoned him." His jaw clenched. "But I knew she didn't. If she left him, it was because of their creating a rift between William and Lola."

Well, that explained the tension between his parents and Gary. Their interference may have caused Lola to leave Uncle Will, but it didn't explain her death. "That doesn't explain why she stopped all contact with her family. Lola and her sister were very close."

Gary eyebrows rose. "How do you know that?"

He avoided his prying gaze. "Josie showed me their letters," he said with a wave of his hand.

"You're working together?"

A quick nod was his answer.

"Good. I hope that helps you make the right decision about the will."

"I hope so, too." He hoped to God they could come to an agreement that wouldn't hurt either of them. The thought of Josie severing all ties didn't sit well with him. He wanted her in his life.

"She looks beautiful all dressed up. It's no wonder the men are so interested."

Patrick ground his teeth and clenched his fists as he watched her laugh at a joke and take another glass of champagne handed to her by one of the men surrounding her.

"Yeah," he grumbled.

Gary chuckled and patted him on the back. "Looks like she needs rescuing."

For the first time, he noticed her looking up to the ceiling and rolling her eyes as she took a sip of champagne. She was bored.

After giving Gary a quick thank you, he made his way through the crowd. He didn't know whether to shout in relief or storm over to where she stood and push the men around her out of the way. He took his first step toward Josie and felt the weight of someone's arm on his. He turned to find his mother looking at him.

"Don't even think about doing what I think you're about to do," she warned.

He sighed. "And what to do you think I'm about to do, Mother?"

Icy blue eyes didn't waver. "You are about to make a fool of yourself again."

"Again?"

"The way you danced with her was not...proper," she said carefully.

He put a hand in his pants pocket. "It was your idea for me to dance with her."

"I wanted you to dance with her, not grope her like some teenager on prom night! Decorum, Patrick."

The point was made without her raising the normal pitch of her voice. How she did it, he'd never know. "Very well, Mother," he replied and took a glass of champagne from one of the passing waiters. "I promise not to grope her."

Elsa gasped.

"Josie is not Lola, but don't make the same mistakes your uncle did," his mother warned. Before he could ask what she meant, her attention turned to another senator's wife.

• • •

"Enjoying the party?"

Josie turned to find Gary standing behind her. "Yes, I am." She smiled politely. Patrick didn't say anything about talking to Gary. "Nice to see you again, Mr. Williams."

"Please call me Gary."

"Okay, Gary."

Although he was not high on the list of suspects, Josie happily entertained the possibility of anyone but Myles being responsible for Lola's death. There was nothing to rule him out, especially after Lola and Patrick established his knack for getting the Pullmans out of trouble.

"How are the renovations coming?"

"Fine. On schedule." She knew he was the family lawyer, but she didn't understand his vested interest in the renovations. "You knew my aunt, didn't you?"

"Yes." Gray eyes moved over her face. "You remind me of her."

What that a good thing or bad? "You helped William look for her?" she asked, without saying the words outright that Lola had disappeared.

"Yes," he replied, even as walls went up behind his eyes.

"How did you end up being the Pullman's family...lawyer?" she said, despite another word coming to mind. Calling him a henchman wasn't likely to get her on his good side.

"Our fathers were friends, so we grew up together and our friendship remained. Will and I went to college together."

He didn't answer her question. "What about Myles?" she asked offhandedly, taking a sip of champagne and letting her gaze move around the room. It found Myles, who watched her like a lion ready to attack its prey. Did he know she was talking about him? She looked away, flustered. It'd been like that all night. Every time she felt someone's eyes on her, it was him.

"Not as close as Will, but yes, we were...are friends," he corrected.

Guarded eyes watched her carefully, making her realize no matter how many questions she asked him, she wouldn't find out what she really wanted to know. He was a master at keeping secrets. Was he keeping Lola's killer a secret, or maybe his own crime?

"Did you ask Lola to leave William?" she asked bluntly. Perhaps she could shock a response from him. He'd certainly been shocked when he saw her at the club.

Astonishment flickered in his eyes, but disappeared quickly behind years of composure. "No. Will loved her."

"Did Myles?"

Gray eyes settled heavily on her, as if trying to read her mind, or perhaps discover her secrets.

"You don't know, do you?" She took a sip of her champagne and gave him her best smile. "Or perhaps you do know, but don't want to say," she taunted.

He took a step toward her and grasped her arm, his eyes dangerous. "You don't know anything," he hissed. "You may look like Lola, but you're not her." His eyes moved around the room as if they spoke of nothing significant. "If you try to hurt this family, you'll regret it." As quickly as he grabbed her arm, he released it.

Her heart raced as she attempted to regain her composure. She'd been on the fence about her suspicions of Gary. Patrick's insistence that he'd always steered him and Noah in the right direction gave her pause. Gary's actions tonight, however, were making her reconsider jumping off the fence completely. Fear crept up her spine as she remembered his daunting stare and threat.

"Are you monopolizing Elsa's special guest, Gary?" Myles asked when he reached them.

Josie felt the tension between the two men fill the air, like two young bucks ready to fight for the female doe, as their eyes met and held. If she didn't know better, she would have thought Myles came to her rescue, but that was ridiculous.

"I was just leaving." Gary smiled politely. "A pleasure to see you again, Josie."

She gave him a half smile. It hadn't been a pleasure, and she hoped she wouldn't have to speak with him again anytime soon.

He gave a curt nod. "Myles."

"Gary," Myles said as coolly.

For someone who was the family lawyer, he certainly didn't fit in, making her wonder how he'd gotten, and kept, the job. He was obviously protective of them; perhaps a little too protective, she thought with a shiver. Did he know a secret that kept him there?

"You certainly know how to make trouble." Myles' gaze moved over her face in the same manner Gary's had, trying to read her mind.

"That's not my intention."

"You have a funny way of showing it," he mocked. "But I must say I've never seen anyone ruffle Gary's feathers before. Not even Patrick and Noah during their college years." A small grin tugged at his lips.

"I'm usually quite charming." Did he just crack a smile?

Myles laughed. It caught them both by surprise. "So Patrick keeps telling me." His solemn expression returned. "What did you say to upset him?"

Had she really made him laugh? There was no evidence of it in his eyes, so maybe she imagined it. "You don't want to know." She didn't want to lose the little ground she'd gained.

"Ah, but I do."

Patrick's green eyes stared back at her with as much intensity as his usually did. "I asked him if he bribed Lola to leave William."

An eyebrow rose. "And what did he say?"

"No, but he didn't answer me when I asked him if you did," she answered in a hushed tone. She held her breath, waiting for his response or his anger, not sure which one she'd get.

His eyes snapped to hers. "Why would you think that?"

She shrugged. "It was an important time in your career and people weren't as...tolerant of mixed marriages as they are now." She took a sip of champagne. "Besides, your connections weren't the most reputable."

The muscle of his jaw worked into a frenzy as his gaze moved about the room. It wasn't the right place to talk about Lola, but she wasn't about to pass up the opportunity to ask a question or two.

"I loved my brother and thought he could do better," he said matter of factly.

She cringed inwardly at his bluntness. "That's a matter of opinion. Everyone loved her and thought they were good together," she exaggerated. She had no idea if everyone really loved her; she was only going by what Joe and Gary had said.

"She didn't know the first thing about being a lawyer's wife, especially one as prominent as Will." His tone tried to convince her it was a good reason.

"You might be right, but she wasn't given the chance to prove it, or even offered help, was she?"

"You can't learn what you didn't grow up to," he said coolly.

Annoyance etched her face. "Really? So, Elsa's parents were senators, too?"

His face flared red. "Elsa was different."

"You mean white?" Damn! This conversation was not going the way she planned or hoped. So much for getting on their good side. She'd shot it to hell.

"What? That had nothing to do with it." His voice raised.

Before either could speak, Patrick came to stand beside her, and Elsa next to Myles. Was their conversation on their faces? It must have been for both of them to show up.

"Myles, you haven't danced with me tonight." Elsa tugged on his arm.

He grunted.

"Josie, my husband's library is in need of restoring. How would you like to give it a try? I'll stop by tomorrow to discuss a time and place. It'll give us time to talk, and you and Myles time to discuss the office. Agreed?" Implying the conversation was over and everyone had to do as they were told.

Josie and Myles looked at each, and then at Elsa and nodded.

"Good. Let's go dance," she said, pulling Myles toward the dance floor.

Josie turned to find Patrick's narrowed gaze on her and knew he was mad. She couldn't blame him; she'd done the one thing he asked her not to.

"How does your mother do that?" she asked in awe, hoping it would distract him from the scolding that was coming.

"Is it too much to ask you to keep your promises?"

"He came to me."

He shook his head. "And I suppose he started the questions."

Her mouth opened to say he did, but she decided against it when his gaze bordered on a scowl.

"I told you I wanted to talk with them," he insisted. "This wasn't the place, Josie." The disappointment in his voice made her wish it was anger instead.

Her eyes lowered; a child caught with both hands in the cookie jar. She didn't want to cause more of a scene than she already had tonight. "I should've waited for you," she conceded.

He lifted her face to his. "See? That wasn't so bad, now, was it?"

"Harder than you know." She pouted. Was it over already? Not so painful. Maybe he was saving it until they were alone and no one could hear them arguing.

To her surprise, he laughed. "Come on. I want to show you something." He took her by the hand, walking her through the crowd of people to a door at the back of the room. It led to the kitchen, which buzzed with people either bringing trays in or taking them out. She followed him through the back door, down a long bowing metal corridor to large arched metal door.

The door opened to a solarium. She gasped when she reached the middle of the room; it was beautiful. A solarium was something few homes had anymore, and those that did were nothing like this. It was a sanctuary for plants large and small, with flowers of every type and color imaginable and art made of metal and stone, from tiny animals to human-sized sculptures. It smelled of spring and summer rolled into one, with the gurgling of water in the distance. If the roof had been left uncovered, it would have been invaded by birds and other animals wanting to make it their home.

"It's breathtaking." Her voice was giddy with excitement.

"I knew you'd think so. This was my favorite place as a child." He spoke so quietly that if she wasn't standing next to him, she wouldn't have heard him.

She took his hand in hers. "Thank you for sharing it with me."

His free hand touched her face.

"What are you two doing out here?" Myles stood at the entrance, his arms folded across his chest. A scowl etched his face.

"I was showing her around," Patrick answered, but didn't put space between them.

"So I see," he said quietly. His eyes moved from Josie to Patrick and back to Josie. "You certainly have a way of making trouble, don't you? Must be a family trait," he grumbled.

She opened her mouth to answer him, but decided against it. It was only when Patrick squeezed her hand did she realize her hand still held his. She tried to remove it, but he held it tightly. She looked up to find his eyes twinkling mischievously, and she found herself smiling.

Myles studied his son for a moment. "Patrick, why don't you and Josie take the limo home? I'll arrange for your cars to be delivered before tomorrow morning."

Patrick nodded.

"Thank you," Josie said.

Stern eyes bored into her. "Don't thank me yet." To Patrick, he said, "Son, be careful."

Chapter 16

Silence was their companion as Josie followed him across the yard to the garage. Their fingers remained laced, even after leaving the solarium. He watched the light make shadows through the canopy of trees, playing across her face. It felt so right for her to be here with him, just another night at his parents' house before they made their way home.

Tonight told him what he'd doubted for months. What he felt for Josie wasn't from Lola and William. They were away from the house, and his heart still raced when she smiled at him or touched him without realizing it. Could he convince her the emotions between them were real and not a result of an outside influence? He hoped to God he could, because he wanted her in his life.

His father's driver was standing at the entrance when they reached the garage. "We'll be taking the limo."

He tipped his hat and headed inside.

"Ever ridden in one?" His heart swelled to bursting when she leaned into him, resting her head against his shoulder.

"No."

"Not even for prom?" He caressed her back in long slow strokes, and the silk beneath his fingertips left him to wonder if the rest of her would feel the same.

"I didn't go to my prom."

He didn't need to ask why. She wouldn't have left her mother to attend something he knew she considered trivial, even if she wanted to. He ached at how much of her childhood she must've missed by taking care of her mother. How many nights had she said no to friends who asked her out? Did she have friends?

Between caring for her mother, college, and working on her career, there wasn't time for much else. He wished he could give her part of that childhood, but he couldn't. He was glad his personal reference would help her business.

Lights flickered along the gravel where they stood and moments later, a black stretch limo parked in front of them. The driver got out and opened the door for Josie to get inside.

"You can ride with your head out the top and pretend it's prom night." He gave her a sideways grin.

She chuckled. "No thanks."

"Or you can roll down the side mirror and moon the passing cars," he dared.

"You first."

He shook his head. "The tabloids have enough photos of my butt. They don't need any more." He could laugh about it now, but twenty years ago, it wasn't so funny.

Her eyes searched his in question.

"A night in college—one I'm none too proud of. I'm surprised you didn't keep those in your file." He winked cheekily.

"I was only interested in your house," she said in a disinterested tone as she looked down at her fingernails.

"Ouch."

Their gazes held after their burst of laughter ended.

Reaching across the seat, he took her hand. His heartbeat skipped at the longing in her eyes. With his other hand, he rolled up the connecting window of the limo and shifted his position in the seat so he was pressed against one side of her body.

"Did you enjoy the party?" He ran his fingertips along her arm.

"Yes."

"Did Sharon give you a hard time?" His caress moved to the middle of her back to the patch of bare skin above her dress.

"No. She wanted me to make you happy." Her voice was a whisper.

"Really?" Well, that was unexpected, even for Sharon.

"What really happened between you two?"

He shrugged. "I wanted the love my uncle had with Lola. She wanted the marriage our parents had."

"I'm sorry." She caressed his cheek.

He smiled. "I'm fine. Deep down, I knew she wasn't capable of it. She kept people at arm's length, but I hoped things would be different with me since we grew up together. I was wrong."

"I know what that's like," she whispered.

"What?" he asked as he nuzzled her neck.

"Keeping people at arm's length." Her voice hitched. "I told myself I wanted a family, but I was scared."

He squeezed her hand. "Why were you scared?"

"I knew my mother loved me, but sometimes..." She took a shaky breath. "It seemed no matter how much love I gave her, it wasn't enough." Tears streamed down her face, tugging at his heart. He pulled her into his arms and stroked her back as she regained control. "I didn't want to take that risk again."

Is that why she fought their attraction as hard as she had? Did she think he wouldn't return what she felt? What exactly did she feel? He wanted to ask her, or confess his own feelings, but fear squeezed around him, filling the small space of the limo.

"Why is it every time I'm close to you, I either burst into tears or I want to rip your clothes off?" She sniffled. Her eyes shot to his as she realized what she'd said.

"Maybe we could work on you just ripping my clothes off." He grinned mischievously.

• • •

Josie was mortified. She'd told him she wanted rip his clothes off. It was true, but not something she planned to admit. She should move away—they were treading on dangerous ground—but his touch felt too good.

"Why don't you just say the words?" he whispered in her ear.

He pulled the shawl off her shoulders and delight ran like fingers up the back of her spine when the silky material exposed her bare skin. She'd tell him anything he wanted to keep him touching her.

"What words?" Her voice trembled.

"You're crazy about me." His tongue ran along the edge of her ear.

She shivered, but laughed to cover it up. He was pressed against her and she sat next to one of the doors of the limo. She'd have to either crawl over him or move to the other side if she wanted to get away, but she didn't. "Are you this full of yourself with other women?" she teased.

He lifted her chin to meet his gaze. "There are no other women, Josie. There haven't been since the moment you stepped into my house."

Her heart flip-flopped. Was it true? No women had called the house, but what about the time he'd spent away from her? His emerald eyes told the truth. "Patrick...I," she whispered.

His mouth was warm and soft against hers. Her knees turned to pudding at the tenderness of it. His other kisses had been so full of heat they'd consumed her, but this kiss was gentle. He nibbled her lips before his tongue moved inside her mouth to caress her tongue softly, the way his hands had her skin. It was filled with all the words he didn't say out loud. *I want you. I need you.* She wrapped her arms around him and kissed him with the same abandon and emotion that filled her. His hand stroked the back of her neck before his fingers went into her hair to caress it. It became hard to breathe, and she couldn't think—only feel the heat from his hands and mouth on her skin.

A knock from the other side of the window jarred her back from the haze of desire swirling around her.

"We're here, sir."

"Thanks."

To her disappointment, he moved away from her. The distance left her empty, missing him. Moments later, the door opened and he stepped out and extended his hand for her.

"Good night, sir, ma'am." The driver tipped his hat.

Patrick nodded and a friendly smile was all she could muster; he hadn't let go of her hand. The warmth of his hand in hers was oddly more intimate than the kiss they'd shared, and her heart was a thunderstorm in her ears. Would they continue what they started in the limo? Did she want him to? *Was that a trick question?* She didn't want him to stop now that they were home without worry of interruptions. Home. The word was a welcoming old friend and she wished it was her home—their home.

He opened the front door and she followed him into the darkness of the house. Light flooded the room when he turned on the switch. His dimple winked at her when he turned, and her heart shot to her throat. She swallowed deeply to return it to its rightful place, but knew it never would. She loved him.

Removing her hand from his, she headed toward the kitchen. "Would you like some coffee?"

He followed her and stood on the other side of the counter, studying her. "I don't need coffee." His voice was low and deep.

The heat of his gaze made her hands shake as she took the tin of coffee from the refrigerator. Even with her back to him, she could feel his eyes on her, watching her, undressing her. "What do you want?"

He walked around the counter to stand before her and put his arms around her waist. "You," he whispered against her ear, his hands running along the back of her neck.

Oh God, yes!

She squealed when her feet disappeared from beneath her and she found herself cradled in his arms. "What are you doing?"

"Taking you upstairs before we have time to change our minds."

Had she said the words out loud, or had he read her mind? It didn't matter. She wrapped her arms around his neck and buried her nose in the crook between his neck and shoulder, inhaling his scent. When her head rose, he was smiling.

"Is that a victory grin?"

His brows knotted before he got her meaning. "No. I'm just happy. Really happy."

She returned her head to the crook of his shoulder. "Me too." Happier than she'd felt in a very long time—ever.

Each step up the stairs took her closer to the bedroom and closer to being with Patrick. Even though she'd dreamed about this moment for a long time, she couldn't help feeling nervous as he opened the bedroom door. Their attraction was a constant rollercoaster, going from intense heat to a warm glow. Would their lovemaking be like their hot kisses or the soft gentle caresses they had shared?

He set her feet on the floor. Her eyes devoured him as he removed his tuxedo jacket. His hands moved to loosen and remove the cravat and open the top buttons of his shirt. She didn't look away; he was too delicious to look at. If not for the distractions and crowd at the party, she would've watched him all night. Most men looked good in a tuxedo, but he'd devastated her in his.

He slid his shirt off, revealing his naked chest. One that still knocked the wind out of her each time she saw it. Unlike the other times she'd seen him bare from the waist up, this time she'd get to see what lay below the waist, and for the first time touch his skin to her heart's content.

His pants fell with a soft swoosh to the ground. Her breath stopped when she saw his underwear went with it, leaving him completely naked before her.

Her hands trembled as they slid the straps of her dress from her shoulders and let it fall in a rumpled heap at her feet. Feminine joy shot through her at the male appreciation in his eyes as she stood half-naked in front of him.

He took her hand in his, kissed it softly, and walked toward the bed, pulling back the comforter. The soft folds of the sheets enfolded her when she sat down. He eased down next to her.

His hand moved slowly over her face, touching the top of her forehead, making a slow pace down to her eyelids, her nose, and across her lips, as if he were memorizing every line and every curve his fingertips brushed over.

"So beautiful." His voice croaked as he took her face his hands. Emerald eyes watched her hotly, and she quivered under the intimacy of his gaze. He lowered his lips and kissed her softly, slowly, until she was drowning in the heat of it.

His mouth moved from hers to place small kisses from her neck to her shoulder, where he proceeded to nibble at the flesh before moving to the other shoulder. Heat radiated through her, and every pore of her skin tingled painfully.

Her hands reached out to touch his skin that had tormented her from the moment she'd laid eyes on him. Sparks shot through her fingertips as she ran them along the surface, loving the taut silky feel of it.

His hands moved over her arms, her hips, and the length of her legs, leaving a trail of fire everywhere he touched. His mouth continued its sweet torture over the surface of her skin, and she arched toward his mouth. With every caress, he was drawing her into him, and she didn't fight him; she was willing to give him everything he wanted.

"Oh...Patrick," she gasped.

He grinned against her skin. "I haven't even started yet, sweetheart," he promised wickedly as his hands removed the rest of her clothing.

She moaned when he touched her.

"Oh man, you're already wet." His voice was raw.

His mouth continued to kiss her skin while his fingers stroked her again and again, the pressure increasing and decreasing as he teased her.

"Patrick, please."

He answered with a kiss, his tongue invading her mouth in deep, slow strokes, fanning the embers of the passion hotter and stronger until she thought she'd burst into a million pieces. Her body bowed with each rush of pleasure that rippled over her in every direction at once.

Her hands were in his hair even as he moved to kneel over her. She arched her back and opened herself fully to him.

He moaned as he eased inside, pulling out a little each time before he was fully in her. "It's like heaven."

She couldn't agree more and lifted her hips, meeting the rhythm of his long, slow strokes drawing him deeper. Her fingernails sunk into his skin. "Oh, my goodness," she rasped.

Every stroke was not only a sweet invasion to her body, but pulled at her slowly, softly. He wanted everything from her—everything she had. She reached out and touched the parts of him he kept hidden, and he gave them to her. Their eyes met as he moved within her.

It was too intimate. She wanted to look way, but the intensity of his gaze and the emotions scorching her soul were too strong. They moved closer to each other and the ecstasy that was waiting. Their hands entwined and locked as they rode on the swells of pleasure consuming them. Release crashed over her and she shouted his name as it tumbled over her again and again, like waves against jagged rocks, powerful and unforgiving.

The weight of his body pressed down on her moments later and she heard his gasping breath in her ear. She wrapped her arms and legs around him as their breathing calmed. The words

'I love you' hovered on her lips, but she didn't let them out. She'd given him so much already that she couldn't risk saying out loud what her body already said. She fell asleep with the weight of him between her legs, her hands stroking the hair at his temple and his lips kissing her neck softly.

When her eyes opened hours later, contentment vibrated through her. She found him grinning at her. She shifted to untangle herself from him, but he held her close.

"Who knew the composed Ms. Fagan would be so noisy?" he teased.

Heat flushed her cheeks and she buried her face in his shoulder. His jokes put her at ease, but she couldn't help but wonder if he'd felt the same intensity she had last night. His face certainly showed no signs.

"I'm not complaining. Not one bit," he whispered huskily in her ear. "It's soothing to my ego."

She snorted. "Since when do you need your ego stroked?" she joked.

His eyes darkened. "Actually, it's not my ego that needs stroking." He chuckled wickedly and rolled them over so she sat on top of him.

She pushed the thoughts aside as his hands worked their magic on her skin.

• • •

"Will you ever run for office?" Her back was to him as she prepared scrambled eggs.

He paused in the middle of biting a piece of watermelon. "Where did that question come from?"

She shrugged her and gave him a sideways glance. "Just curious." *Please say no. Please say no.*

"It's my brother's dream, not mine." His eyes didn't leave her.

"He's going to run against your father?" Her eyes widened in surprise.

He shook his head. "My father is running for governor next year; Noah will run for the Senate." He sat up on the barstool and folded his arms.

She knew what that meant. Discussion over. "We need to review the design and samples for the new bathroom. I want Danny to pick up the items tomorrow so the guys can get started." She leaned against the kitchen counter.

"Sure." He got off the barstool and walked behind the counter to stand before her. "Although I had something better in mind." His gaze settled on her lips.

"Oh." She peeked up at him. Her skin grew warm as she remembered the feel of his hands and mouth on her last night, and earlier this morning.

"I thought about fulfilling a fantasy or two." His hand reached out to trace her collarbone, and her breath caught in her throat when his fingertips moved to caress her neck.

She shrieked when he lifted her onto the kitchen counter. "Are you planning on cooking me?"

"No. Just having you for dessert." His hands touched her bare calves.

"It's a little early for dessert, don't you think? Besides, how do you plan to get up on the counter?"

Hands moved farther up her legs so they caressed the tops of her thighs. "I don't need to be on the counter." Fingertips roamed up the inside of her thighs until he reached her underwear and stroked the silkiness of the material.

Pleasure raced across her flesh in ripples and heat rushed to her cheeks when she got his meaning. So much for breakfast! Who cared? His hands moved to her hips to tug at the edges of her underwear.

The doorbell's chime rang through the kitchen.

"Damn!"

She couldn't agree more.

He gave her an apologetic smile and helped her off the counter. Before she could step away from him and straighten her clothing, he pulled her against him and crushed his lips against hers. His tongue delved into her mouth, showing her how he would explore all corners of her body once they were alone again. Delight ran its fingers down her back at his heated gaze when their mouths parted.

He squeezed her hand quickly and left her standing in the kitchen with nothing but her underwear and the shirt he'd given her this morning, even though her clothes were in the next room. She hadn't argued, liking the feel of it next to her skin and the smell of him on the fabric.

She scrambled to regain her composure. It was ten on a Sunday morning. Who could be at the door? *Don't let it be Danny.* The last thing she wanted was another lecture.

"Mother?" She heard him grumble when he opened the front door. "This had better be good."

His mother! She looked down at her bare legs. If she tried to sneak upstairs, she was bound to be seen. As she looked around her, the only option was a couple of dish towels. Not good. What would his mother think when she saw her wandering around the kitchen half-dressed? She knew exactly what she would think. Their voices got closer to the kitchen, even though she heard Patrick attempting to keep her in the living room.

"This really isn't a good time," he insisted again.

"It's a perfectly acceptable time. It's after ten."

"That's not what I meant, and you know it."

"All right, why is it a bad time? What could you possibly be doing that you can't talk to me now?"

Josie scooted right against the counter, hiding her legs just as Elsa came into the kitchen.

Elsa saw her right away. "Oh, I see," she observed. "Isn't that your shirt from last night?"

Josie and Patrick looked at each other and blushed.

Elsa looked at them both before turning her attention to Patrick.

"Well, I hope you've at least discussed the conditions of the will before you embarked on this...relationship." Her blue gaze was solemn. There was no disappointment in her eyes, nor was it in the tone of her voice, but it radiated from her stiff posture and crossed arms.

What did William's will have to do with anything? As she glanced at Patrick, her breath stopped. "Patrick?"

"It wasn't your place to tell her, Mother," he said through gritted teeth.

Elsa's hands dropped to either side of her hips. "True, it was yours, and should've been done before..."

"What does William's will have to do with me?" Josie asked quietly, as dread descended on her. She wasn't going to like what he had to say.

Walking into the kitchen, he went to stand before her.

"I'll let you talk it over. Josie, I'll be back later this afternoon—say, two?" Elsa gave them both a last look before leaving them alone.

Josie nodded numbly, wondering if his mother had come over to prove her suspicions about their sleeping together or to stir up trouble with her announcement. Whatever the reason, it was done and there would be no going back.

They listened to her leaving and their gaze held, even after the door closed. The moment Patrick told her his secret, things would never be the same. It hovered above them, menacing, waiting to crash down and ruin their intimate moment.

•••

"You have something to tell me?"

The weight of not telling her sooner squeezed around him at the quiver in her voice. It was because of him. Gary was right. He should've discussed it with her as soon as he found out.

"One of the conditions in my uncle's will was that anyone related to Lola would have a share of the inheritance..." He paused, expecting her to ask how much, but she merely looked back at him with her heart in those beautiful brown eyes. "Along with ownership of the house, if they want it."

Surprise danced in her eyes and then contemplation. She loved this house almost as much as he did. Would she ask for it?

"You knew and didn't say anything?"

"Say what, Josie? 'Hey, do you want to take the only home I love? So what if you just found out about the aunt that gives you that entitlement a few months ago. Heck, while you're at it, why not help yourself to the money. My brother's dream can wait.'" His tone was harsher than he planned.

"You could've told me," she said gently.

"I didn't know your intentions. You could've come to destroy my family's reputation, or for the money." He regretted the words the moment they left his mouth and felt worse when hurt filled her eyes.

"I wouldn't have put my company in jeopardy by applying for this job if my intention was to ruin your family's reputation. If I wanted money, I would've gone to your parents, not you," she said matter of factly.

"I know that," he mumbled.

"I told you what I wanted. Peace for my mother and a reference to help my business." She took a step back, putting distance between them.

It pained him that she was right, and there was nothing either of them could do about it. His parents might acknowledge her as a business associate, and maybe even a friend, but there was no chance of them admitting she was family without tainting their own, especially if Lola's killer wasn't revealed.

"We could share the house," he offered. Share? The tabloids—not to mention his parents—would have a field day with that arrangement. He didn't care; she'd be with him.

Surprise flickered in her eyes at his offer before it was replaced with a look he knew well: controlled and professional. "This was a bad idea. Things were bound to get...complicated," she murmured, using his word.

He didn't need to ask her what "this" was. She meant them, and what happened last night. Swallowing a lump the size of Texas lodged in his throat, he focused on his anger.

She stood before him, arms crossed, shutting him out. He longed to close the distance between them and put his arms around her, forcing her to work out the conditions of the will, but he didn't, and knew any effort he made at this point would be met with the same coolness reflected in her eyes.

"You're right." He put his hand in his pockets and went to the kitchen entrance. "Last night shouldn't have happened," he said coldly, pushing aside the pain squeezing his heart.

Chapter 17

Josie opened the bedroom door, slipped out of Patrick's shirt, and headed for the shower. She'd hoped the last few months with Patrick would be an opportunity to enjoy his company, his body, and create memories she'd take with her when she walked out of his life. Who was she kidding? She wasn't good at normal relationships, much less casual ones. Was that all she wanted from Patrick? No, she wanted more, had hoped for more.

Last night shouldn't have happened. The words rang in her ears like a broken record, piercing her heart each time it repeated. Keeping the conditions of the will from her was a cruel betrayal. It said he didn't trust her enough to be honest. Walking back to her room, she sat down on the bed, not caring that it got wet. From the beginning, their relationship seemed built on lies: lies about their attraction, then secrets about Lola and William. The obstacles were more than she could handle, and continuing to turn a blind eye to them was not possible.

When she'd said it had been a bad idea, she was talking about them working together. He misunderstood, but she hadn't corrected him, despite her protesting heart. Fear made her hesitate: fear of his rejection, of the events that could unfold with Lola's disappearance, of all the things that made it impossible for them to be together.

The front door closing echoed downstairs and she knew Patrick had left the house. She was still in his room, so he had no sanctuary to escape to. His room would be finished by the end of the week. She'd return to hers and stop fantasizing about being more to him once her head wasn't buried in his pillow, inhaling the lingering smell of him.

After slipping on a cotton floral dress, she laid on the bed and closed her eyes and ears against the silence of the house. The loneliness that pressed down around her reminded her of the nights she'd spent alone in Detroit, listening to the sounds of the television coming from her mother's room.

The doorbell rang. She pushed herself off the bed and headed downstairs.

Elsa stood in the doorway. Josie smiled in welcome, thankful for the company to distract her from her melancholy thoughts. She hadn't had time to fret about talking with her and Myles.

"Hello." Elsa greeted her warmly. It wasn't warm in the traditional sense, but warmer than any greeting she'd received since meeting her. It was especially unexpected after her mention of the will this morning.

"Hello, Mrs. Pullman...Elsa," she said as Elsa gave her a correcting look.

Elsa made her way through the living room, admiring the changes since the disastrous dinner visit. There was no opportunity this morning. Josie had been too busy trying to hide the fact she'd slept with her son.

"You did a wonderful job," she observed, circling the room. "Everything is to Patrick's taste, but you've taken the edges off so it's not a bachelor pad. You've made a home for him."

"Thank you. I sensed it was what he wanted." She neglected to add his comment that it was the only home he'd ever loved.

Cool blue eyes studied her. "You have a way of reading people and knowing what they need." Her words implied Josie gave people more than just their design needs. Elsa moved to the leather couch and tested its stiffness before sitting.

If only she knew. "I get it right most of the time." Did she know about her connection? Had Patrick said something to her and Myles? They hadn't asked her about it, but she couldn't see them keeping quiet about something so bizarre. He probably thought they wouldn't believe him if he told them.

"Perhaps you'll give Myles what he needs, too...with his office," she added, but Josie sensed it wasn't his office she was talking about. What could she give Myles? He'd told her she was nothing but trouble. She definitely didn't want to give him more of that.

"I'll try."

Across from her, Elsa sat on the edge of the couch, as though she were ready to pounce at any moment. *Doesn't the woman ever relax?* She released her own posture when she realized she was sitting just as stiffly. Well, that was the pot calling the kettle black.

"Where are my manners?" Josie stood up. "Can I offer you something to drink?"

"A scotch would be lovely, thank you. Neat."

Josie didn't know whether to smile or bow before she headed to the kitchen. She decided to do neither.

She felt lighter with every step that put distance between her and Elsa. Would she ever get used to being in the presence of a Pullman? They didn't intimidate her so much as make her feel like a germ beneath the microscope of their investigative eyes. She never knew if they liked her or were merely tolerating her presence until she left. Lola must have felt the same.

She returned to the living room. Elsa nodded her thanks and took the drink.

"I almost forgot." Elsa picked up a plain white envelope beside her on the couch. "This was stuck in the front door." She handed it to Josie.

Terror spread through her like a fire through a dry forest as Josie glanced down at the envelope. It could be nothing—another invitation like the one from Elsa—but something inside her knew otherwise. It'd been in the front door. Since the security system was installed, there was no way to get inside without drawing attention or keys that only she, and Patrick had.

With shaky fingers, she opened it. Inside was a picture of Joe, Pearl, and Lola. Lola's face had been partly burnt off. She turned over the picture. 'LAST CHANCE' was written in large black letters.

She eased onto the leather loveseat next to Elsa. It was a month since someone tried to run her over, and despite the occasional nightmare, she had been lulled into a sense of relief that no more threats would come.

"Are you all right?"

Josie didn't answer, numb with fear.

"What is it?"

"A photo."

"Of what?"

"Not what, who."

"Oh? Who?"

"Lola and...friends." She chose carefully. It wasn't a complete lie. Lola and Joe were friends.

Silence filled the air as if it was an unpleasant odor that couldn't be ignored.

"How well did you know Lola?" It might be the only time she'd have to speak with Elsa alone. She pushed aside visions of Patrick's disapproving eyes. Elsa said last night that they could talk, right? Now was as good a time as any.

Elsa looked at her over the rim of her short glass. "You don't beat around the bush, do you?" She took a sip of her scotch.

"I know the Pullmans prefer directness," she said tentatively.

"To an extent, yes, but there are exceptions," she replied, her tone flat.

She waited on pins and needles as Elsa contemplated the glass in her hand and her answer. Her study was slow and deliberate. "Not well. We only met a few times."

"I guess that's understandable; it was Myles' first time running for office, wasn't it?" she said offhandedly. "And he was being backed by...important people."

The air crackled with the tension of someone who'd just been asked to the boss' office at the end of the day on a Friday. Elsa glared at her with her famous 'you need to do what I say' stare. Josie met and held her gaze with her own controlled 'I'm not going to back down, so don't bother' stare, even as visions of another Pullman reference disappearing flashed before her.

Surprisingly, and thankfully, Elsa conceded. "I admit I could have made a better effort to know her, but I was new to the family..." It was a sorry excuse, but Josie understood. It was easier to go with the flow than rock the boat.

"It didn't help that your husband didn't like her." And urged William to end the marriage.

Elsa didn't deny it or try to defend Myles. Why should she? He never denied it himself.

"Do you think it's the same person who left the other photos?"

Patrick had told them more than she thought. How much, was the real question. Did they know she suspected them? "Yes."

"May I see it?" She held out her hand.

She gave Elsa the photo and watched her face carefully for any signs of recognition or emotion. There was none, but, then, she knew how to control herself.

"It's hard to see her face. Are you sure it's her?"

"Yes. I know the other people in the photo."

"What is this on the back? Was does 'last chance' mean?" Elsa's leveled gaze searched her.

"It's a threat."

Elsa's expression didn't change as she carefully regarded her, then the photo. "What other threats have been made?" she asked as calmly as if they were having tea and crumpets with girl talk.

She shifted in her seat. "Patrick didn't tell you?" Elsa knew about the other photos, but Patrick apparently hadn't told her about the poster or nearly being run over. It was easier not to answer. It might lead to her hinting she suspected Myles. If Patrick hadn't told them, he wouldn't be happy that she did.

"Patrick told us many things, but I'd like to hear it from you." She pressed in that polite, but firm, way she did so well.

Time was running out and Josie had to find out as much as possible before it was too late. She carefully relayed all the threats, pausing between each one to allow Elsa time to absorb them, making sure not to imply that she suspected the Pullmans. Elsa's eyes lifted in what she assumed was surprise when she told her about someone attempting to run her over.

"Did you see what kind of car it was? Why didn't you go to the police?" Her tone was stern and disapproving.

"I thought it best not to get them involved. It would hinder my own investigation if the police were asking the questions instead of me."

"Myles has contacts in the force; it would have been discreet," she offered.

That was another problem, getting help from someone who was on the suspect list. "Patrick insisted he'd go to them if another threat was made. I'll speak with him later about putting it off just a little longer."

"I don't think—"

"Getting the police involved will scare them off," Josie interjected.

A perfectly curved eyebrow rose. "You're using yourself as bait?"

A brave smile carefully hid the fear that rose each time she thought of it. It wasn't the best plan, but it was a plan nonetheless.

"You should discuss it with Patrick."

"He wouldn't approve."

Elsa let out a frustrated sigh. "I know that family is important, Josie, but is finding out what happened to Lola worth your life?"

Josie pushed herself off her seat. "Yes, in ways you wouldn't understand." Nothing in Elsa's eyes said she was insulted, but she wasn't happy about it, either. It didn't matter at this point—Josie needed things to end. She couldn't live her life wondering if Lola's killer would jump out of the dark at any moment and take her out. She suspected that whatever they had planned for her would be done before she left Patrick's house.

"What are your plans when the job here is finished?" Elsa asked, changing the subject.

"I'll need to find somewhere to live."

"You won't be staying?"

Josie eyes snapped to hers. "No," she stammered. "Why would I stay after the job is finished?"

"I saw the way you watched each other last night, and after this morning, I assumed—"

"I won't be staying," she interrupted. Sorrow threatened to choke her.

Her sculpted eyebrows rose. "Really?"

"It's not what you think." God, she hoped she didn't sound like she had casual relationships with all her clients. Not something to put on your resume.

Elsa gave an unladylike snort. "There's definitely something between you. My son is infatuated with you."

"You're wrong." She wasn't convincing enough. Elsa's expression made that evident.

"No, I'm right. A mother knows these things. My son has never looked at another woman the way he looks at you—not even Sharon. It's obvious he adores you, and you him. I see it in your eyes, even if you won't admit it."

Josie remained silent for several seconds. "I don't get involved with clients." It was only thing she could think of. She couldn't say the real reason.

"He won't be your client much longer."

Damn! So much for Elsa letting her off easy. "Our relationship would be...complicated."

Elsa nodded in agreement. "Relationships are always complicated, my dear, but I wouldn't let that stop me. Did you know that Myles was seeing someone else when I met him?"

"No." Josie smiled as she saw Elsa confronting the woman, and doing it without raising her voice. It was almost comical. Almost.

"She wasn't right for him, and I knew he was meant to be mine the moment I laid eyes on him. I was a sophomore in college, he was a senior: handsome, popular, and quite the catch."

"I'm sure you were a catch yourself."

Elsa gave her a half smile. "No, I was beautiful, but nothing more."

"Myles doesn't strike me as the type of man who'd marry a woman just for looks." His family wasn't likely to either, but she kept that to herself.

"I was ambitious and driven, but it took a bit more to convince his family," she said with a wave of her hand.

"Really?" She couldn't imagine Elsa, the epitome of perfection, not being welcomed with open arms by any family, even one as prestigious as the Pullmans.

"They didn't think I was suitable for their son...at first." Her jaw tightened. "I didn't come from a...wealthy background."

"But I thought..."

She shook her head. "My mother was a drunk who lived in a crumbling shack in Louisiana where my father left us." As she finished, her voice was as brittle as the jagged edge of a rusty knife.

Josie didn't respond, finding it hard to imagine Elsa as anyone other than the wealthy, politically connected socialite she knew. "How'd you convince them?" she asked, sensing Elsa didn't want her sympathy.

"They could see I was good for him. His father knew I would help him get where he needed to be in life." Her composure returned and the lines that strained her face earlier smoothed over.

"How did the woman Myles was seeing take it?"

Cool blue eyes glassed over. "I took care of her."

Josie's heart stopped beating. *What does that mean?* Elsa's words created unpleasant thoughts that perhaps she was the one who'd made Lola disappear, not Myles. Did that reserved and controlled exterior hide more than just emotions?

She shrugged off the thought. The idea Elsa would get rid of someone to marry Myles was ridiculous. She wouldn't want to tarnish her perfect reputation. Elsa was many things, but Josie couldn't picture her as a murderer.

"We were married after he graduated and Myles became the youngest man elected to the Senate, and years later, we had two beautiful children."

"A happy ending, then?"

The light in her eyes that had sparkled as she spoke of her and Myles' lives dimmed. "We should go. Myles is expecting us," she said and stood.

Josie followed her out the front door, her mind filled with questions of why Elsa's story didn't have a happy ending, and if it had anything to do with Lola.

•••

Myles' gaze burned her as she circled his office space and took pictures. It didn't look in need of renovation, but she didn't mention that. She'd use this time to speak with him, as Elsa said. Another chance might not come her way.

His sour expression said he wasn't thrilled to see her, but she expected no less. Their conversation at last night's party hadn't ended on a happy note. "What would you like done?" she asked, taking another picture.

"You and my wife haven't made that decision?" he said snidely.

She smiled in spite of his rudeness. "It's important to me that the person occupying the space has some input. You'll be spending the most time here."

He didn't respond. Elsa stood silently by his desk, watching them.

"What did you and my wife have in mind?" he asked tentatively.

"No wooden ducks and pictures on the wall of men fishing, I promise." Josie winked.

To her surprise, a smile cracked his face, but it didn't last long.

Elsa excused herself, leaving them alone. The tension in the air expanded like a balloon.

"My wife tells me you are moving out of Will...Patrick's home when the renovations are done."

She nodded. What else had Elsa said while she waited in the entryway for Myles to know she'd arrived? "I never intended to stay."

"Patrick says you love the house, so I thought you'd share it with him."

She did love the house, but how could she stay with Patrick when he didn't feel the same? His emotions were from William, and hers...she still wasn't one hundred percent sure it wasn't Lola. "I have a business to run."

"Is that what my son is to you, a reference to promote your business?" The venom in his voice surprised her.

"He made the decision to hire me knowing the conditions. It was clearly laid out in the contract he prepared."

"And you'll just move on and forget about him?" He regarded her with narrowed eyes.

Confusion knotted her brows. What was with Patrick's family? One minute they wanted her to leave, and the next minute she was being chastised for leaving. "I thought that's what everyone wanted."

He moved to stand behind his desk. "You won't find your aunt."

"Why not?" Her breath caught in her throat. Was he about to confess? Could he get rid of her in his office? No one but he and Elsa knew she was here.

"She doesn't want to be found."

"What does that mean?"

"She abandoned my brother. Took what she could and left in the middle of the night!"

The pain in his voice took her by surprise, and for the first time, she saw him for who he was: a man who'd lost his only brother and was angry at the woman who'd broken not only his brother's heart, but his life. Hatred and every other emotion he'd felt for Lola was directed at her—a woman who had her face and was making him remember.

"Gary told me she loved Will, that she wouldn't have left," she said softly. "There was nothing in her letters to my mother to say she was unhappy, only that William's family disapproved of their relationship."

His cruel laughter sent chills down her spine. "Love? Why would she steal from him if she loved him?"

"Patrick told me you think she stole his grandmother's jewels, but I don't believe it."

"It was my mother's jewelry, expensive pieces!" he said with conviction.

"Why would she leave all her things behind? Clothes, shoes, everything? It doesn't make sense."

"She could buy anything she wanted with the money she'd get from selling the jewelry."

"She stopped all connection with my mother, her only relative. That's extreme for a few expensive jewels. They were very close. My mother never recovered when she disappeared, and when my father died, she slipped into a severe depression until the day she died," she said bitterly.

He remained silent, her comments appearing to make him doubt what he'd held onto for so many years.

"Your family wasn't the only one that suffered when Lola disappeared, Myles. You need to open your eyes and see that," she finished quietly, pushing back the tears that beat against her eyes. Jeez. What was it about this family that made her emotions spiral out of control?

"You expect me to believe you didn't come here to destroy my family by accusing us of her disappearance?"

"I didn't even know about Lola until after I took the job with Patrick!" she insisted.

He didn't answer.

She sighed. "I never wanted to destroy your family. I thought Lola was the only family I had left. I wanted to find her for me, but mostly for my mother." She'd also hoped they would be her family. They were the closest she'd have until she got her own.

Silence hung in the air between them.

"Patrick said that was the reason you were searching for her, to find family." His tone was less brittle.

"I guess we both had misconceptions of each other, and perhaps Lola, as well."

His brows knitted. "What do you mean?"

"You always thought Lola only wanted William for his money and position," she said tentatively.

Myles was pensive before answering. "I knew William loved her; I was never sure about her. Their relationship happened so quickly."

"Gary's certain she loved him," she added carefully.

Myles snorted. "Gary was in love with them as much as they were in love with each other."

Josie raised an eyebrow at his accusation.

Myles waved a hand in front of her before she could speak. "I don't mean it that way," he corrected quickly. "I merely meant he was obsessed with them. He introduced them and helped to keep their relationship a secret from the prying eyes of the press. It would've been a scandal back then if someone found out," Myles said. His eyes reflected a moment of shock before it disappeared.

He hadn't intended to tell her so much.

"Yes, it wouldn't have helped your campaign, either," she said plainly. "Your brother being married to a black woman and a jazz singer."

Myles' eyes went instantly to her and held hers with his intense scrutiny. "You know they were married."

"Yes."

Patrick had certainly picked and chosen what he shared with his parents. He probably had his reasons, but would they work against her now?

"How?"

A prickle of fear tickled the back of her neck as she contemplated telling him. The documents were carefully under lock and key, but they could easily be removed. They could disappear as easily as she could—as Lola had. "I have photos of their wedding."

His eyes reflected surprise before he contained it. Her gaze moved nervously to the door, her only means of escape.

"Lola was one shrewd broad...lady." He corrected himself.

Her heartbeat's tempo increased as she imagined him killing her in his room without anyone knowing about it. No one had seen her enter the house with Elsa earlier, and she had told no one where she was going when she left. Had that been their plan? Elsa would lure her here with the promise of work, and Myles would make her disappear. Is that what happened to Lola?

"What's the matter?" Myles asked. "You're about to turn blue."

She let out the breath she didn't realize she was holding.

"What's wrong? Are you okay?"

The concern in his eyes calmed her a little. He wouldn't care if he was about to hurt her, would he? She took a deep breath. "Yes. What do you think happened to her?"

"For years, I thought she abandoned Will. That she was only with him for the money, but what you've told me only confirmed what Will was trying to tell me all those years. Someone killed her."

William hadn't said that to her, but then again, he thought she was Lola. "That's what I've been thinking for a while now, but what I can't figure out is who or why. To be honest, Myles, your family are the only suspects who had a motive."

Myles ran a hand through his salt-and-pepper hair. "That's what Will said."

"What? He accused you of getting rid of her?" She shook her head in disbelief.

He smiled. "He sure did. He claimed it was my questionable connections backing me at the time. He felt they did it to ensure nothing would get in the way of me winning."

"What do you think?" she asked tentatively.

He was pensive for a moment. "I adamantly denied it at first, but after I got to know them, I'm not so sure," he said quietly. "Are you certain there's no one else?"

"There was her friend, Pearl. They had a falling-out over Joe."

"Joe?"

"The bartender and owner of the Jazz Joynt."

"It seems my son left out a few details."

More than he knew. "He probably didn't want to upset you." Or have you interfere with our investigation.

"Is there anything else I need to know?" With Patrick, that meant the conversation was over, but with Myles it seemed to mean 'you need to tell me what I want to know.' She had no intention of taking the bait.

"We're still exploring all the leads."

He waited, expecting her to say more. "Keep me better informed from now on, okay?"

She gave him a thin smile. It appeared Patrick's bossiness didn't all come from his mother.

The door of his office opened and Elsa walked back in. Josie was grateful for the interruption and to elude further questions.

"Have you two decided to play nice?"

Myles and Josie looked at each other, and then Elsa.

"We've come to an understanding," Myles said.

That was an understatement. One minute he'd been upset she wasn't staying at the house with Patrick, then accused her aunt of stealing, and then demanded to know the details about the disappearance in which he was a suspect. Truthfully, she didn't know where she stood, with him or Elsa.

Chapter 18

Firelight flickered on the walls of the living room. The sound of wood crackling echoed in the room. Josie sat on the couch, a book in her hand, but gave up after she realizing she'd read the same page twice.

She returned from the Pullmans' hours ago to an empty house. Part of her hoped Patrick would be home, just so she could see him. It'd only been a few hours, but she missed him. How pathetic was that? Lola's killer was probably planning her death at this very moment, and she was thinking about Patrick. Boy, was she was in for a world of hurt when this job was finished.

The sound of a key in the door made her heart thunder. She'd gone over and over what she'd say when he got back, but she went blank when she saw him standing in the entryway with wind-blown hair and heartbroken eyes.

"Hi."

A wall was behind his eyes when they found hers. "Hey," he said softly, setting his keys on the metal tray by the door.

He walked into the living room where she sat. He fidgeted, as if he couldn't decide if he would head upstairs or stay and talk with her. She made the choice for him.

"I got another photo today," she said. Would he make her call the police as he promised? Could she stop him?

"Why didn't you call me?" He held her gaze for several seconds, his brow knotted in annoyance.

"I thought your parents told you." Why hadn't they? "You shared information with them. I assumed they'd do the same with you."

The muscle of his jaw line moved frantically. "They didn't. You should have." He walked across the room and sat down on the couch next to her. "Where is it?"

She handed it to him and watched his face while he studied the photo, flipping it over to read the words that had wrenched fear from her when she read them. "Where was it?"

"Your mother found it in the front door."

His lean fingers raked through his hair and gripped his neck. "At least it wasn't in the house. I don't want you leaving the house without me, okay?" His intense gaze held hers, saying he wouldn't take anything but yes as an answer.

"Okay." Her heart swelled with love at his concern and she longed to lean into him and rest her head on his shoulder. Would he put his arms around her?

"Who are the other people in the photo?"

His questions jerked her back to reality. "Joe and Pearl."

Squinting, he looked closer at the photo. "Get dressed. We're going to the club."

The club? Did he mean to question Pearl? "Are you sure that's a good idea?"

"I want to get this over with. The sooner we eliminate all the suspects, the better chance we have of that happening. I'll meet you back here in half an hour."

I want to get this over with. His words were like a sword in her heart. Despite his concern, the walls behind his eyes said he was going to keep her at arm's length until she was gone. Sharp pain stabbed her heart until it ached. There was no one to blame but herself. Instead of showing him her heart, she'd chosen to keep it to herself.

Keeping the conditions of the will from her had hurt, but he'd made an effort to correct it, and had even offered a means for them to work it out, but she'd been a coward and ignored it. She'd used Lola and her suspicion of his parents as an excuse, but the truth was, she'd been afraid.

She pulled herself off the couch and headed upstairs, wondering what Patrick would ask Joe and Pearl, and whether they'd answer.

• • •

The neon sign of the club blinked sporadically. Patrick and Josie made their way through the crowds on the street and down the stairs leading to the club.

Josie had remained quiet the entire car ride, and he wondered if she was scared or silent because of their argument about the will. Sadness filled her eyes, making him frustrated and lamenting the fact that he couldn't do anything about it. She wouldn't let him.

It was a reminder of another problem that plagued her that he couldn't do anything about. Anger tore through him when he saw the photo with the threat. It took all his strength not to call the police, as he'd insisted he would the last time she was threatened. He knew it wasn't what she wanted, and not just because his father had contacts in the police force.

He wasn't a fool, however, and had called his father when he went upstairs and told him about the other incidents, enduring his criticism for not telling him sooner. His mother hadn't told Myles about the photo, which was strange; didn't they tell each other everything?

He also called Gary, telling him what he wanted to do about the conditions of the will. Both Gary and his father told him to call if they needed anything. *They.* The word was bittersweet. There was no "they" and wouldn't be if they couldn't find out who killed Lola and was threatening Josie.

As they made their way down the concrete stairs to the club, he noticed the change in her. A sensual smile curved her lips and her frame relaxed into her clothes. He half-expected her appearance to change before him, as it had the last time he was here. It didn't.

He followed her to the bar and sat on the stool next to her. Behind the bar, Joe turned and graced her with a smile that would've made him jealous if Joe was years younger.

"The usual for me, Joe." Her gaze met his. "What do you want?" The words rolled off her tongue in a way that made him wonder if she was talking about a drink or something else.

Soft caramel eyes met and held his in a seductive manner that shook him as hard as the other emotion he saw there. Love. His heart ached because it wasn't Josie, it was Lola with her love for William. Unlike when his uncle took over his body, Josie had remembered what she said and did. He wished he'd had that luxury. He would've loved to have been a fly on the wall that night in his bedroom to know exactly what they talked about. He was certain she left out a thing or two.

"Just a beer, Joe. Whatever you have on tap." Inquisitive black eyes raked over him, as if trying to decide if he was worth his attention. Had his uncle been scrutinized as harshly?

Moments later, a beer appeared before him along with a friendly smile. "Welcome."

Patrick gave a quick nod. *I guess that means I passed the test.* Too bad he wouldn't get to reap the rewards his uncle had. There was nothing he'd like more than having Josie in his arms and in his bed tonight, and every night after that.

"Where's Pearl?"

Patrick gave her a sideways glance. She didn't waste time, did she? He would've taken a more diplomatic approach himself. It appeared Lola and Josie had more in common than he thought.

One dark eyebrow raised in surprise. "She's backstage getting ready." He nudged his chin toward the door to the right of the stage.

"Thanks." Patrick took her by the arm and led her there. She didn't move away, instead leaned her body closer to his until it caressed his with each step they made across the room. Damn!

His uncle didn't stand a chance. He hadn't been able to resist Josie with her cool demeanor. He'd have gone crazy if she had been this seductive and alluring while under his roof.

The room was dimly lit and smelled of old dust and mothballs. Boxes lined the walls, except for the space in the far corner where a small wooden seating area was set up for Pearl.

She didn't turn when they walked in, but watched their reflection in her mirror. "Joe told me you'd be back, but I didn't think you'd bring him with you." She twisted around so she faced them.

There was no trace of fear or apprehension, just annoyance and a hint of amusement in the curve of her bright red lips. Clad in knee-length purple sequined dress and thick makeup, she was dressed to go onstage from head to toe, except for her shoes, which were only a foot away.

Pearl stood to meet Josie halfway across the room. They were two adversaries going head to head, neither intending on backing down. Would fists start flying?

"You know why I'm here." Josie took a step toward her.

Tension, thick and heavy, filled the room, suffocating him nearly as badly as Pearl's strong perfume.

"I know why," Pearl shot back. "Joe told me she's talking to you." The word *she* was said with so much venom he could taste it. "You can fool Joe, but you don't fool me!" Her gaze ran down the length of Josie as if she was no one of importance. "I told you before to leave him alone. You and your family have caused him enough pain."

"You're the fool, Pea."

Her eyes narrowed to slits. "Where did you hear that name?" she demanded. "No one calls me that!"

"Lola did. You used to like it." Josie's tone softened.

Shock and revelation moved in waves across her brown face. "Lola?"

Pearl was given a smile that wasn't Josie's. Patrick knew them all. "No, but she's here."

Painted-on eyebrows rose. "How?"

"She doesn't actually speak to me," Josie clarified. "Put simply, I sense her emotions, and pick up things here and there."

The answer wasn't the one Pearl expected.

"We're here about this," Patrick said. He held out the burned photo to her. He wished Lola did talk to Josie. It'd make everything a lot easier. She could tell Josie who killed her.

Pearl looked at the photo and relief spread across her face. Why did she think they were there? "Look on the back," Patrick said.

Her eyebrows rose in question. "What does 'last chance' mean?"

"You don't know?" Josie added.

"If I did, I wouldn't have asked." Pearl placed her hands on slim hips.

"Someone's been making threats against me."

That statement surprised her. "Why?"

"Because of Lola. We think it's her killer." Patrick held her with a firm gaze as she digested his words.

"Killer? I thought..." The emotions playing across her face said that she'd thought Lola had merely disappeared, not been killed. "Who do you think killed her?"

Their gazes settled on her for several seconds.

"Me?! Why would you think that?" Pearl took a step back.

"You left right before she disappeared. That's a little too convenient, don't you think?" Patrick said, closing the space she tried to be between them.

Her mouth opened and closed like a fish gasping for air and her eyes filled with fear, and then anger. "I didn't kill her!"

"Why should we believe you?" Josie took a step toward her. "Lola's emotions for you are conflicting. She cares for you, but is also angry at you. How do we know that anger is not because you killed her?" She took another step closer. "She stayed here, instead of going to the house with William. Why?" she pressed. She was right in front of Pearl, who'd sat back down on her stool in retreat.

"You told me finding out the truth would hurt Joe, and you wouldn't let anyone hurt him. That sounds like a confession of guilt to me." Josie's hand rested on her hip, leaning farther over Pearl.

"It wasn't guilt the way you think," Joe said from the doorway. Relief washed over Pearl's features at the sight of him.

"What do you mean?" Patrick asked. What else could Pearl feel guilty about?

Josie looked at Joe, then Pearl, when he didn't answer right away. Pearl's head was bowed, avoiding all their gazes.

"She didn't want me to know why she really left. She was afraid," Joe started. "Afraid I would find out Pearl had kept my child from me," he said quietly, as if it would hurt them both less.

Josie looked at Patrick in surprise and then back at Joe and Pearl.

"She left because she was pregnant and thought I was in love with Lola."

"You were," Pearl insisted.

Joe shook his head and walked to where she sat and knelt before her. "Only in the beginning." He took her hand in his. "I told you she became a sister to me, but you wouldn't believe me, stubborn woman." He kissed her hand.

Jealousy gripped Patrick. He envied them. It couldn't have been easy for Joe to forgive her for keeping his child from him all those years, but he had, and they'd moved past it. Would Josie be able to do the same when this was all over? Would he, if Lola's killer turned out to be one of his parents?

Joe turned his attention back to them. "Pearl may've wanted to strangle Lola for what she thought was selfishness, and for our relationship, but she'd never actually hurt her. She loved her like a sister."

"That explains why Lola stayed here. She knew about the baby, didn't she?"

Pearl nodded. "She told me I was a fool to leave him, that Joe was just a brother."

Josie turned to Joe. "She didn't want to leave you alone."

"Lola stayed here?" Joe asked, surprised.

She nodded and gave him a warm smile.

Patrick raked his hand through his hair. "We're still no closer to finding out who killed Lola." Pearl was no longer a suspect at this point. He hadn't expected a confession, but hoped for another clue. Something.

"Are you sure it wasn't William's family?" Pearl said tentatively, ignoring his harsh gaze at her accusation.

"We haven't ruled them out completely." Josie went to stand next to him. "Lola's presence is strongest here, and I don't sense anything when I'm around them. Whoever killed her may not have been as close to her as we thought."

"I don't believe that," Patrick interjected. "Every threat they made was at the house, or close to it. That means they knew where she lived and have a reason for you to leave. They want to keep what they did a secret."

"But I didn't know about Lola. If it weren't for the photos, I wouldn't have even started this whole thing." She covered her chest with her arms protectively.

Patrick ignored the urge to put his arms around Josie and give her the comfort she needed. If he did, he wouldn't be able to let her go.

Joe walked over to them and put his hands on each of their shoulders. "You have to forget the past." He looked at each of them in turn. "If you don't, you'll miss out on your future, and that's all that matters." He held Patrick's gaze longer than Josie's, as though he had the answer to the questions they were seeking. He wished to God he did.

Pain, fear, and apprehension moved across Josie's face. It's wasn't easy for her to just let it go; Patrick knew that. She needed this to put her past to rest.

"Don't let anyone or anything take away what you want," Joe said to them both, but he was looking at Patrick. Were his feelings for Josie so transparent that even Joe could see them, or was he merely guessing? He wished she could see them as easily.

"The same goes for you, Lola," Joe said out loud, but didn't look at Josie. He walked over to Pearl and put his arms around her. "We found each other again, and it's time for you to move on, too." Pearl rested her head against his shoulder. "Find William."

Patrick looked at Josie, but her face was unreadable. She'd put up her wall again. Was Lola gone? She didn't meet his searching gaze.

• • •

Josie followed Patrick into the house. The fire was gone and the room had grown cold. She watched him walk over to the fireplace and restart the fire. Her heart twinged at the sight of the locks of hair that fell across his face.

Emerald eyes stared back at her, searching, and she looked away, not wanting him to see the love that filled hers. Tears beat at the back of her eyelids and she bit the top of her index finger to keep them from falling and making a fool of herself.

"Josie." He closed the space between them. "We need to talk about what'll happen if we don't find out who killed Lola."

"I know." She sat down on the couch, putting distance between them.

"We're going to have to involve the police at some point. I don't want to risk anything happening to you." He put his hands into his pockets. "I know it's not what you want, but will you at least consider getting a patrol car to circle the neighborhood when I'm not here?"

Her heart swelled at his concern, but there was one important thing he was forgetting. "What happens if the renovations finish and we still don't find out who made the threats?"

"You could stay here," he offered.

She gave him a fragile smile. "I can't stay here forever, Patrick. I'll need to leave at some point." How long would he let her stay if she agreed? What if the killer didn't strike and they never found them? As much as she liked the thought of staying with him, there was still the issue of the will. She loved this house, but so did Patrick. It was more a part of his history than hers. He'd invited her to stay, but as what? His girlfriend or the permanent, freeloading tenant he couldn't get rid of? What happened if the killer was someone from his family? She couldn't bear to see the little he felt for her turn into hatred because she'd destroyed his family.

"I know, but..."

"No buts, Patrick." Her stern gaze met his, telling him she was right and he needed to accept that she wasn't going to change her mind. "I have another idea other than waiting around."

Hope filled his eyes and she nearly changed her mind about not staying. "I stay here alone. If the killer noticed you were gone, they'd likely make good on their final threat." She didn't need to say what she really meant: 'they'd try to kill me.'

"No!"

"It's the only way."

"I won't agree to that!"

"It's not your choice."

"It damn well is!"

She got up from the recliner and closed the distance between them. Her hand rested on his shoulder. "Patrick. I need to do this. I have to end it." Her finger covered his lips when his mouth opened. "Please."

He moved away from her and paced for several seconds. He sighed deeply and took her hand in his. "I insist that a police car patrols the house at night, inconspicuously."

She smiled. "Agreed."

The heat of his hands enveloped hers, reminding her that he still held it. His other hand caressed her face. Her breath hitched as his lips covered hers in gentle possession. Her mouth opened beneath his, welcoming his tongue's strokes and caresses against her own. She clung to him when he pulled her closer to his frame.

"Josie, I..."

"Don't." Her voice strained. Her eyes told him what she wanted—what they both wanted. She closed her eyes and took a small step away from him. She couldn't be with him again, no matter how badly she wanted him. She couldn't take sharing so much with him for it to be brushed aside so casually. He cared about her, but she wanted so much more.

"The crew will be here early tomorrow. They'll be finishing up the other room, so you can move back into your room in a couple of days." She smiled, despite her heart breaking inside. Not that it mattered. They'd just agreed she would be leaving.

The muscle at his jaw clenched and she didn't know if it was from anger or something else. He didn't reply, merely gave her a curt nod before she went upstairs, leaving him alone in the soft glow of the firelight.

She sat on his bed and loneliness filled her until she thought she'd burst from it. It was worse than the months that followed her mother's death, before she left Detroit. The hurt throbbed in her heart and she closed her eyes to keep the tears at bay. Tears were something she didn't need right now. Strength was what she needed to get through the coming days, to lure—and hopefully catch—Lola's killer.

The hard part would be after the renovations, when she had to walk out the door and say good-bye to Patrick and the house, forever. She shook herself mentally. There was no sense thinking about it now, or ever. It would drive her crazy.

She ran a hand through her hair. She still hadn't decided what to do about the will. One phone call to Gary was all she needed—to find out how much money she was entitled to—but each time she reached for the phone, she couldn't bring herself to do it.

The money would help keep her company afloat if things went sour with Patrick and his family, or it could go toward relocating. Putting distance between them would be the best choice, but there was only one problem with that option. She didn't want to leave. But if the killer was who she suspected, she and Patrick could never be together.

Chapter 19

Patrick knocked on his father's office door and walked in without waiting for a welcome.

Myles looked up from the paperwork on his desk. "What brings you here?"

Walking over to the couch, Patrick flopped down on it, weighing it down with the same weight he felt. "This business with Lola." He rested a hand on top of his forehead.

"You'll drive yourself crazy with it, son, just like William did." Sadness filled his eyes as he set down the pen in his hand. "Have you spoken to Gary? He and Will chased endless leads without success."

"No."

"Why not?" Myles was clearly surprised.

"Gary is a suspect." So was Myles, no matter how badly Patrick wanted to think otherwise. It was no secret that he didn't want Lola in their family.

A smile cracked his father's face. "Why is that funny?" He certainly hadn't thought it was funny.

"Why do you think he's a suspect?"

"I didn't at first, but Lola mentioned something in her letters about him that couldn't be ignored. He had access to the house, photos, and everything else in the house used as a threat against Josie."

"So did your mother and me. Is that why we're suspects?" His eyes said 'don't bother denying it.'

"One of her reasons, but there were others. Someone attempted to run her over the same night she confessed to us she was related to Lola."

"Your mother told me she didn't want to call the police." Myles leaned back in his leather chair.

Patrick raked a hand through his hair in frustration. "I know! She still won't, even after the last threat. She's using herself to bait the killer." God, how he hated leaving her at the house alone. It took all his strength to do it, but she was right. It was the only way to draw out the killer, and quickly. The sooner they knew who they were, the sooner Josie would be his.

"What?"

"Crazy, right?"

Myles got up from his chair went to stand by the window. "Not so crazy." His tone was low.

Patrick straightened his position on the couch. "You agree with her?" His father's face didn't give anything away. Did he know who the killer was? His stomach lurched that it might be his father. They didn't have the best relationship, but they loved each other.

Myles shrugged.

• • •

Josie shifted her weight on the couch so she was sitting up instead of lying down. Setting her book aside, she reached for the glass of wine on the coffee table.

Patrick left the day after she suggested dangling herself as bait for the killer. He still tried to talk her out of it, but she stood her ground. Lola's murderer had roamed free for fifty years, and she had no intention of letting them silence her like they had her aunt.

A knock on the door got her attention. Her breath held, she walked to the door, not bothering to look out the peephole that Patrick insisted Danny install before he left. No matter who was outside, she had to let them in to discover the truth. *Or be killed.* She gripped the pepper spray in her pocket, a gift from Patrick.

"Gary, come in." Her hands shook as she closed the door behind him. Since his threat to her not to hurt the Pullmans, she had moved him to the top of her list of suspects. Finding out her movements, and that she was alone, wouldn't take much effort.

"What are you doing here?" It was a rhetorical question, but more diplomatic than 'Are you here to kill me?'

He walked into the living room and looked around with appreciation. "I came to discuss the will. Elsa mentioned Patrick told you."

"It seems everyone knew but me," she said bitterly.

"You could've called me."

Heat colored her cheeks and she looked away. He was right. She still hadn't decided what to do. She let out some of the breath she was holding, but kept her guard up.

"I suspect Patrick withheld the information for the same reason. He was unsure what to do after the shock wore off," he offered, taking a seat on the couch she motioned to.

That should make her feel better, but it didn't. "Would you like a drink?"

"Thanks, but I don't drink."

She went to stand behind the loveseat across from where he sat. If he did try to get at her, he'd get a face full of pepper spray and she'd be out the door before he could touch her.

His relaxed posture on the couch showed no indication of wanting to attack her, or even reach for her. In fact, he sat there, silently assessing her in that way the Pullmans did, as if trying to read her mind. Was he going to start talking soon? He didn't seem in a hurry. Was that better or worse? Maybe he merely wanted to intimidate her with the drawn-out silence. Talk already!

"The will entitles you to eighty percent of the money Will left, and the house, if you want it."

At last! She shook her head. "Patrick loves this house. I couldn't take that away from him." She bit her bottom lip nervously. "How much money is it?"

A graying eyebrow rose. "Patrick didn't say?"

She shrugged.

"You didn't ask?"

"No." It was the last thing on her mind at the time. "It didn't seem important when he mentioned it," she mumbled.

"The total inheritance is eight million dollars."

Even without calculating the eighty percent, she knew it was a lot of money. Her fingers dug into the leather of the couch. It was more money than she'd see in a lifetime. She could pay off the bank and not have to worry about her business again—ever. Her hands shook with excitement and dread. Taking that money would mean taking away everything Patrick wanted to do with it. "I see," she managed, hoping to sound calmer than she felt. She loosened her vise like grip on the edge of the couch. Had he noticed?

"Do you need my answer tonight?"

"No." For once, he didn't try to hide what reflected in his eyes; right then, it was surprise.

"Good. Was there anything else?" What was he waiting for? Was he merely biding his time until she relaxed so he could catch her by surprise? Whatever his reason for not making his move, it was frazzling her nerves.

"The moment I saw you, I knew you were related to Lola. Part of me hoped you weren't, but in the end, it doesn't matter."

Finally! Here it comes—his confession and the truth about what happened to Lola. She hadn't met Gary until Patrick introduced them. The advertisement for the renovation had been emailed to her. Realization hit her like a ton of bricks. She hadn't given it much thought at the time, since she got email requests for jobs all the time. "You emailed me about this job?"

"Yes. I recommended you to Patrick, along with one other so he wouldn't be suspicious. I also left the photos of Lola in your room." He said it so casually, she wondered if he had planned Lola's death the same way.

Her pulse raced as she met his gaze. "That was you?" Would the police hear her if she screamed loud enough? Would that make a difference? Myles had connections in the force; did Gary?

"Why would you want me here? If you were trying to cover up Lola's...disappearance..." she said tentatively. Saying the wrong words could make him angry. She'd learned that the hard way at the party, and wasn't going to take the chance. Not until she figured out a way to get outside, out of his reach. Fear tightened her chest until she could barely breathe. *Pepper spray! Don't forget the pepper spray!*

"What are you talking about, covering up Lola's disappearance?" He got off the couch and stood in front of her. She half-expected him to shake the answer out of her.

"I know Lola was killed." The words hung in the air while his eyes raked over her face in contemplation.

"How do you know that? William and I couldn't find a trace of her."

"It's difficult to explain, but I know." She took a step back, putting distance between them.

Despair etched his face, deepening the wrinkles around his eyes and mouth. "You think it was me? I...I loved her. I would never have hurt her." He sunk down on the couch next to her, his composure sinking to the floor as he cradled his head in his hands.

"Then why did you leave the photos and the poster threatening me?" She placed a hand on her hips. Should she mention his attempt run her over? The pain of her accusations was blaring, making her doubt her suspicions.

"I left the photos so you'd know about Lola and find out about the will. Your business needed the money. It was something I could do for Lola." Sharp gray eyes met hers. "Poster? What poster?"

His surprise couldn't be ignored.

"You didn't leave one of Lola's posters in my room with the words 'leave or die' on it?"

She held her breath. He wouldn't admit to the photos but not cop to the threats, would he? Part of her wished he'd just kill her already, if that was his plan. The waiting and not knowing was driving her crazy. Okay, maybe waiting to find out if someone was going to kill you wasn't such a bad thing.

His spine stiffened instantly. "Someone threatened you? Who? When? Why didn't Patrick tell me?" He paced before her, not pausing to give her time to answer him.

The coiled tension in her body that was ready to sprint to the door relaxed a little. His questions made it clear that he hadn't been told and didn't like it. "You were a suspect," she said, although Patrick probably had other reasons for not telling him that she didn't know about.

Confusion and then anger flashed in his eyes before they retired behind years of practiced composure. "I see. Are there other suspects?"

"Yes. Patrick's parents, Joe, and Pearl; but we've eliminated Pearl and Joe."

Deep in thought, he sat back down. "Why would someone threaten you? You don't know what happened to her, no one does."

They must think she did, otherwise why make threats? She didn't remind him she knew Lola was dead. Her reason for knowing would be difficult to explain. Lola couldn't tell her who the killer was, just that she was dead. If Lola was at the house, she could just parade everyone in and out until Lola reacted to them, but that wasn't an option.

"Who were your suspects at the time?" Josie asked.

"Myles' political connections were at the top of the list, but we questioned the neighbors and people at the club. No one saw anything. If they did, they were too scared to talk." He ran his hand down the length of his face. "I just wish we could've found her. A body, something. It was the not knowing that drove Will crazy and broke his heart."

Had he wondered to the end that she'd left him? If he did, he kept it hidden from his family. "She loved him and wouldn't have left," she declared. She couldn't tell him how she knew, but sensed just hearing the words would make him feel better.

"Thank you."

She smiled in return.

"What are the police doing about the threats? Is there anything I can do to help?" He took her hand in his.

If she told him her plan, he would be furious and, unlike Patrick, would insist on staying and getting the police involved, and ruin everything. The reasons she gave Patrick wouldn't pacify Gary. "There's a patrol car outside making rounds, and investigations are being made." It wasn't a complete lie. She was doing the investigations and not the police, but he didn't need to know that.

He breathed deeply, seemingly relieved. "Good."

She nodded.

He stood up. "You still have three weeks to make a decision about the money...and the house. I'm a phone call away if you have any questions."

She walked with him to the front door. "Thanks, Gary. For everything." Even leaving the photos that started this whole crazy ride. Her life might not be threatened, but she wouldn't have learned what she did about her family, and she wouldn't trade that for anything.

"My pleasure." He kissed her hand in a way that made her wonder if he didn't see Lola each time he looked at her.

After locking the door behind him, she went to the kitchen for a drink of water, her mind going over their conversation. Gary wasn't the killer, but that fact didn't comfort her. That only left Myles and maybe Elsa; however, she suspected Myles loved his brother too much to take away the woman he loved. That left Elsa, but what were her motives? Would she kill someone for her husband's political gain? There was no denying she was ambitious. Josie's stomach, along with her heart, lurched at the killer being either of Patrick's parents. There would be nowhere for them to go from there.

She leaned over the counter, her hands cradling her face. She thought of Elsa's answers, how she got rid of the woman Myles was seeing. It was very creepy. Elsa and Myles wouldn't try to kill her while attempting to convince her to stay with Patrick, would they?

She tugged at her hair in frustration. Every suspect on the list was either innocent, or she had overlooked something or someone. Gary left the photos, which could mean she inadvertently alerted the killer with her questions. She went through the faces of the people she questioned after finding the photos. It would exclude Patrick's parents, but not Joe and Pearl. They didn't have access to the house, so that eliminated them leaving the poster in her room.

Her hands went up in defeat. Was this how William and Gary felt as they'd attempted to find Lola? No matter what direction they went, it led to a dead end.

The doorbell rang.

Tonight was one busy night. Maybe she'd have more luck with this visitor.

...

Patrick paced the floor in his father's home office. "It's driving me crazy that she's there at the house, defenseless."

"Isn't there a police car patrolling?"

"Yes, but what good is that if the killer is inside the house and she's alone with them?" He raked a hand through his hair.

"Have you told her you love her?"

His eyes snapped to his father, who gave him a knowing smile. "Am I that obvious?"

"Only to those who know you," Myles said with a shrug.

He flopped back down on the leather couch. "Until this thing with Lola is resolved, there's little use in me telling her. She's obsessed with it, and so is her stalker." He didn't say the word 'killer', couldn't bring himself to say the words that might mean Josie leaving his life permanently.

A dreamy expression lit his father's eyes. "Did you know your mother pursued me?"

He gave him a sideways glance. His mother? He could imagine her doing many things, but pursuing someone—even his father— was not one of them. "How?"

"I was seeing another woman at the time, but your mother managed to maneuver her way around her—or, rather, through her." He grinned sheepishly.

"How did she manage that?"

"I'm not certain, but the woman called me one night saying she didn't want to see me anymore, and that night, your mother showed up at the door with a picnic basket. We've been together ever since."

He gave his father a cheerful smile, but his thoughts raced. His girlfriend called to break up with him, and then suddenly his mother appeared? Had she threatened her? If so, what could she have said to make her break up with her boyfriend?

He took a deep breath. He was overreacting. His mother might be cool and calculating, but threaten someone? "What happened to the girl?"

Myles eyebrows narrowed. "I don't know. I didn't see her again after that. She must've transferred or something."

Panic ran through him like a stream of cold water over a waterfall, fast and furious. "Where's Mother tonight?" He prayed to God his voice was calm.

To his dismay, his father noticed the change in him. "Your mother knew what she wanted and went after it. She wasn't crazy or anything. Not like Mrs. Anderson." His body shook with shivers. "Oh, your mother is at some fundraiser meeting."

"Mrs. Anderson? You know her?" How did the sweet, albeit strange, old lady know his father? His uncle never mentioned her, and she'd never come over until Josie moved in.

"I didn't know her, but Gary and Will did. Did you know Will had a restraining order against her? If he wasn't waiting for Lola to return, he would've left that house years ago."

"I didn't know that." Patrick's heart raced. Just because she liked his uncle didn't make her dangerous. Besides, why leave photos of Lola and bring attention to herself? It didn't make sense. He remembered her apple pies and cheerful laughter and found it hard to believe, but it had given her access to the house. Could sweet Mrs. Anderson be the one stalking Josie? As farfetched as it was, he liked it better than it being his mother.

"I need to go." He stood up.

"Tell her how you feel, son," his father said as his hand reached for the doorknob. "Life's too short not to be with the people you love."

The regret in his eyes surprised Patrick. He knew then it was because of the times he'd argued and distanced himself from Uncle Will.

"I will," he assured him. He strode over to the desk and put his arms around his father.

They hugged each other before Myles cleared his throat and took a step back.

"I love you, Dad."

Water pooled in his father's eyes and his throat convulsed. "I love you, too, son."

He dialed Gary's number as he left his father's office. "I need a favor." It was the first time in months he'd said those words.

"Name it," Gary said without hesitation.

He relayed his request quickly and got into his car. He hoped he wasn't too late. "Please, God, let her be safe."

• • •

"Mrs. Anderson...Sofia," Josie corrected. A friendly face was just what she needed to distract her from her unanswered questions about her stalker. "Come in."

Sofia walked past her and into the living room, her keen eyes taking in all the changes that'd been made. "You've done a great job. Not my taste, but I'm sure it suits Patrick."

Josie smiled. There was a word for her tastes. Like her, her design style was unique.

"I brought wine to celebrate." Sofia lifted the bottle of red wine in her hand. "Is Patrick not here?" She looked around as if she expected him to be just around the corner.

"No, he's staying at his apartment while we finish up."

"Got tired of the noise, I bet."

She laughed. "Something like that." What else could she say? No, he left so I could wait for my stalker to come and kill me. "Here, let me open that for you." She took the bottle of wine from her.

"I hope you like red. It was Lola's favorite."

Josie caught the last of her words as she entered the kitchen. How did she know what Lola drank? Didn't she say she didn't know her that well? Fear prickled the hair at the back her neck. She ignored it. Obviously, she'd misunderstood her. Glasses in hand, she left the kitchen and handed Sofia a glass. "Good guess. I like red. I take it you do, too."

Full shoulders shrugged. "I tolerate it."

Unlike most days, she wasn't wearing her signature strawberry wig. In fact, the one she wore was a lot darker and made of better quality hair. It was the same color as her hair in the photos with her husband.

"How did you meet your husband?" she asked when Sofia didn't speak. Strange. She was usually a chatterbox.

Pain filled her eyes. "I was a nurse at the hospital he was admitted to." Light replaced the pain. "He was so charming. We had our first date when he got out, and were married three months later, before he was shipped out. I never saw him again." Her voice trailed to a whisper.

Josie put her hand on her shoulder. "I'm so sorry. You never remarried?"

"No. I came close once."

"Really? What happened?"

Sofia set her glass down on the coffee table and stood up. "Please excuse me. I need to use the bathroom."

"Of course."

Josie sunk into the couch and let the taste of the wine soothe her. She missed Patrick—the sound of his voice, his presence in the house, but most of all, his touch. The night before he left was torture; she hadn't slept, listening for sounds of him moving about. He'd offered her comfort in all ways possible, and she'd rejected him. At the time, it seemed like a good idea, but now she was scared.

Gary's visit had been unexpected, but needed. Now she knew that he was the one who left the photos, but not the poster. Neither did he attempt to run her over. She twirled a strand of hair at the base of her neck as she recalled everything he said. He and William had searched for Lola and found nothing. The only thing she'd managed to do was put her life in danger by baiting the killer. She'd questioned everyone, like they had—but unlike them, she'd discovered something.

Her hand stilled on the glass of wine. Gary said they'd questioned the neighbors and people at the club, but they hadn't remembered anything. Sofia hadn't remembered anything at first, but she'd remembered Lola leaving the house late at night. Had she told William? Why, then, had Gary said no one remembered anything? He wouldn't forget something like that.

A sharp prick nipped her neck. She turned to find Sofia standing over her, a syringe in her hand. The friendly light in her eyes had been replaced by menacing shards of blue ice.

Realization hit her in waves. Sofia had access to the house, knew which nights she sang at the club, and what time she came home. "Why?" It was the one thing she didn't know.

"It was bad enough I lost Will, but then you showed up and started shoving Lola's victory in my face! Even after she left, he didn't forget about her so we could be together."

Josie didn't know what had been injected into her system, but her eyelids felt heavy and the skin on her face felt as if it was going to slide off until there was nothing left but exposed bloody muscles. "Is that why you killed her?" Sofia hadn't said she killed Lola, but the hatred in her eyes and voice left no room for doubt.

Sofia paced before her like a predator stalking its prey. "William was as sweet and charming as my husband. I knew he'd make a good replacement, but Lola took him away from me." Her jaw clenched. "I thought once I got rid of her he'd want me, but he didn't."

Panic seeped through her at the madness in Sofia's eyes when she looked at Josie. She saw Lola. "You don't have to do this, Sofia," she pleaded. "What did you give me?"

Her once-sweet laughter was now as harsh as jagged rocks. "Just a little mix I concocted from my garden."

She went to the front door, put the chain on, and then walked over to the windows to close the blinds. "Just in case that pesky patrol car decides to come by before I leave. I would've been here sooner, but I wanted to know their schedule first." She sat in the chair across from Josie. "It was so nice of Patrick to leave you alone.

I guess he doesn't like you as much as I thought." She shrugged her black-covered shoulders. She wasn't wearing her usual vibrant colors. Another trick she used to disguise herself.

"He'll find you," she whispered. Her head was a ball of lead on her shoulder.

Cruel laughter rolled off Sofia's lips. "No he won't. I fooled everyone fifty years ago and I'll fool them again. Who'd suspect the sweet old lady next door who brought over pies and other treats?" She batted her eyelashes, which years ago would have attracted men; today, however, it only added to the danger that lay behind them.

"You could've continued to keep your secret and no one would've been the wiser."

"I thought a simple threat would make you stop your search, but it didn't. You're as tenacious as Lola. I knew you wouldn't give up."

"So you did know her?"

"I knew her. She thought we were friends." A Cheshire cat grin curled her lips. "You should've seen the look on her face when I shot her. Like you, she was easy to fool with a friendly smile and a slice of apple pie."

Josie's gaze moved across the room to the front door. Her legs were as heavy as metal, and her head felt it would fall off from the weight. She'd never make it. Sofia was not only very dangerous, but calculating. Fright paralyzed her nearly as much as the drugs. Would the police notice the blinds were closed and knock on the door to inquire? She was stupid to think she could trap someone who'd covered her tracks for fifty years.

Sofia picked up the photo on the table—the one she'd left with Lola's half-burnt face. "It still shocks me how much you look like her." She chuckled creepily. "I almost lost my composure the day you showed up at Patrick's house, and again when you came to tell me about the renovations. I thought you were a ghost."

She tossed the photo down on the table. "You should start feeling the final effects any minute now." Her eyes were those of a nurse inspecting her patient.

"I was expecting something more dramatic," Josie mumbled. Her mouth opened to scream, but Sofia wagged a finger at her as if she were a naughty child about to do something she shouldn't. It didn't matter—she had no more strength. Weight, like an elephant, rested on her chest.

Her lips closed, along with her eyes. The words 'you can't get away with this' formed in her mind, but they would be wasted. Sofia had already gotten away with one murder, what was one more? Josie struggled to move, but could only manage to open her eyes. A light in the corner of the room flickered. When her eyes focused in on the figure, it was Lola. Just like the figure of William she'd seen in the house the first night, she was translucent and dressed in a sequined red dress. Rage flared in her eyes as she stepped toward her and Sofia. She reached out to touch Sofia, but her hand went right through her.

Sofia didn't sense her presence or feel her touch. Her expression remained emotionless as she watched Josie grow weaker. Lola moved past her and went to stand next to Josie, touching her.

"I don't want to die," she whispered weakly.

"You have no choice, my dear," Sofia said coolly.

"I do."

Eyes half-closed, she heard Sofia scream as Lola went from translucent to a physical body—not solid, exactly, but visible. She hadn't aged a day past the photos Josie had seen, and her eyes burned with the fire of revenge.

Sofia lowered her hand from her mouth as Lola place a hand on her hip.

"How..." Sofia whispered, but it was an observation more than a question.

"I told you it wasn't over," Lola spat.

Sofia stared back at Lola, stunned. "This can't be happening."

Lola laughed. "It's real, and it's happening." She took a step toward Sofia.

"Stay away from me!"

"Or what? You'll kill me again?"

Lola took another step toward her. "You made me believe you were my friend!"

Sofia found her voice and sneered at Lola. "You didn't belong with William. He just couldn't see that."

Lola strode up to her and closed every gap she tried to put between them. "You ruined my life, hurt my family, and for what? To replace your dead husband with someone who didn't want you."

Sofia didn't reply, her eyes wide with fear.

Lola's hands reached out to her, but instead of passing through her as they had the first time, they came in contact with flesh.

A look of surprise washed over them both before Lola put her hands around Sofia's throat and squeezed. She screamed as the flesh beneath Lola's hands smoldered.

Sofia's eyes were wide with terror as she pushed against Lola's hands. They didn't budge. The stench of burning flesh filled the room and small pieces of bloody flesh fell on the floor.

"Lola, stop." The words were just above a whisper. Another figure materialized. It was William.

Josie struggled to keep her eyes open, knowing that if she closed them, it might be forever. Patrick's face flashed before her and she clung to its image, praying desperately it wouldn't be the last thing she saw.

"No, she took away our lives!"

"Killing her won't make us better than her," he reasoned.

Lola released her, as though she was disgusting to touch, and Sofia's body landed with a heavy thud.

The wetness of a single tear streamed down the side of Josie's face. It was sadness for her unfulfilled life without Patrick, along with happiness that she'd soon see her mother.

"You really do look like me." The cold touch of Lola forced her eyes open. "Hold on just a little longer," Lola urged. "Stay awake for him."

There was no need to say whom she meant.

"Stay away from me!" Sofia screamed when William and Lola stood before her.

"Josie?"

It was Patrick! The chain was on the door, so he wasn't able to get in.

Her mind screamed 'help me!' but she didn't have the strength to say it out loud.

There was a loud bang and then Patrick was at her side. "What have you done to her?" he yelled at Sofia.

He stormed over to Sofia and yanked her to her feet. "Tell me what you gave her!" His eyes were narrowed to dangerous slits.

"Curare," Sofia stammered. "Just keep them away from me!"

He dropped her roughly—and she edged herself back and cowered in the corner, her eyes wide with terror, and blood dripping down her scorched neck. Josie wondered what she saw, as Lola and William were no longer visible; at least, not to Josie.

Sofia thrust out her hands before her and screamed, "No, no!" over and over again before her eyes became colorless and vacant.

"Hold on, Josie," Patrick whispered. "Please don't leave me. Please."

The figures around her blurred as her eyes grew so heavy she couldn't keep them open. Her heartbeat, already a staccato drum in her ears, slowed until long seconds seemed to pass before she heard it again. Patrick's muffled voice was in the background, and then there was nothing as emptiness descended around her.

Chapter 20

Josie's eyes opened cautiously at the feel of someone squeezing her hand. She hurt in places she couldn't identify. Her throat was raw cut meat, and her tongue was heavy cotton in her mouth, and the back of her throat tasted of plastic.

Patrick sat on the edge of the bed, his eyes red and filled with worry. More stubble covered his chin than she'd ever seen and his clothes were rumpled, as if he'd slept on the chair in the corner of the room.

"Hi," she whispered.

He squeezed her hand. "Glad to have you back."

She didn't ask how close she came to seeing her mother. The relief in his eyes that she was awake gave her the answer. "What happened after I blacked out?"

"I rushed you here and told the doctor what Mrs. Anderson had given you, and prayed that she wasn't lying."

Part of her wanted to ask what it was, but mostly she didn't want to know. She was just thankful to be alive and that he'd been there to save her. "What brought you back to the house?"

"Something my father said."

"So you knew it was her when you got there?"

"No. I also suspected my mother, so I had Gary find her to make sure she was where she said she was."

"You found out about the woman Myles was seeing before her." What would he have done if it'd been his mother behind the door and not Sofia? She was glad they didn't have to find out.

"You knew about that?"

264

She nodded. "She told me the day I went to see your father's office."

He took hold of her other hand. "Josie, I..."

"Hello there, Sleeping Beauty." Standing in the doorway, with a bouquet of flowers, was Danny.

Patrick released her hand and stood up. "Danny. Thanks for coming."

"Wild horses couldn't keep me away." Worry edged lines around his face. "Why don't you take a break? Looks like you need one." His eyes roamed over Patrick's face and shambled clothing. He wrinkled his nose for good measure.

"I could use a shower and a change of clothes. Take good care of her until I get back."

"I won't let her out of my sight."

He looked at her, and then Danny. "I'll be back as soon as I can."

"Thanks, Patrick." She gave him the brightest smile she could muster.

He walked back to the bed, took her hand in his, and kissed it while his eyes held hers. "You're welcome." His eyes said he would do it again, anytime.

Her heart hammered in her chest and she knew she loved this man, and it wasn't because of Lola or anyone else. It might have started that way, but not anymore. It hadn't been that way for a long time. The heat of Danny's stare pulled her gaze from the door Patrick walked out of.

"Why aren't you at work?" she teased.

"This is no time for jokes." His voice croaked. "I thought you were a goner."

"You can't get rid of me that easily."

His hand squeezed hers. "Good."

The love in his eye made her heart sink. She'd hoped arranging for him meet Sharon would help him forget about their kiss. He'd returned to his old self, but it hadn't been as successful as she'd hoped.

"Danny, you know that I care for you, right?"

"Yeah, and I care about you."

She removed her hand from his carefully. "But I don't care about you in that way."

To her surprise, Danny laughed. It wasn't the reaction she'd expected.

"That's good to know, because I don't care for you that way, either."

"What? Then why did you kiss me?"

He grinned. "I saw Patrick coming back inside the house, and I figured he'd find us. He's the first guy in years who's rattled that brick wall of yours, so I thought it would help you along. You were dancing around each other and it was driving me crazy. Kissing you was torture," he teased. "It was like kissing my sister." He stuck out his tongue.

She punched his arm, then winced in pain at the movement. "What about those lectures?"

"I couldn't make it too easy, now, could I?"

"I thought you didn't like him. Pullman with the reputation, and all that."

He shrugged. "I could see he really liked you, and that was enough for me."

She gave him a weak smile. Another person telling her Patrick cared about her should make her happy, but it didn't. They didn't know the truth. His attraction was because of William. When she tried to sit up, the events at the house came flooding back to her and she fell against the pillow as her body protested in pain.

"Knock, knock," Gary said from the doorway.

"Come in, Gary."

"How are you feeling?"

She gave him a sideways glance. "Like I was run over by a truck—a really big one."

He laughed. "You still have your sense of humor. That's good." He shook Danny's hand. "Can you give us a minute?"

Danny nodded. He paused at the door. "I'll check on you later, JoJo."

She smiled. It was the only thing that didn't hurt. When the door closed, Gary pulled the only chair in the room close to the bed. "How much do you remember about what happened?"

She looked down at her hands. "Too much," she mumbled. The sounds of Sofia's terrifying screams would haunt her dreams for days to come, as would her cruel smile.

"When Patrick called and asked me to check on his mother and told me about his suspicions of Sofia, I didn't know what to think. Half an hour later he asked me to meet the police arrest Sofia so he could take you to the hospital." He shook his head as if he still couldn't believe it. "I knew she wasn't all there, but I never suspected murder. All these years, she was just next door."

Josie touched his hand resting on the bed. "No one suspected her. She planned it that way."

Gary nodded. "I'm just glad it's over. I only wish William could have lived to see it."

"Me too." Josie squeezed his hand.

He cleared his throat. "I did damage control with the press, so your name won't be in the papers."

"Thank you," she whispered. It really didn't matter, but it was better than having her name and company tied to a murder attempt.

"I still don't understand why she tried to kill you."

"She was trying to cover her tracks. I questioned her about the photos you left and Lola being in the neighborhood. She hated Lola, and I have her face."

"I caused this, didn't I?" He squeezed her hand as if to say 'sorry'.

"We'd never have found the truth if you didn't." She smiled in assurance. It was over, and that was all she cared about. The weight of it was gone. Now if only her crushing heartache would leave.

"Patrick told me he wants you stay at the house to share the ownership with him, and the money. I'm glad you were able to work things out."

Her heart jumped at his offer and then sunk as she realized he hadn't asked her. He'd made that offer before, but she sensed it wasn't what he wanted—just an attempt to keep her happy and forget that his parents were suspects. What was his reason this time? Guilt? Obligation? Or maybe a bribe. She didn't want anything but him. If it was for anything more, he would've talked to her directly about it.

"I don't want it." They were the hardest words to say.

Silence hummed like a rotating fan.

"Are you sure?"

"Very sure." Not having the money would hurt, but it would hurt less than staying with Patrick and watching him grow further apart from her now that Lola and William had found each other and wouldn't need to haunt them anymore.

"Tell him no thanks."

"Really? I thought you wanted to be with Patrick."

She gazed out her room window as she choked back tears. "There's no relationship."

He snorted. "A blind man could see there is something special between you."

"It wasn't us, it was William and Lola." That's all it was for him. For her, it'd been so much more, and the thought of being little more to him than an unwelcome tenant tore her insides apart.

Graying eyebrows narrowed. "What do you mean?"

"They were haunting us with the emotions of their unfinished relationship. The emotions we felt were all from them. At the house, and at the club. William and Lola were there the whole time." His expression said he didn't buy her story. Who could blame him when she and Patrick had a hard time believing it?

"What about at the charity event? Were they there, too?"

She looked down at her hands. If she spoke, she feared she'd burst into tears. It was better than saying the truth out loud. Patrick didn't want her. If he did, he'd have asked her to stay with him. He'd have felt the emotions she had the night they made love. She was a fool. That was probably Lola and William, too.

He ran a hand through his gray, thinning hair as wrinkles made waves on his face. "How? She's dead—has been for nearly fifty years."

"She appeared in the room, saved me from Sofia, took her revenge, and found her peace," she finished softly.

He ran his hand slowly through his hair as he digested her words.

She leaned back against her pillow and let the tension drain from her body, along with the pain, as a new dose of drugs came from the drip attached to her arm. "It doesn't matter now, it's over. All of it," she said sadly. Like the mystery, her and Patrick's time had also come to an end. "Can you help me with something, Gary?"

"Anything."

"I'd like to have a headstone for Lola placed next to William's. She'd want to be next to him." She didn't mention she was already with him spiritually. It might be a little too much for him to swallow.

"I'll make the arrangements."

"Thank you," she said quietly. Tears welled in her eyes, and she was no longer able to keep them at bay.

"I loved them and I'd be glad to bring them together again."

"Thanks for everything, Gary."

"My pleasure, doll."

• • •

Josie picked up her last bag and headed out the bedroom door. It'd been three days since she was released from the hospital. The renovations to the house were completed, and there was no longer a reason for her to be there. She and Patrick couldn't talk during the day with the crew cleaning up, and they'd tiptoed around each other at night. It confirmed what she suspected. He was relieved she hadn't taken his offer. He didn't want a relationship with her and was starting to put distance between them. She cried into her pillow every night.

She paused at Patrick's door for a minute before continuing downstairs. Her fingertips touched the cold wall as she made her way down the stairs. Sadness overwhelmed her when she reached the bottom, and with each step she took into the living room. The living room she and Patrick had designed together, one she'd hoped to cozy up on the couch with him and talk about their dreams. A thick lump formed in her throat, threatening to choke her unless she swallowed it.

"Need help?" Patrick asked from the kitchen entrance.

Her heart lurched at the sight of him and she wished she could tell him it wasn't just Lola's emotions drawing her to him. She loved him, wanted to be with him. Her resolve tightened at the solemnity on his face; she wouldn't survive another rejection.

"Thanks, but this is the last bag." She managed a small smile.

"Let me walk you to the car," he offered.

She wanted to leave quickly before she made a fool of herself, broke down, threw her arms around him, and confessed she didn't want to leave him or the home they'd come to share. "No thanks," she said politely. "Bye, Patrick." She prayed the tears beating at the back of her eyes wouldn't fall before she got out of the house.

"Bye, Josie." His eyes searched hers before she moved away.

She walked slowly to the front door, her heart filled with hope that he'd stop her, but silence followed as she walked out the door and out of his life. He didn't care. She was right. If he cared, he would've stopped her—something.

The tears she'd been holding onto since she finished packing her final bags fell down her face as she closed the car door. She slammed on the brakes when Patrick stepped in front of her car.

"What the heck is this?" He waved an envelope before her.

"It's your reference," she said quietly.

Anger flared in his eyes. "You don't need me now that you have your millions?" he shouted.

She rolled down the window. "What're you talking about?"

"Gary told me you accepted the money, but not the offer to stay at the house with me."

"What? I didn't accept any money! I told him you should have it."

He crossed his arms. "Really? How do you plan to keep your company going without any money or a reference?"

"I planned to sell my mother's house! I don't want or need your money. As for the reference, I'll find my own way," she insisted. She didn't mention that she hadn't been able to sell the house when it was on the market a year ago, that his mother promised to recommend her when Myles' office was done, or that she was dead broke. She'd used all the money he paid her to cover renovating his home.

"Get out of the car," he barked.

"No."

"Now, Josie!"

She jumped at his tone. She'd never seen him that angry before, not even when she accused his family of murder. Slowly, she got out the car.

"You were going to walk away, just like that?"

"You were letting me go just as easy," she shot back.

"What else could I do? You didn't want to stay with me."

"You didn't ask."

"Gary told me you said no." His eye filled with pain. "He said you wanted the money but didn't want to stay with me."

"I didn't!" she insisted.

His eyes lit up. "So you'll stay with me?"

If he'd asked her the same question a few days ago, she'd have gladly said yes and jumped in his arms, but things were different. "Too much has happened," she said quietly.

"Stay with me, Josie," he said gently.

"I can't," she whispered, although her heart screamed yes. She wanted more from him, even if it meant losing him.

"Why?"

"Stay with you as what? Your tenant? Your girlfriend?" Being his girlfriend wouldn't be such a bad thing, would it?

He closed the distance between them and took her hand in his. "Fine. Marry me."

She froze. "What did you say?" Had he just asked her to marry him with a very pitiful proposal?

"I said, marry me."

"Just like that?" she asked, annoyed. "Don't do me any favors." She was being picky, but she didn't care. A girl had certain expectations when it came to things like that.

"What?" He looked at her as though she'd lost her mind. "I ask you to marry me and you tell me don't do you any favors?"

She placed a hand on her hip. "Fine, I'll marry you." She mocked him.

He took her hands and held them firmly. Her heart stopped in mid-beat when his finger stroked her hands and his eyes held hers firmly.

"I wanted you the moment I laid eyes on you. I thought it was because of Lola and William, but that changed the night of the fundraiser when we made love. I want you in my life, Josie, and if that means marrying you now instead of later, it makes no difference to me."

Tears welled in her eyes. "So what you're saying is that you love me?" Her tone was heavy with sarcasm.

"Your sense of humor was better when I first met you," he teased.

She threw her arms around him and rested her head against his chest, inhaling the scent of him she'd come to love so much.

"Is that a yes?"

She nodded into his chest.

"Why?" He tilted her chin upwards.

"Because I love you."

He kissed her forehead. "See how easy that was?"

She laughed and lifted her lips in invitation.

Flickering movement from the upstairs window caught her attention. Behind the window, William stood with his arms around Lola. Lola's hand touched the glass of the windowpane, leaving an imprint. Although she couldn't see her face clearly, Josie knew she was smiling. The figures disappeared moments later.

"Everything okay?" Patrick asked, looking in the same direction.

"Everything's great."

About the Author

Elke Feuer was born and raised on Grand Cayman. She lives there with her husband and two wonderful kids (one of each) who keep her on her toes. She has a sarcastic/quirky sense of humor not every gets and loves using checklists for just about everything.

For the Love of Jazz is her first published novel. She stumbled into writing suspense and found she really enjoyed it along with writing about serial killers. She writes time travels, contemporary, and historical romance to even out her dark side, but no genre is safe because characters keep telling her their crazy stories and she's a sucker for a crazy story.

For more information about Elke and her upcoming works, visit her at: *www.elkefeuer.com*

In the mood for more Crimson Romance?
Check out *Playing with Fire* by Molly Kate Gray
at *CrimsonRomance.com*.